OTHER TITLES BY SUSIE BRIGHT

THE BEST
AMERICAN
Erotica
1997

EDITED BY

SUSIE
BRIGHT

A TOUCHSTONE BOOK

PUBLISHED BY
SIMON & SCHUSTER

TOUCHSTONE
Rockefeller Center
1230 Avenue of the Americas
New York, NY 10020

TOUCHSTONE and colophon are registered trademarks
of Simon & Schuster Inc.

Designed by Barbara M. Bachman

Manufactured in the United States of America

1 3 5 7 9 10 8 6 4 2

ISBN 0-684-81823-X

ACKNOWLEDGMENTS

Thank you, Jon. Thank you, Bill. Thank you,
Jo-Lynne and Joanie.
This edition of *Best American Erotica* is dedicated to
the pioneering editors of erotic fiction in this country,
without whom there would be no contemporary erotic
genre to speak of: Amelia Copeland, Jack Hafferkemp,
Marianna Beck, Joe Maynard, Michael Ford, Thomas
Roche, Laura Antoniou, Max Airborne, Cecilia Tan,
Michael Lowenthal, Bill Brent, Marcy Sheiner, Lily
Pond, Mark Pritchard, Pat Califia, Shar Rednour,
Tristan Taormino, and David Alan Clarke.
As I write their names, I marvel at what outstanding
writers all of them are as individuals. But in this
instance, it is their talent to acquire, develop, and
publish other artists' work that inspires my feelings of
kinship and admiration. We have indeed changed the
world of writers and readers, and you all have my
deepest respect for it.

CONTENTS

INTRODUCTION

GIVE ME THAT OLD-TIME RELIGION,

GIVE ME THAT OLD-TIME RELIGION,

GIVE ME THAT OLD-TIME RELIGION—

IT'S GOOD ENOUGH FOR ME

LAST YEAR, I wrote an introduction for *Best American Erotica 1996* in which I gleefully and somewhat Grinchfully announced that "erotica is dead." I warned all the Whos down in Whoville that if they weren't ready to embrace the gothic, nihilistic, leather-noir-supernatural gestalt of the moment, then they weren't ready for the end of the century.

When I reached the end of my iron(y)-clad rant, I took another breath and acknowledged that as we still have a couple of years to go before the millennium I honestly didn't know what to predict would happen next. There's no shock button that hasn't gone stuck from overuse; there's no otherworldly possibility that hasn't already been plumbed to its psychic depths.

Almost as an afterthought, I concluded my essay with a prediction—"After death only comes one thing: resurrection." I had no idea that my Catholic training in clichés would prove so spot-on in the coming year. In 1997, something different did indeed start crossing my desk, something beautiful and new, and I didn't even know what it was until I'd already been swept away.

My first hints were manuscripts from a couple of friends who told me that they were writing some revisionist fairy tales, adult erotic stories based on tales we'd last heard aloud in our nursery schools. I heard titles like "The Butch's New Clothes" and "The Little Macho Girl," and I thought, *What fun!* It's obvious to me now, as I read fairy tales to my own grade-school daughter, that there is plenty of sex and gore driving every page of Mssrs. Grimm, and I've often wondered what the originals sounded like before publishers got out the pastel crayons and made them appropriate for a little girl's bedtime.

Many of my authors told me that their goal was to restore the sex to fairy tales gone soft (the violence has never diminished) and perhaps add twentieth-century kink or kick in the pants to the original plot. Other writers I admired seemed to be looking at mythic inspirations other than those of old Europe and were inspired instead by legendary American Indian figures like Old Man Coyote, who rarely learns or gives a lesson without scatological and explicit sexual misadventures. (See "How Coyote Stole the Sun" by M. Christian). Author Simon Sheppard wrote a story I nominated called "A *Puja* to Ganesha," the Hindu elephant god whose generosity has obvious erotic dimensions. Another new writer, Loana d.p. Valencia, pays some well-lubricated lesbian homage to Her Majesty La Luna, the moon. Michael Lowenthal put his remorseless and erotic biblical spin on the price of sex when AIDS is calling out chapter and verse.

Other writers I nominated for this year's edition were not faithful to any particular deity or scripture, but instead were just intoxicated by the notion of long-dicked wizards ("Dictation"), insatiable ghosts ("The Case of the Demon Lover"), and the spell of gender-free or even gender-subversive possibilities ("What?," "Mate," and "Queer Punk").

What was this mythic outpouring all about? I think I found my answer while skimming one of those "Change your life, get rid of everything" books that are so popular in gift shops and bookstores these days. I don't know if I was reading the manifesto designed for your closet or your freezer, but the boldface command, repeated on every page, was "Get back to basics." After ten minutes of review, I resolved to have a garage sale and stop eating Marie Callender chicken pot pies once and for all.

More than that, I wanted to make an inventory of what I really couldn't live without . . . not because I *have* to, but because I want to. I'm sick of being a prisoner of my stuff, my debts, my social obligations, my generation's expectations—flush it, I'm constipated as hell and I can't take it anymore.

Now, for a long time, the "basics" activists have been of the Old Testament sort, talking about Adam and Eve and ten little rules to figure out everything in your life. But I think that as we grow closer and closer to the year that begins with a 2 and follows with all those unfathomable 0-0-0's, people of every philosophical persuasion are feeling close to their elemental selves. We're less cynical about all the excess and dross—not because we've become more naive or forgotten what the score is, but because we have rejected all the big bang theories and charismatic-leader solutions to the world's insanity, and now are thinking about what it means to ever so simply and gracefully Be Here Now (thank you, Ram Dass). Or to Be Accountable Now—do I have to thank a neocon policy wonk for that?

Since American erotic fiction is as much a rectal temperature reading of all American prose as anything else, it's not surprising that resurrection is the theme of this year's collection: the rebirth of sexual identity, the dedication to what makes sex so essential and rapturous to us in the first place. When I saw titles like Rose White and Eric Albert's "She Gets Her Ass Fucked Good," I knew erotic fiction was ready to ride hard and be put up wet.

Not every story in this collection is a fable reimagined; we have randy schoolgirls with late-century cheekiness ("My Professor"), superb S/M craftsma'amship by Selena Moloch, a good washing and rubdown in "Soap and Water." But then honoring lusty women has always been "back to basics" in my book.

I'll admit it now: when I first mentioned resurrection last year, I was just spouting off a little tarot card bullshit that I hoped everyone would interpret more wisely than I realized at the time. Then I read the Back to Basics Cliff Notes and saw how the perfume companies were using words like "essentials" to get their smelly point across.

Their cheap commercialism helped me get the point that our dear culture was poking at me, without a lot of hints. Resurrection *is* the order of the day, and here's what the Easter Bunny didn't tell you: to live again is to fuck again, and everyone, right down to the last fundamentalist, gets to go into the Great Wash and get licked clean.

—*Susie Bright*

MAY 1997

Mate

*Being a tale of love, pain, sex, relationships,
and boring government jobs*

Lauren P. Burka

On WEDNESDAY TERRY lost at chess.

He sat back in his chair and stared at the game board as it faded away. The program recorded his losing score. Terry didn't lose often. His console prompted him with several unread mail messages, which he ignored. Removing the headset, Terry blinked as his eyes adjusted, and stared about the office.

The C3A building, where Terry worked, was a modern, terraced office building a bit smaller than a football field. The lowest and most central area held a fountain, grass, maple trees, and a small bit of carefully reconstructed parkland. The walls were lined with the balconied offices of those important enough to merit privacy. High above, the polarized ceiling admitted the glare of the yellow, polluted, northern Virginia summer sky.

As Terry sat in his low-walled cubicle in the center of that glass cavern, he could never know who was staring down from a curtained window, smiling in triumph, knowing something that Terry did not. The winner need not even be in the building, though the metachess server ran off a C3A machine. Access was easy to arrange from a remote site. Terry's conqueror could have been at Caltech, for all he knew.

Terry was disturbed. Who on the Net was that good? Was it Daphne?

Packing up his things for the day, Terry locked out the console and headed for the underground, deep in thought. Once out of the Classified area, Terry passed few people. On weekday nights, the stores were nearly empty. Bored doormen lounged about the hotel entrances. A small pack of young punks clad in tight, old leather and bright new chains had spilled out of the Sense Arcade, daring the security guards to chase them away. One of them, vampire pale and androgynous, turned and gestured a sexual come-on so blatant that Terry missed his step and walked into a potted plant. Stung by their laughter, and certain they could smell his confusion, Terry hurried down the mass transit entrance.

Metro had finally gotten climate control fixed in the subway. The station was cool and pleasant and smelled only slightly of sulfur. The aseptic walls and crisp advertisements were familiar and reassuring.

Terry's train whisked out of the station and over the Potomac River. He looked back at the spidery mass of Crystal City, its hotels and DoD offices, restaurants built on expense account dining, and the hulking air-conditioned fortress of the Communication Authority. Terry wondered again about the metachess wizard who had beaten him. If it wasn't Daphne, could it have been the same person who cracked the Gateway?

Daphne was already home, but scarcely lifted her head from her console when Terry came in.

"How was your day?" he asked.

"Shitty."

Terry sighed and went to microwave dinner.

He knew why Daphne was so busy. Hers was the first class to graduate since the phone system disasters of '12. The Government had been riding the new generation of computer geniuses hard, offering them unlimited loans if only they'd build the talent and discipline to keep the Net in one piece. After Daphne passed this last set of exams, she'd be bound to a civil service job for the next three years. How good a job depended on her GPA. Daphne was brilliant, first in her class, and likely to graduate with all honors.

Sometimes Terry wished she still had the time to love him.

At length, Daphne logged out. She tipped her chair back against the wall and tapped her fingers against her knee. Her face was pale and her blond hair greenish in the fluorescent light.

"I aced Queue Theory," she said. "One more exam to go."

"That's good. I lost a game of metachess."

She chewed the end of a stylus idly.

"I don't know who to, either. They left no ID."

Terry was watching Daphne. It could still be her. She had been known to lie.

"You ate?" he asked.

"Yeah. Ordered a pizza."

Terry finished dinner and dumped the plate down the recycle bin.

"They're bringing in the big guns on the Gateway security problem," he offered. When she was silent, he continued hopefully. "They hired lots of outside consultants and are turning the whole Authority upside down. All staff have been asked to submit to scan. My turn is tomorrow morning."

She nodded as if to be polite.

And then, since words were useless, Terry went and knelt and pressed his head against her knee. She was quite still for a long time. He stole a glance upward at her face, and wasn't sure what bothered him more, his sexual hunger or her indifference.

At last Daphne pushed him away and walked to the closet. Standing, she was taller than he, even in bare feet. Terry scarcely drew a breath as she dropped a handful of stuff on the couch.

"Come here and take your shirt off."

Terry obeyed. Daphne clasped his wrists in a pair of handcuffs, then, pulling Terry down to his knees, padlocked them to the eyebolt set in the bottom of the couch. Daphne dropped down to sit in front of him, her denim-clad legs spread wide, and pressed something unyielding against his lips. It was the rubber handle of her whip.

"Eat this," she ordered.

Terry opened his mouth. Instantly Daphne shoved the whip handle against the back of his throat. He tilted his head and swallowed, feeling the tears drip down his face. He was never really sure what she got out of it, aside from the obvious dominance kick. Maybe that was enough. His own jeans were becoming unbearably tight.

Daphne fucked his mouth a few more times, then pulled the whip out, wiping the handle on Terry's shirt. Then she stood up.

Terry rested his head against the edge of the couch. No matter how much he begged to be beaten with her three-tailed whip, the moment of terror before it struck was almost too much to bear. After she began, the rising adrenaline rush would wipe out his fear. Now he chewed his lips to keep from asking for mercy. One word and she'd release him, lose interest, and return to her console. And that wasn't what he really wanted.

*   *   *

The first stroke of the whip bit into his back with the lazy deliberation of a cat at a scratching post. Terry cringed and closed his teeth on the couch. He could smell the oiled length of the whip as it cut the air, then his flesh. Blow followed blow, regular as clockwork. Daphne wasn't strong, but her whip was nasty artillery. The fire in Terry's skin consumed doubt and confusion like some live and hungry thing. Terry was getting hard, faster than the stoned feeling was emptying the thoughts out of his brain.

Then Daphne stopped. Something bounced on the cushion before his face. It was the key to the cuffs. Behind Terry, a door shut, the door to her bedroom, with her on one side and him on the other.

Terry knelt there, panting, not quite believing. He snagged the keys with his teeth, brought them down to his fingers, and started working at the locks. When he had freed his hands, he didn't stop to take his jeans off, but pressed his erection against the edge of the couch. He came so hard that his foot cramped and he had to step on it until the pain went away. It wasn't the kind of pain he wanted.

Dropping his clothes in the corner of his tiny room, Terry went to the bathroom to check his back. He was bleeding in a couple of places, with an impressive set of welts. Terry showered briefly and then tried, with partial success, to spread disinfectant over his back.

Terry's room was actually a closet with a bed. It had no windows. Most summer days he slept on the couch to catch the breath of Daphne's air conditioner as it leaked under her door. Once he used to sleep in bed with her.

Terry lay down on his stomach and stared out the

window. The pollution made the sunsets beautiful, deep and red. It almost made up for air too hot and harsh to breathe.

Did he really think himself lucky for having Daphne? She did let him stay in her place, a boon in the midst of a severe housing shortage. And Terry couldn't exactly afford to be picky. Femme dominants were in short supply, and men like him too numerous to count.

Daphne used to love him. After that, she had hurt him as a favor. Lately, she did it out of simple cruelty. He considered, as he did every night, dumping her for someone vanilla, someone less brilliant and preoccupied and more personable, who talked to him once in a while.

It was just Terry's misfortune to turn on to intelligence harder than to anything else except, maybe, a touch of leather.

"Montiero! Get in the conference room now. They're waiting for you."

Terry glanced at the console clock as Johnson's abrupt verbal message thundered in his ear. It was 8:15 in the morning.

"But I'm early. I thought—"

"Someone ahead of you canceled out. Get moving. We're paying the team by the hour."

Paying them a good four times as much as I make in a day, Terry thought.

That someone had decided to pass on the scan did not surprise Terry. Their employer could not legally fire or deny promotion to them because of it. But if Terry didn't get his raise, he wouldn't be able to prove why.

A frustrated ACLU had tried to outlaw scanning. But they couldn't explain to the middle-aged members of the Supreme Court, who had never had a pickup planted next to their skulls, and never played a coin-op VR game or lost their sight from poorly tuned equipment, how a scan really felt. There was no objective measurement for that kind of feeling. Besides, this wasn't a polygraph test. Terry's employer didn't really think he had anything to do with the security problem, only that he might have something buried in his subconscious that would help them find the guilty party. Or name a scapegoat?

Terry took a right turn at the glass-fronted machine room. Behind the clear wall and sprinkle of condensation, the Gateway itself, a compound entity of Digital and SG / C machines, worked silently, routing all the communication traffic on the East Coast, switching impulses to Michigan via satellite, overseas to Europe, underground to Boston, and to a matching gateway in Palo Alto. The whole world in a fish tank, Terry thought. Or all the world that counted. The building's architects had left the computers visible because they really were beautiful. There was a symbolic map on the wall that showed traffic all over North America. Terry remembered after the big earthquake, when the lights tracing traffic to Boston had grown too bright to look at as everyone phoned their relatives in that city to see if they were safe.

A harassed-looking secretary was working a transcription set outside the conference room. She glanced up and pointed to a chair. Terry sat. And waited. He'd been told to hurry. Were they trying to keep him off balance? It was working.

Just before ten, the conference door clicked open. The secretary pulled her wire from under her hair and took her coffee up from the warming pad.

"You may go in now."

The conference room was paneled in wood, and

could have held twenty. There were only two. One was partially hidden in a corner behind a bank of consoles and a box of doughnuts. The other was a woman, red-haired, dressed in a suit and heels just high enough to be formal. She stood as Terry entered, and smiled the exact degree calculated to be soothing.

"Welcome." She came around the table and shook his hand. "Terry Montiero. I'm Louisa Arnold. Would you like some coffee before we begin?"

Terry hated coffee, but his mouth was dry. "Sure."

Arnold nodded. "Grey? Coffee for us both."

Terry glanced around. Grey wasn't a description of the coffee, but the name of the second person, who emerged from behind the consoles. He was small, dressed in denim, an old rock concert T-shirt, and a cowboy hat. Terry blinked. Technicians didn't have to dress up, but they usually did when paid as much as this pair was getting. He transferred his attention back to Arnold, who was taking her coffee from Grey.

"You should already have read the disclosure form on synch scan. We're going to ask you to read it again, and sign it."

Grey put the other coffee cup down on the table by a paper and indicated that Terry was to sit.

Paper was an expensive old habit of the federal government. Terry took a mouthful of the coffee, grimaced, and swallowed. The disclosure informed him in dry language that he was not entitled to sue for any damages caused by synchronized neural scan, and that any injury that prevented him from working was covered by his health insurance. Terry had read it before. He signed.

Grey took the paper and dropped it into a folder. The tech pulled a box out from under the table with his sneaker-clad foot, reached down, and picked up a handful of contacts. His hair was black and shoulder-length, Terry noted. Techs usually had a collection of skull sockets, and would either shave their heads to show them off or grow their hair for camouflage. Out of context, this tech would look like no one special.

"Please finish your coffee now," Arnold said.

Terry took another small swallow and then pushed the cup away.

Grey reached for Terry's right wrist. There was a shock at the contact. Terry jumped. It was just that, a shock from the dry air and friction on the carpet. He watched Grey's face as the other wet Terry's right wrist with saline from a squeeze bottle and clipped the band around it. Grey's eyes were blue and sharp under his hat. His mouth was softer, slightly open in concentration. He smelled faintly of soap.

Grey put a matching band on Terry's left wrist.

Arnold said, "Please leave your hands on the table."

Terry hastily put his palms upon the polished wood. The chair beneath him, he noted idly, was made of leather. This conference room was usually reserved for other, more honored guests.

A hand on the back of his neck encouraged him to tip his head forward. Instantly he felt something cold behind his right ear as Grey held a lead against the socket set in his skull. Something in Terry's brain clicked. He felt / heard the familiar whisper of data traversing the wire. He glanced up briefly. Arnold had taken a seat at the opposite end of the table and connected to the table console. Grey made his way back to the corner, dropped into a chair, and shoved his own wire into place behind his ear.

Instantly Terry's vision went blank.

"Please relax."

The voice was no voice, data on the wire. It didn't

sound like Arnold, but then it didn't sound like anyone in particular. Generic voice, genderless, constructed for a commercial. Nonthreatening. The blindness resolved to a soft fall of snow, as if seen through a window. Terry felt himself sitting back in the chair.

He gave a sharp, involuntary gasp as his welted back, almost forgotten, hit the upholstery. Instantly something cool dripped into his veins. Terry was safe. There was no pain. He was held as loosely as a puppet with no strings. He couldn't hurt himself, not even, in a fit of panic, rip the contacts away from his body and burn out the nerves. Time passed.

"We will ask you questions. You will answer them truthfully, and at length."

Terry nodded. Or something to that effect.

His assent was noted, recorded. Terry's brain, unoccupied, reported a scent of leather from the chair. Smell wasn't important. They'd left him that. This was like the time Daphne had left him tied to the bed in the dark.

"What is your name?"

"Terry Montiero."

"Where do you live?"

"1800 Kensington Street 14A, Silver Spring, Maryland."

"What is your job title?"

They would have this information in his file, of course. But they asked him anyway, to get a baseline response.

"Assistant to Daniel Johnson, director of Gateway East."

"What does your job entail?"

"I . . . manage Johnson's correspondence. He dictates into a pickup, and I have to clean up his letters to text. I edit out the random thoughts about his kids, his feud with the Transportation secretary, and having sex with his wife. Johnson's wife, not the Transec's."

And such boring sex it was, too. So few people in the world really knew how much sweeter a kiss tasted after the sting of leather. Terry pulled his thoughts back on track.

"It's still supposed to cost less than having him type it out himself, even though the pickup records everything he thinks."

As you're recording everything I think. Do you hear this?

"Obviously," Terry continued, "my job requires a lot of discretion, as well as good comprehension of written English. I had a minor in literature in college. . . . "

"Do you like your job?"

"Yes. It pays well—"

"Terry, we asked you not to lie."

Terry felt the first touch of real fear. Something tugged at his mind, like a trainer jerking a dog's choke chain. It was a warning.

"Okay. I don't like my job. The hours suck. I'm not a morning person. And Johnson, for all that he's in charge of the most important computers in the Capital area, is a remarkable technophobe. He can't even reboot his own console. I'm not the least bit surprised that things don't always work quite right. It's frustrating, and often an insult to my intelligence. And if I hadn't fucked up my final exams last year—I broke up with a girlfriend and got drunk the night before—I'd be over in NASA programming something useful. Satisfied?"

"What do you think doesn't work right about Gateway East?"

Terry noted the condescension implicit in the wording. To criticize the Authority, even so obliquely, had the slimy taste of treason.

"We're generally over budget by a good seventeen percent. Johnson could have gotten the last cable laid through the Amtrak tunnel, but then he got in a fight with Transportation. It was all political. The consoles are all IBM models and cost too much and don't work nearly as well as the same thing made by Northern Telecom. They also crash the SG / C machines. Then there's the security thing. This is why we're here, right?"

"What security problems?"

This was the hard part. Terry thought, *I didn't do it*. He wondered if that made him look guilty.

"You know . . . well, first there was the data leak. A certain amount of electronic mail just wasn't getting to its destination. As if someone was reading what was in them and accidentally messing up the addresses. That stopped really quickly after we noticed it. But then there was that bidding scandal over the new weather satellite, and we figured someone was still reading the mail. That's about all I know."

"Who do you think is doing it?"

"I honestly have no idea."

"Who do you know outside of Crystal City Communication Authority who might have the skills to crack government security?"

"No one."

"Who do you know who works with the Net on a regular basis?"

"No one. There's Daphne, my girlfriend, but she's still in grad school."

Terry thought about the player who had beat him at metachess.

There was a long pause, noticeable even in Terry's disoriented state.

It was scary, yes, but far from intolerable. Compared to Daphne's whip, synch scan was just a nuisance. Terry hated to beg for pain, and resented the possibility of mercy. Seen that way, this nonconsensual mental strip-search was almost interesting.

Terry told himself not to get too interested. He still had to finish up work for the day.

"Open your eyes."

Terry blinked. Grey was sitting still behind the console, chin on hand, staring at him. Grey blinked once, then stood up. Arnold was keying her console. Grey got up and pulled the contacts off Terry.

"That's it," Arnold said. "Thank you for your cooperation."

Terry stood up and stretched clumsily, never taking his eyes from Arnold.

"I hope you enjoyed it."

Arnold glanced up. "You may go now."

Terry gave a sarcastic bow and backed out the door.

"Top of my class," Daphne was saying. "I really did it."

"Work was a pain today. After the scan, nothing went right."

"Um. How was it?"

"Like having my brains sucked out my nose."

Daphne nodded. The buzzer for the door downstairs rang.

"That's the sushi," she said.

After paying the delivery person, they sat down for dinner.

"So tell me about the scan."

Terry was startled a bit. Daphne didn't usually care enough about his life to ask.

"They asked me lots of questions, of course. There

were two of them, a woman named Arnold and an assistant named Grey."

Daphne chewed and swallowed her tuna.

She said, "Grey. Short guy, wearing a Stetson?"

"Yeah. You know him?"

"They put one over on you. That was no assistant. That was d'Schane Grey."

"D'Schane . . . oh." Terry swallowed. "Oh. Wow. I feel pretty stupid."

Daphne favored him with a rare smile.

"Yeah, he does that to people. He was a visiting professor at Georgetown, on leave from MIT, when I was a sophomore. Taught a class on security. One of the best classes I ever had, and the hardest."

She paused for another bite.

"First lecture he came in, in jeans and that hat, and told us that computer security was a myth. But a marketable myth. George Lucas got rich selling myth, and so could we. Our final exam was to find a security hole and to exploit it. Any security hole. This one student charged seven thousand bucks to Grey's Citibank card. Grey thought it was pretty funny, but only gave the guy a C because he figured out who it was without asking, though he let the money slide.

"His whole philosophy was that it didn't matter how well you knew your operating system, though knowledge certainly helps. If a computer is connected to the Net, any high school student can find holes faster than you can patch them up. It's all psychology and intuition. You have to know how they think before they hit you.

"Then he quit academics and went to work as a consultant. He's only twenty."

"And the government hired him to sniff out C3A," Terry finished for her.

"Looks like it. Who do you think did it?"

Terry shrugged. "I think Grey did it. He broke it, now he wants the government to pay him to fix it."

They ate in silence for a moment.

"The government of Mexico bought out my loan contract."

Terry blinked. "What?"

"I'm not working for Uncle Sam. I'm moving south of the border to program a nice new cellular system for the 'burbs of Mexico City. The rent on this place is paid up until the end of July. You can stay here if you want. I'm leaving in two weeks."

Terry sighed, feeling the strength go out of him with his breath. That was it, then. He hadn't left her when he had the chance, so now she was leaving him.

"Well," he said, "have a good time."

Three weeks later, Terry finished up work and logged onto the metachess server for a game. Terry was using his own ID. This tended to discourage casual players who had lost to him before. There was a short pause as the server matched up a player good enough to be a challenge, one who did not flash ID. Terry stiffened and felt his pulse pound distantly.

The metachess board looked much like a traditional chess board. Only, one of the white pieces housed Terry's heart, and one of the black, his opponent's. Terry picked a knight.

It was possible to win metachess on the basis of strategy alone or on the strength of reflex and combat skills. Terry had both. Serious challenges to his chess abilities were both rare and welcome.

Terry moved a pawn; then, from his vantage point as the knight, watched black do the same. The first few moves were simple. Terry sent his king's bishop after a black pawn. There was a brief contest, a flash of light, and the pawn lay bleeding upon the board, then vanished. Which black piece was real?

Terry lost two pawns in rapid succession, then took out another black one. Metachess was faster than its parent game. The object wasn't to take out the king, but the mate piece, the one that held your opponent's heart. You couldn't find that out by accident. You had to know how your opponent thought.

A pawn slew Terry's bishop. There was a certain chance of this happening anyway, even with a real pawn. Terry risked another pawn to find out. But the black pawn, weakened, toppled before his own piece. It wasn't black's heart. It had just been lucky the first time.

Then Terry found the knight, his own heart, up against a black castle. It was an inevitable risk, for surrounding this piece with defenders would bring attention upon it, not to mention lose him a good view of the board. Terry blocked the castle's missile of light with an electron sword, moving his piece a half-dance to the side of the square. Castles were big, but slow. He forced himself to take a hit, a numbing shock that made his arms tingle, then landed a flurry of lunges. The castle crumpled.

Good, Terry thought.

All of black's pieces had moved, and none were obvious. It was a smooth job. Was this the same player who'd beaten him before? It sure felt the same. Could it be Daphne, like a ghost in the machine, logged in from Mexico? It felt like her, just as it had that time three weeks ago. Wishing it almost made Terry certain. Daphne usually picked the queen.

Terry fired off a text note to his opponent: "Who are you?"

Two moves later, he checked for an answer, and found none. Terry got slow and careful. Avoiding small battles, he eased his queen into black territory, then closed with the black queen. The battle drew from him an admiring sigh. Deadly force, even in a game, had a certain beauty of its own. The black queen toppled.

Terry had guessed wrong. It wasn't the queen.

A black knight challenged his square. As Terry was bringing up his sword, the black piece laughed.

For two, maybe three seconds, Terry froze, just long enough for the black knight to strike him a damaging wound. The game wasn't supposed to do that. Someone had tricked with the server.

The black sword danced before Terry's vision.

The server warned him of imminent checkmate, then forwarded a yield request from black. That was the polite thing to do. Virtual death tended to cause a headache, though the visual effects were interesting.

Terry sent back, "Tell me who you are."

He received another one-word message: "Yield."

In another world, Terry bit his lip. "I'll do anything to know who you are."

A message from black: "Lounge, Crystal City Marriott, 21:30."

Terry yielded.

The game recorded mate.

Daphne could have taken a jump-plane up from Mexico that quickly. Terry hated himself for wishing it. It wasn't Daphne. But what if it was?

Terry was in the lounge by nine, a half hour early. He got a cola and waited. And waited. By ten, no one had shown up. He wondered if this was a joke, but then reminded himself that the chess player had only said that Terry should be there, not that anything would necessarily happen. It was late, though. Terry had to work the next morning. He decided to leave at 10:30. If it was Daphne, she would just have to deal.

At 10:20, Terry glanced up in time to see a slight figure in a cowboy hat drop into the chair across his table.

"D'Schane Grey," he said.

Grey flashed a wide, feral grin. "You're quick on the uptake. Buy me a strawberry daiquiri." His voice, more than anything else about him, was startling. Terry hadn't heard him speak last time.

"What?"

"You heard me. I won't pass an ID check, and a drink is a subset of 'anything.'"

"Oh." Terry signaled the waiter and ordered. He could smell the merest breath of d'Schane Grey's scent, soap and sweat and denim. "You play dirty chess."

Grey's grin settled into a small, sweet smile. "Thank you. Just remember: the first time I beat you was a clean game."

"So what else does 'anything' include?"

"Haven't decided yet." Grey folded his arms on the table and leaned on them.

The daiquiri arrived. Grey sipped at it contemplatively.

Terry asked, "Why are you taking such an interest in me? You think I cracked the Gateway?"

"No. In fact, I know you didn't. Your girlfriend did."

"Daphne?"

"Daphne Lawrence. Unfortunately, she's in Mexico,

so we can't indict her. Mexico doesn't recognize data theft."

"And they have her working on their phones?"

"That's what she told you? She lied. She hired out to the same combine she was working for when she cracked the Gateway. The Authority wanted to string you up in her place. But I know you didn't give her your password on purpose. If I push them, they can't do a thing to you with my data. License laws and all that."

Terry took five slow breaths under the burning glare of Grey's amusement. To be at someone's mercy like this was almost worse than knowing Daphne had tricked him.

"I ask you again. Why are you taking such an interest in me?"

"Because you went under my scan with fresh, hot whip kisses on your back."

Terry closed his eyes. "What do you want?"

Grey emptied the daiquiri. "Chill. Masochism isn't a federal crime, though you should watch out how you let people use you. For now, I want you to stop cutting your hair for a while. I'll let you know when I think of anything else."

"Why my hair?"

Grey wagged a finger at him. "You ask too many questions. Thanks for the drink."

Terry, feeling distinctly appalled, watched d'Schane Grey leave the lounge. The man walked like a twenty-year-old, loose and a bit hurried. And he dared order Terry around like that? Terry sighed. What did he have to lose?

*   *   *

Terry found a new apartment. It was even farther from the Metro than Daphne's had been. The fifteen-minute walk out in the open air did his health no good.

Nothing happened at C3A, not a whisper more about security problems. Terry got his microscopic raise on schedule.

He dated a woman named Janet for a month. Janet worked in another department, and was very nice. Too nice. Terry couldn't face the inevitable look of horror on her face when he asked her to hurt him. So he never mentioned it, and neither of them was happy. They went out to movies, slept together on occasion, got bored, and stayed friends after it was over.

Terry mostly forgot about D'Schane Grey, but he did not cut his hair.

One Monday in January, Terry was at work at C3A when his console cut out abruptly, leaving him blinking in the fluorescent lights. Terry looked up to see d'Schane Grey sitting on the corner of his desk, finger on the disconnect switch.

Grey held up a narrow leather strap. "Let me see your neck."

Terry interposed a hand. "No!"

Around him, people were pausing in their work to stare.

Grey was smiling. Terry was starting to hate that smile. He didn't say, as Terry expected, "I could have you fired," or "I could destroy your credit rating with a wish."

"Are you good for your word, or aren't you?"

Terry bit his lip. "But . . ."

"Aren't you?" His blue eyes narrowed, hard and bright as diamonds.

"Yes."

Grey snapped the collar around Terry's neck. It was thin and soft, with cold metal along part of the inside surface and a D-ring set in the side.

"Come with me. Or do I need to leash you?"

It was only 2:30. Leaving work would not please Johnson, especially since Terry had three megs of notes to transcribe by tomorrow morning.

Terry stood and followed Grey from the office. Grey was the smaller of the two, Terry noticed with a start. They went first to the underground garage, to a nice new Pontiac parked in a reserved space.

"Get in the back. Do you have a preference for a radio station?"

"No," Terry said, and struggled into the seat harness. The upholstery was leather. Brushing his nails against it gave Terry chills.

Grey took the car out of Crystal City and onto 395. Once they had settled into the express lane, the highway's automatic navigator pulled them along gently at 110 miles per hour. Grey fiddled with the radio, then popped a chip into the player. Ten minutes later, they pulled off the highway into a far suburb of Virginia.

Terry glanced out the window. The streets were narrow and winding. Houses were set back on hills, surrounded by careful plantings and kept lawns, brown with winter. These were luxury homes built back in the 1980s on what once was farmland.

Grey pulled into the driveway of a comparatively small house. It was built of brick and had a fantastic glass-sided tower at one corner. Grey shut off the car.

"Last stop," he said.

Inside, the house was empty of people and sparsely furnished.

"No servants?" Terry asked. He walked through a doorway into a large living area.

"No. I just bought this place. A housekeeper comes in once a week when I'm not here. Want something to drink?"

"Just water."

Grey vanished into the kitchen and came back with two glasses of ice water; he handed one to Terry and sat down on a couch.

"Now."

Grey wasn't smiling. Terry swallowed, feeling his throat move against the collar.

"You hair is passable. See, I don't usually do men, though I was apprenticed to a male top two years ago. By the way, you can be sure anything I might want to do to you has been done to me at least twice over. I wanted to see if long hair would soften your face a little bit. I think it does."

Terry did not like the direction of this conversation.

"A couple of things about that collar you're wearing. It doesn't come off easily. It's leather, but with a mylar-and-steel core and a permanent snap closure. I figure if you want it off enough to take bolt cutters to it, then you can have it off."

"This is too far, d'Schane Grey. Tell me what you want."

Grey laughed. "You know what I want. And you know what else? There's a pickup chip inside of your collar. It's very sensitive. Needs no saline, just your sweat. And you're sweating quite a bit, aren't you, Terry? You can't fool me with your coy little protests. You put up a really good show of fighting the scan last summer. The whole time you were just itching for me to hit you harder. I would have done it, but the Authority wasn't paying me to get their employees off."

D'Schane Grey pointed to the ground in front of his feet. "On your knees."

In that instant Terry learned something Grey already knew. Terry knelt before one who was younger and smaller, but infinitely more sure of himself. Fingers tapped his chin.

"Look up. You have a pretty face, and I want to see it. That's better."

Terry looked up into the blue eyes, narrowed with concentration. A finger stroked Terry's cheek and circled the outside of his ear. Terry shivered. Grey set his hat aside and reached behind his own ear, checking for the lead that matched the one at Terry's throat.

Kiss me, Terry thought.

The corner of Grey's mouth twitched with amusement.

"I approve of your change in attitude. But I won't kiss you yet."

Grey hooked his finger in the top button of Terry's shirt.

"Nice arms. Nice upper body," he said, unbuttoning the rest. "What do you do besides sit in front of a console all day?"

"I swim, mostly. C3A has a pool."

Grey drew a line with his finger down the center of Terry's chest. The cold air tightened the flesh of his nipples. Grey took the shirt the rest of the way off and dropped it on the floor.

A hand supported the back of Terry's head as Grey leaned forward and brushed his lips against Terry's own. They held there for the longest moment. Grey kept his eyes closed when he kissed. His tongue gently pressed between Terry's lips and teeth and into his mouth. A hand stroked his back, trailing nails along his ribs. Grey tickled the roof of Terry's mouth and sucked on his upper lip, then broke the kiss.

"Let me see your back."

He turned Terry so he was draping his upper body across Grey's left thigh. Terry's mouth, empty, tingled. He licked his lips and circled the leg with his arms as Grey inspected the old scars.

"You've played rough. Daphne did this?"

"Yes."

Grey whistled. "Six months old and I can still see them." He tugged Terry's hair. "I will love you so much better than Daphne did. No matter how you cry, there will be no mercy."

Terry sighed and pressed his cheek against Grey's leg. Grey was reaching over. He hooked a finger through the ring on the collar, holding Terry pinned halfway over his lap. Something touched Terry's back.

He froze, trying to tell what it was from sense of touch. The hand on his collar kept him from looking. The touch vanished.

The first blow of the riding whip was louder than it hurt. Terry gasped. The muscles of his back tightened like bowstrings. Nothing happened for a moment, and Terry started to relax again. The second blow fell. Terry screamed.

Grey laughed, leaned over to kiss Terry's ear, and whispered, "You aren't as hurt as you are scared, you know that?"

The toe of Grey's other foot pressed between Terry's legs to the spot right behind his balls. Blows three and four fell abruptly. Pain and heat washed over Terry's skin.

Daphne used to whip until she got tired. Grey spaced it out more, letting Terry savor most of it, occasionally pushing him off balance with a flurry of blows that kept getting harder and harder as his resistance broke down. Terry wept and clawed at Grey's leg, twisting the flesh between his fingers. This was a mistake.

Grey peeled his fingers away and pulled him around by an arm. The whip bit Terry's chest, catching his nipple. Grey smacked Terry across the face twice, then concentrated on his chest and belly. The last blow fell upon Terry's crotch and the erection that pressed against his jeans. Terry's body snapped. He sobbed. Grey put down the whip.

Breathing hard, Grey forced his tongue into Terry's mouth again. The kiss was violent and sloppy. Grey was unbuttoning his jeans with one hand. With the other, he pushed Terry's head down to his crotch.

Grey's erect penis was much thicker than the handle of Daphne's whip. It was hot and tasted of salt and something sweeter. Grey gasped and swore as Terry went all the way down on it.

"I didn't think you could do this." He clutched at Terry's head. "Slower!"

Terry backed off and teased the head with his tongue, stroked the balls with his fingers. Grey took his hair and forced his head up and then back down. They both moved slightly, changing angles. Terry wrapped his arms around Grey's hips and sucked.

He sucked until Grey's back arched and he cried out and his hips bucked so hard that Terry almost choked. He swallowed. Grey relaxed one vertebra at a time, slowly sinking back down into the couch.

Terry reached for where he had left the glass of water and drank, savoring the cold in his throat. Ice clicked against the side of the glass. Grey took the water away, then shoved Terry down on the floor.

"Your turn," he said.

Grey pinned Terry's hands over his head and unfastened his pants. Terry lost himself in the sensation of the carpet on the rawness of his back until Grey's hand on his penis jolted his eyes open.

"Now don't move your arms," Grey said, "or I'll stop."

Terry's body twisted involuntarily as Grey stroked him. Grey tsked and took a swallow from the water glass. He bent over to suck on Terry's sore nipple, and his lips burned with ice. Grey licked his way down Terry's body, leaving a trail of cold water behind. It was so hard not to move. A hand clasped both of his, fingers intertwined, giving something to hold on to. Grey lay down next to him and touched him very softly, and then a little harder, until at last Terry came, crying into the mouth that kissed him.

Grey was shaking.

"I've never read anyone climaxing before. Ah. That was sweet."

They lay on the floor, silent, until the sun vanished from the window, leaving them in darkness. Grey stood up, flipped the light switch, and stretched.

"Well, I may as well show you the rest of the house. Like the bathroom. And I've got some food in the fridge. Are you hungry?"

An hour later, showered and dried, they were sitting on Grey's bed eating fried chicken. Terry felt the bruises on his back and chest when he moved, sharper than the sweet feeling of sexual satiety. He wanted to be held. Grey teased him with that comfort, stroking his hair until he sighed.

Grey was saying, "The pickup in your collar is keyed to the lead I'm wearing right now. It's short range, and I won't wear it often."

"So, Grey," Terry said, fingering his collar, "depending on Johnson's mood, you may have just gotten me fired."

"Was it worth it? Don't answer that. I'll have my pet lawyer draw you up a contract tomorrow, and you can join Grey Consulting Enterprises. By the way, my name is d'Schane. Use it."

"Don't do me any favors, d'Schane."

"This isn't a favor. I looked up your school records. The government isn't paying you half of what you're worth. And anyone I've fucked is entitled to call me by my first name."

Terry smiled. Daphne only got to work for data thieves in Mexico. They'd be on opposite sides of the business now. He knew how she thought. Perhaps their spoiled relationship would work to his advantage?

He wondered if d'Schane liked having tables turned on him, and how his lean, small body would feel pressed down on the bed, beneath Terry's weight.

D'Schane looked up sharply. The excitement and the fear in his eyes were clear to Terry, even without a wire to his mind.

"I'd like to see you try it, love. If you can checkmate me, well, then, you can have me."

MY PROFESSOR

Ivy Topiary

MY DEAR READER, understand that I scarcely know how I came to be here. I—young, lovely—have been cruelly transported from the wilds of my sylvan Northwest to this East Coast horror-school, a college made up of, God forbid, all girls.

I, so skilled at being all things to all people in secondary school: piano recitals, straight As, literary magazine, secret mistress to my hoodlum beaux, wild nights, things I cannot here recount. What irony to find myself here, at eighteen and one-half, amongst these rotting, moneyed virgins, and the only men available more rotting, moneyed virgins at the men's college nearby. What have I done to deserve this purgatory, this wanting, waiting?

To be fair, there is my roommate Sophie, a rich, patrician beauty from Connecticut, blue-eyed, innocent, just my age. Besides her loveliness, I felt she had little to recommend her until I witnessed her practicing her cello; she played with the most intriguing mixture of concentration and wild euphoria on her face as she sawed the bow back and forth. There was that, and there was the way she watched me covertly when I undressed.

I surprised her upon my return from the library one

night, as she was changing her clothes. It was raining an autumn downpour, and in I came, rivulets running down my face. Here was Sophie, feigning modesty, clutching her L.L. Bean flannel nightgown to her breasts.

"Sorry, Soph," I said, approaching her slowly. "I didn't mean to startle you," closer and closer now, and I licked my lips and kissed her fully, insinuating my tongue into her mouth to graze her orthodontically perfected teeth. I pulled her nightgown away and cupped her breast, rubbing the nipple against my wet rain slicker.

"I don't think we should be doing this," she whispered, pulling her mouth away, but arching her back to bring her body against mine.

"You don't think?" I breathed into her ear, kissing my way down her cheek, stopping to suck on her neck, and bending quickly to take her nipple into my mouth. Licking, sucking like a baby, I unzipped my raincoat and dropped it to the floor. I began unbuttoning my blouse one-handed.

I reluctantly let her go, but only to pull my blouse open and my black lace bra down. "You don't think?" I asked again, quietly, looking at her eyes, her body. Her breasts were full, mine smaller; but our nipples were spaced precisely the same distance apart, I noted as I circled the tips of mine against hers. She looked down and watched, breathing hard. "What *do* you think, Sophie?" I said, as her arms went around me.

"You're all wet," she said. And I was. I leaned back against her bureau as her hands slid down to my hips, lower still to my thighs, then back up under my plaid skirt. I made a resolution to stop wearing underwear as she cupped my ass through the black lace overlay.

My hand went down between us, between two flat,

flawless stomachs, to reach her blond nether hair. My index finger opened her pussy and found wet softness, then riding back up, fingered her clit. I rubbed myself, through the lace, with the back of my hand. "Do you think you'd like to take those off?" I asked as she felt my ass through the underwear, and obediently she slid them down, her hands trailing fire on my bare flesh. She bent her head, moaning, as I pushed another finger into her cunt, and began licking just the tip of my nipple. I watched her tongue flickering between her even, white teeth, my nipple getting hard, and I felt a spreading hot wetness of desire between my legs. I increased the pace of my moving hand, and she responded, sucking my tit with force, her hips rotating, her fingers finding my snatch, pushing recklessly inside me.

Sophie threw her head back and I beheld the look of strangely focused abandon, her eyes almost closed, the muscles in her neck straining. I wondered what music she was hearing. I held her around her waist, pressuring her clit the way I like to do my own, sawing my hand back and forth inside of her. She convulsed and bit her lip with one pearl tooth till it bled. She faltered in my arms and I trailed my hand up from her cunt to her mouth to wipe away the red drop; but she took my finger in, tasting herself, her blood.

After one still, singing moment, she slid down to her knees, spreading my legs and pulling up my skirt. Shyly she kissed my inner thigh, her eyes watching my face. I looked down at her, smiled, and she trailed her mouth across the fur. My knees went weak, and I leaned on the dresser as she licked and sucked and ate me. She traced my ass with her fingers and finally put one, two, then three up inside me, moving them gently, then fiercely, until my mind was gone and there was only me, burning bright, coming to the extinguishing, the measureless brief throbbing bliss of nothing.

So there is Sophie. We climb in bed with each other now and then, which is nice as the winter grows closer. We love each other like sisters, one of us turning around under the covers and fitting mouth to cunt, cunt to mouth, so we can come at the same time. Even so, it is never quite like the first time, and Sophie, well, as I say, I love her like a sister.

So, to the library to study. Ninety-nine percent of time spent "studying" is actually spent thinking about sex. I think, as I gaze at Manet's *Olympia* in my art history text—o! that cool fire, that forthright look of desire. I want to be her, a whore laid out for viewing, to view, full breasts, the object of lust. My hand finds its way inside my sweater, fingers squeeze and rub my nipple; I creep my other hand up under my skirt, pushing my underwear aside (it grows too cold here, I have found, to go without), pressing my fingers against my clit. I look around, finally; no one is near, stacks of books, an isolated desk: let the mewling maidens find me here, anyway, pleasured, who cares? I flip through the book with one hand, fondling myself, stopping at Michelangelo's *David*. Ah, that cock, beautiful inside me, alive, yes—*but what ugly hair!* a little voice in my head mocks, as I come, sighing. After a moment I turn, reluctantly, to the poems of Wordsworth. He's pretty dry, and maybe that will take my mind off fucking, I think; plus, the old bag who teaches Romantic Poetry is giving a quiz tomorrow. Hellfire and damnation.

*   *   *

But lo and behold, the next day the old bag is gone, dead of a heart attack. The entire class is horrified, devastated, and secretly pleased, none more than me as I look upon her replacement. Our new professor is virile, young, handsome. He is saying he regularly teaches upper-division classes, but in the event of this tragedy, here he is, to try to help us go on. *Help me go on,* I think, staring wide-eyed at him. He meets my gaze, briefly, looks for one instant unnerved, quickly looks away. My professor.

I watch him, his crotch, undress him with my eyes for fifty-five minutes; then at the end he says he has read over our Coleridge papers in an effort to get to know us (*Get to know me!* I think) and would like to see the following students during office hours this afternoon, *Me,* I think, *me,* and miraculously, my name is called, and I cannot believe it. "Did he call me?" I ask the girl next to me. Yes, she nods, and the look in her eye says, *You lucky bitch.*

I run to my room after the bell. I know just what to wear: white—virginal white—garter belt, white stockings, white cotton underwear (over, not under the garters), short plaid skirt, soft white button-up sweater (not buttoned up very far, and no bra, so my nipples will show through), and my reading glasses. Hair in a bun, red red lipstick. I grab a pen and whirl around: Sophie is sitting on her bed, reading, "Oh, hi Soph, gotta go," I say, and run out.

Outside the door to his office I breathe, pinch my nipples hard through my sweater, and, glancing up and down the hall, quickly reach up under my skirt and pull off my skivvies. Can only get in the way, I think, stuffing them in his mailbox that hangs by the door. I knock. "Come in," his voice answers.

I open the door, step in. "Well," he says, "Miss . . . " As I turn to shut the door I drop my pen, bending deep from the waist to pick it up. I know he can see the tops of my stockings, maybe more, I hope. I straighten up and turn around. "Pardon me," I say, looking at him sitting in his big leather chair, a tent already being pitched in his pants. I want to laugh. The walls are lined with books; his desk is massive; a radiator clanks under the window. Dusk is falling. He coughs. "Miss?"

"Forester," I say. "Miss Forester, but you may call me Emily."

"Please have a seat, Emily," he says, swallowing, and I sit, subtly hike my skirt up, and lean forward.

"Ah, Miss Forester," he says, shuffling papers, "your paper had a most, well, interesting, how shall we say, slant, hmm . . . " He flushes red, looking at it. "Very sophisticated, very . . . complex." He puts the paper down and stares at me. "I see in your file that you are from Portland, Oregon, and a freshman, and this paper is just, well, very engrossing, well written, and, eh, sophisticated, yes . . . " He is breaking a sweat. I spread my legs so he can see, darkly, my fur, my lips, which begin to burn at the thought.

"We are not completely bereft of culture, or of stimulation, out west, Professor," I reply. "What is the point you are trying to get across?" I ask, toying with the pen.

"Well, yes, I see . . . " he says. "Well, I suppose the point, er, the thrust, well, it is an interpretation of 'Kubla Khan' that is very well sexualized, yes, interestingly so . . . " he says. He leans back in his chair; sweat shows on his shirt in his armpits, and the bulge in his crotch has grown to interesting proportions.

"Well, Professor," I say, "what really could that 'deep

romantic chasm' with its 'cedarn cover' represent but the woman wailing for her demon-lover's deep, wet cunt?"

He stammers.

"Professor," I continue, "that mighty fountain exploding, the writer's desire, the sexual impulse, the milk of Paradise, it's all hot come out of a hard cock to me."

My professor chokes a bit. I look him straight in the eye and stand up. "Ah," I say, glancing at the wall, "Blake's illustrations of the Inferno; beautiful, aren't they?" I turn to them to give him a moment to compose himself. "And here is my favorite, Canto Five, the poor hellish lovers . . . her words are so poignant . . . " I hear him come up behind me.

He breathes in my ear, "' . . . and when we read of the longed-for smile that was kissed by so great a lover, he who never shall be parted from me, all trembling, kissed my mouth.'" My professor presses against me; I can feel him, the specific pressure against my lower back; I turn my head and he roughly kisses my mouth.

I whirl around and push him away. "Professor!" I say, shocked. He retreats, quickly, in disbelief, behind his desk. "I am so very sorry," he says, "I must have misunderstood . . . " His voice falters, but as he sits I can see the bulge in his pants is unaltered but for a tiny stain.

I follow him back behind his desk.

"You could at least quote the Italian. And don't you know, with the climate as it is in academia nowadays, that this type of so-called misunderstanding could ruin your career? Don't you know what could become of your reputation?" I say, coming around and leaning on his desk in front of him. I ease up my skirt and unbutton my sweater, pulling it down to reveal faultless shoulders, firm breasts.

I cannot quite make out his answer as he clamps his mouth on my nipple: "I don't care"? "I have tenure"? He pulls me down to sit astride his lap, and I reach out to tease his cock through his pants. It is rock hard, and he moans. I undo his belt, unzip his zipper, open his fly—aha! no underwear!—and run my finger down his shaft.

"Oh," he moans into my nipple, pushing his fingers into my wet, wet pussy, "'light of my life, fire of my—'"

"Quiet, Professor," I say, pulling myself further onto him, moving my cunt in a warm stain up his leg to the base of his cock, riding up and down the length of it, before sitting up on it, pushing myself down, gradually, taking it all in, slowing to tease him. He feels good, he feels good, and he is burying his face in my breasts, and moaning, and I ride him, and we come, together: o, the ascent to the heavenly, the descent into hell.

LUNCH

Mark Stuertz

DREW WROTE THE phone number at the top of a car wash receipt, because it was the only piece of paper we could find between the two of us. On the bottom he wrote "Popeye juice."

"Say this when they answer the phone," he said.

"I hate spinach," I said.

When I think of spinach I think of Ellen, a woman who picked me up from a bar and took me home. She wore black lacy stockings with cobras woven into the material, and each snake had red sequin eyes. We were walking down the street slowly, full of smoky lust, when we came upon this man squatting on the sidewalk, propped up against a newspaper box. He had a long, white beard that made me think of Abraham and Moses and Elijah and the other robed men who looked out at me in full, comic-book color from the three-hole-punched Sunday school lessons they gave me when I was a boy.

Ellen pulled a five out of her purse and flapped it near his lips. "Here's five dollars," she said. "Now I want you to take this and buy yourself a spinach salad with hot bacon dressing and a bottle of Chocks vitamins. O.K.?"

"I can do that, lady. Christ, I can do that," he said. I usually don't remember the ones from the bars. But the thing she did with the five and the spinach set her in my mind.

"You won't hate this," said Drew. He rubbed his lower lip with the side of his finger. "If you chew the leaves slowly, the taste will cling to the insides of your cheeks after you swallow. But it's not an aftertaste. It's still in there, moving around your mouth like a fish."

"What's this?" I pointed to the bottom of the receipt.

"You gotta say that or they won't serve it to you. You say you want a spinach salad and they'll look at you funny and bring you something with iceberg lettuce. Just say it." He smiled at me and shook his head. "And another thing. It's seventy-five bucks. Prepaid."

"What, do they sprinkle it with cocaine?"

Drew had a sixth sense for things, the odd things that invisibly float through everyday life like demons from a parallel universe. He would find them, collect them, and bring them to his friends like little offerings. "Would I bother with this unless it was one of life's great moments?"

"What kind of a moment can spinach make?" I asked.

The name of the place was the Dark Corner Café. I called, said the words on the bottom of the receipt, and read my credit card number over the phone twice because they thought I said nine instead of one. My reservation was for 11:30 A.M. They wouldn't give me anything later. Booked, they said.

The Dark Corner Café is in the middle of a narrow street, a link in a continuous row of brick buildings, all attached. The café is painted a dull green that makes the mortar between the bricks look like thick pesto. The door is a blazing 1950s lipstick red.

I was met by a tall, thin man in a red silk shirt. "One?" he asked. I looked around and saw one person in the whole place. He was sitting at a table next to the window dipping handfuls of french fries into a bowl of creamy soup.

"You should have my name," I said.

"Prepaid. This way." He took me to the back of the café and led me through a narrow hallway to a metal fire door. He forced it open and motioned for me to enter. "There's a drop," he said.

The first thing I saw was this wooden platform, like a stage, raised two feet above the floor. A thick, faded red curtain with swirling brown stains along the bottom hung from a beam above. Conduits dropped from the ceiling and stretched over the concrete walls like varicose veins.

The second thing I saw was a single round wooden table near the stage. Gashes and scratches scarred the surface, and stains filled the criss-crossing lines with crusty greens and dried browns. A chair was placed at the table, facing the stage.

Drew liked pornography. He made no bones about this. He was forward and up-front. "I want something with a girl sitting on the toilet, pissing and wiping herself slowly with a wad of Charmin," he would shout to the clerk in the video store. "White Charmin, I don't care about ethnic backgrounds, although Chinese would be nice. And the angle has to be good so the toilet paper doesn't block my view. Very important. What have you got? I don't want anything half-baked." That was how he went about it.

I don't mind pornography, not one bit. But I get jittery when people know that I don't mind. I don't want them to know when I quench this kind of thirst. I have it shipped in a brown Jiffy Pak to my P.O. box. That way, I avoid the stares from the people next to me at the checkout counter renting Disney films.

"Sit," said the thin man, brushing his left hand over his shirt pocket. There were no windows in the place, and the lights were dim. As I sat, I thought about the things I've fished out of those brown Jiffy Paks over the years. "I could bring your carafe of burgundy now, or we can wait until your lunch begins."

"Now is fine," I said. I didn't know that wine came with the spinach.

I can't picture Drew eating spinach. He doesn't eat raw greens of any kind except for the ones in those taco salads they serve in deep-fried shells instead of bowls. He eats the whole thing, the deep-fried bowl, the bed of lettuce they set it on, everything. Other than that, the only green thing I've seen him eat is the eggplant in eggplant parmesan, which he devours with taco-salad vigor.

The dim lights went out when the thin man brought my carafe. Spotlights from the back of the room turned the stage into a red, blue and yellow soup.

When I was fifteen, I made this same soup in my room by screwing colored bulbs into the light fixture in the ceiling. I burned jasmine incense and pumped Deep Purple through my stereo speakers. My dad came into my room with his fingers in his ears, sniffed the air and said, "What are you doing to your eyes?"

The thin man filled my glass. "The carafe is bottomless," he said.

"That's good." I picked up the glass and tilted it slightly, looking at the colored lights through the wine.

The curtain rose slowly with a dull hum pierced by the screams of old pulley bearings. The whole assembly jittered when the curtain came to a stop at the top.

There was this weird collection of things on the other side. A white reclining chair with a polished metal cylindrical base—like you might find in a dentist's office—was on the left. In the center, draped in a white pleated cloth, was a long table with two bowls on top: one stainless steel, one white. The back of the stage was pitch black.

The chef walked onto the stage like an actor, moving with nimble intent to the center. He wore a starched white shirt buttoned up to his throat and a small toque that settled on his head like a wad of sea foam. He touched the top of the toque lightly when he bowed.

Then he moved behind the table, reached below it and pulled out a bunch of spinach and a bottle of olive oil. He set these things on top of the table.

The chef looked out at me, squinting in the soup of light. I saw a smile come to his face in a slow, jerky motion, as if the corners of his mouth were being hoisted by hand-cranked pulleys. He went to work on the spinach, pinching off the stems, dropping the leaves into the stainless steel bowl. I swear I could hear wet, muffled slaps when they hit the metal.

"You know what sound I can't get out of my head for days after I've heard it?" asked Drew. "It's those wet, sticky smacks that batter the air when you're screwing a girl from behind. I don't even hear the cries she buries in the pillow. I blot those out. All I hear is the wet slap that becomes a swampy thud as it works through her flesh, shaking it all the way up to her chin. There's something in that sound—a dousing of kinetic lust, over and over again. I hear an auditorium filled with a roaring applause that's not coming from hands, but from those slaps. It pounds in my head for days afterwards."

The woman moved onto the stage in tiny, quiet steps. She was wearing a thin shimmering silk gown that clung to her like honey glaze. The hem landed just above her knees, and her legs and feet were bare and pale. Her dark hair was tied in a knot at the back of her head. She turned to face me, closed her eyes and bowed.

The dwarf wore nothing but a tiny white loin cloth. He was stocky and muscular and he carried a thick red cushion between his upper arm and ribs. He dropped it behind the woman's legs.

"Don't eat it fast," Drew had said. "The way they prepare it, it's slow and methodical, like a ritual. So don't rush anything. Smell each forkful and feel how it touches your mouth. Hold it there for a while. It'll feel like a warm bath."

The woman lifted her gown and hooked her thumbs into the waistband of her panties. She dragged them down her legs slowly—with her palms flat against her skin like she was covering it with lotion—to her feet. She stepped out of them.

The dwarf stepped back and the woman turned to face the back of the stage. He put his hands on her hips and pushed her gently to her knees on the cushion. She straightened her back and spread her knees apart.

It was the chef who had the long, red scarf. He pulled it slowly from a pocket in his trousers. He pinched a corner in his fingertips and let the rest drift from his pocket to the floor. The woman put her head back slightly as the chef walked in front of her, holding his arm out, twirling the scarf, letting it brush against her face.

"Eating is this thing we do without thinking," Drew said. "We chew and swallow, chew and swallow, feel our bellies fill up with who-knows-what. Auto-pilot. Then we stop. There's no memory of it. How many people can play back a taste in the same way they can run a song over and over in their head?"

"Great chefs," I said.

"But how many great chefs are there? Everyone eats."

I watched the woman's back, her muscles and bones stirring under the gown, while the scarf was dragged over one cheek and then the other. The dwarf dropped to his knees and reached under her legs to take hold of the other end of the scarf that lay twisted on the floor in a delicate heap.

The woman reached down and grasped the hem of her gown, gathering the material up to her waist. Her buttocks were smooth and full. Her vaginal lips puckered beneath her like the mouth of an aquarium fish. I watched that mouth and could see its moist, musky breath wisp against the blackness behind the stage.

The dwarf stepped back, clutching the scarf. He raised it until it touched the crease between her legs and, together, the dwarf and the chef worked the edge of the silk into her fish mouth. She sucked a quick, tiny breath into herself and let go of it slowly, letting her body settle into the contact.

"Please bear with us." The dwarf's voice buzzed with a gravelly rattle. "These things take time, and demand precision . . . Oh, God help us," he said, shuddering, "we're going to begin." And he pissed a stream down his bowed legs, spreading a pale yellow puddle around his tiny feet.

"I tasted spinach the first time from my mother's finger," Drew said. "It was there on her plate, next to a bloody-rare lamb chop, in a fluffy blob of buttery cream sauce. I begged her for a taste. 'You know there's spinach in that butter,' she said, plowing her finger through the yellow-green dab, scooping up a bit of it with the underside of her long nail. 'You know spinach. You spat it out the last time you two met. Do you still want a taste?' The rich creamed green hung from her finger in strands. She pushed it into my mouth and I sucked at her finger. She pulled it out and wiped my lips with the tip before pushing it against my tongue. 'Don't bite,' she said. That is how I fell in love with spinach."

They worked the scarf like a log saw under her pelvis, back and forth. Each sweep seemed longer and slower than the last, working greater lengths of the silken edge through the humid swamp between her legs.

The movement grabbed her like a fast-acting drug. I could hear the gain in her breath. She tightened her grip on the gathered gown around her waist and stretched it outward from her body. Tiny shocks shook her thighs, tugging at the surface of her skin. She rolled her head and swirled her hips to the rhythm of the pulls, breaking her breath with low hums and little cries. Arching her back, snapping her neck behind her, reaching for the ceiling with her chin, she struggled for balance. The edge of silk darkened as it was threaded through her moisture. My mouth watered like broken plumbing.

The chef closed his eyes and let his arm go limp, dropping his end of the scarf. The dwarf gathered it with his free hand and wrapped it around his wrist. He took the woman's hand and helped her from the cushion. She wavered. Her breath was rapid, heaving hisses.

She pushed the gown's straps from her shoulders and let it fall to the floor before stepping out of it. She stood there, smooth and pale, like a boiled bird. The dwarf took her hand again and helped her into the chair. He worked the foot pedal so that it reclined. Then he turned it so that the woman faced me.

She pressed the bottoms of her feet together and drew her legs up, pointing her knees outward on either side, exposing her inner thighs. Her vagina was hairless, swollen and polished with juice. I swallowed hard and felt the spit flow over my lips. Blood flushed through my arms and legs. I felt a shower of hot sparks battering me from the inside.

The chef carried the olive oil, the bowl of spinach, and the white bowl to a tray that swung out from the chair like a wing. He pulled the cork out of a bottle of oil and drizzled it over her body, pouring a shallow puddle on her belly. The dwarf moved next to her and dipped his fingers into the puddle, rubbing the oil into her skin.

I took a drink of wine. Cool shivers scurried through me. I was nervously thrilled. My heart thumped hollow in my chest. It was like the first time I saw stray strands of dark pubic hair coil out of a bikini crotch at the public pool. My clothes felt like they were miles from my body. My bones felt like loose springs. This whole thing was voodoo.

The chef reached into the stainless steel bowl and pulled out a spinach leaf and laid it on her thigh like it was a dab of dough. He did this again and again, one leaf at a time, until a row of leaves striped each thigh from her hips to her knees.

He licked his fingers and gently brushed them over her labia. My cock strained and oozed at the tip like a puncture wound. The force of her humid body came crashing into me, flooding me with the loss of my wits.

He lifted his fingers from her and they shined with her varnish in the stage lights. He put them to his lips and sucked, filling the air with the smacks of his roiling mouth. "It's fine," he said. "We're there."

The dwarf pinched a leaf from her thigh and dangled it in front of her like a piece of rich flesh. She took it from him, wrapped it around her index finger, and slid it through the olive oil on her belly. She stroked the outer folds of her labia, slowly working the leaf into her body.

She held it there, sighing, rolling her hips. Her breath opened up, heavy and deep. She pulled the leaf from her body and let it fall into the dwarf's palm. He turned his hand and let the leaf fall into the white bowl.

She did the same for the next leaf and the next until the rows were gone and her swelling lips, stained green, were dulled with her thickening sauce.

The chef spilled more oil over her body and the dwarf spread more leaves on her legs. She rolled them around her finger and wiped them over her oily skin. She worked each one into her body until it was thoroughly marinated. The folds between her legs swelled and separated; her hole widened with arousal, like a bulging, watery eye.

"More," said the chef.

The dwarf untied the scarf from his wrist. The woman raised her hips from the chair cushion. He threaded the scarf underneath her body—one hand behind her, the other in front—pulling it through her, working it into her thirsty flesh. He moved the silk slowly back and forth until her vagina drooled. He sniffed the damp scarf and tied it around his neck. The chef lined up more spinach leaves on her thighs. She pushed the leaves into herself. The bowl filled.

"Think about how hard it is to taste without swallowing," Drew said. "When you taste, you don't really taste, because what's on your mind is getting it into your body so that you can get more into your mouth.

"When I had my mother's finger in my mouth, I just wanted to taste. I don't remember swallowing the buttery spit. I think I just left it there in puddles off the edges of my tongue to wash against my cheeks. And my mother said, 'If there's anything spinach does, it's make your blood red. And if there's anything a man needs, it's the deepest, reddest blood.'"

It was the dwarf who took my table and lifted it onto the stage. He set it in front of the woman, who was still in the chair, relaxed and breathing deeply. He covered it with a clean, stiff white cloth, set the bowl in the center and put a fork next to it. The chef put two small wooden chairs around the table.

Then they bowed, smiled and walked slowly off the stage, leaving me with the woman. I looked down and saw that one table leg was in the puddle of dwarf piss.

"Come and sit," she said in a thirsty whisper. "It's served."

I stepped up onto the stage with my wineglass and took a seat at the table, my eye still fixed on the piss puddle. I hesitated before the white bowl and took a deep breath. The smell of beached kelp hovered in a fog of olive oil. The leaves were limp with dark green creases from the folding and rolling. My mouth felt twisted out of shape, like my taste buds were lined up in the wrong order. I thought of how red Popeye's blood must have been.

The woman got up from the chair, her body covered with glistening blotches of olive oil, and moved to the table, where she took the chair across from me. Her neck was long. Her breasts hung low from her chest and curved upward, the nipples pointing to a space somewhere over the top of my head. She put her hand on the table and pushed the fork in front of me. I took it.

"Taste," she said smiling, and folded her arms across her chest, leaning forward, gently grabbing my face with her eyes.

I picked up the fork and held it over the bowl, looking into the bed of wilted greens. She brushed her arms with her fingertips and tilted her face a little to the side. I lowered the fork into the bowl and pierced the leaves.

With my eyes closed, I brought the fork to my lips and pulled a shred of green into my mouth. The delicate spinach fabric broke apart and spread thin over my tongue like an oil film. I swallowed. She closed her eyes, rolled her neck and groaned. I heard her release a slow, heavy breath; heard the air pass through her long throat and spread out of her mouth, swirling just past her lips. Then she looked at me, first fixing her eyes on my mouth, then lifting them, trapping me. She worked my eyes hard with her stare, daring me to acquire the taste.

WHAT HE DID

Thomas Roche

JOHN LIKED GUYS; there was no question about that. But in guys, as in everything else, he had perverse, somewhat decadent tastes. And he had always liked to put people in situations that would test their boundaries, destroy their resistance, take away their feigned innocence. He liked to see people, particularly men, lose control.

That's why he did what he did.

Adrienne and I worked the same shift, at the comic shop, five to eleven, four days a week. So she and I were getting to know each other pretty well. Adrienne was a fag hag to begin with, that was for sure. You can always tell by the comics a girl reads. And she knew I was into boys. Maybe she just wanted something safe, a guy who wouldn't want to own her, or maybe just a guy who wouldn't bellyache about wearing a condom. She knew I was bi, not gay, but she also knew John and I were together.

That night John came in, he stayed for the half-hour after closing while Adrienne and I cleaned and locked up and counted out the drawer. The two of them talked like old friends, about Wonder Woman and Captain Marvel, sexual innuendoes periodically drifting into the conversation. I could tell he was baiting her. I was sure that he and Adrienne were flirting, which didn't quite add up.

"That chick has a crush on you, Paul," John told me as we walked home up Haight Street, through the mid-November chill.

I responded without responding. "Maybe she has a crush on you."

"Nah. She's a fag hag, but she's not a glutton for punishment or anything."

I considered Adrienne in my mind's eye. She had the look I so adored, the waiflike black-clad pose, the deathrocker bob dyed black, the studs in her lower lip and nostril and the eyeliner and tattoo of a bat on the back of her neck, the rings of silver around her ears from top to bottom. Her sexuality was just overt enough to snare my interest, not brazen enough to strike me as that of a poseur. Plus, she had great tits.

I like guys fine, and I had been monogamous with John for over a year now. I was totally into him, but of course I still looked. And John knew who got my attention.

"Maybe you should ask her out on a date," I said. "And find out. You could take her to the drive-in and fuck her in the back seat while you watch *I Was a Teenage Fag Hag* or something. I hear it's playing down in Serramonte."

"I don't have a car. Besides—you'd go mad with jealousy," he told me, leaning over and whispering into my ear. "You'd take a meat cleaver to the both of us. It'd be a tragic affair. In all the papers and everything."

I snorted in disgust. We let it drop, and that was that. But the matter didn't leave my mind, and hours later,

I was still thinking of her as John fucked me from be-hind on the futon, the two of us tangled in the black sandalwood-scented sheets, his hands on my waist, groaning his midnight pleasures in a cloud of incense and pot smoke. I thought about her as I came: I imagined her stretched on the bed next to us, my fingers inside her as our tongues intertwined.

And it was afterward, as John lit up our post-sex joint, that he whispered to me, his breath all fragrant clouds and intoxication, "You were thinking about her."

Adrienne was a hell of a flirt. John had been right: she had a crush on me. She wasn't necessarily interested in doing anything about it, though—not at first. At least, that was my reading. She just liked flirting with me, and of course, I responded in kind. Her body continued to impose itself on my fantasies, especially when John whispered to me about her. After a while, I stopped complaining when he did it, and just let the images flow into my mind: John wanting to watch me fuck her, to taste her cunt on my cock. John had never even fucked a chick, and had never expressed an interest in doing so. But it seemed that my desires fascinated him even more than his own.

I began noticing things about Adrienne, little details you only notice about someone when you have a crush on them. Like what sort of bra she wore, how she stood when she leaned up against the counter, where she bought her shoes. How the rings in her nipples would show through her babydoll dress when she moved her shoulders just right. The way she smelled when she got close enough to me. The feel of her ass brushing slightly against me as she squeezed past—maybe just a trifle

closer than she needed to be—in the close quarters behind the counter. The way she would blush afterward.

"You're fucking her, Paul. You're on top of her,
pounding into her pussy. You like that, pussy? I hear it
tastes real good to some guys. . . . You got her tits in
your hands. . . . " This while John was behind me, fucking his rubber-sheathed prick into my ass. His lips up
against my ear, his hand around my cock. Jerking it.
After I came in slick streams all over his gloved hand, he
told me that one day he was going to bring home a
sweet treat and share her with me on this very futon.

"All walk and no talk makes a gayboy dull as fuck."
I sighed good-naturedly. But I didn't take him seriously.

Adrienne became a more and more fascinating creature; the shape of her body seemed more exotic every
day: the curves of her hips like those of some elaborate
statue, the shape of her ass like harem pillows. . . . She
paid more and more attention to me. It had gone beyond a crush. For both of us.

I knew she'd been dumped a couple of months before,
and her boyfriend sounded like a real creep. She had
had a couple of things going with girls, but that was
at least a couple of years back. I knew she was on the
rebound, and rebounding hard, and that spelled bad
news to me. I didn't want to encourage her. It seemed
sort of unfair to do so. Maybe it was just a bit too easy
when I got that other job at the art store. The dollar
an hour more wasn't the draw so much as the fact
that I wouldn't have the perpetual sexual tension of
being close to Adrienne. She seemed sad at my leaving,
and we promised to keep in touch and have dinner
sometime.

I was glad to be away from the desire. It wasn't that I
felt guilty or anything—it was just a perpetual confusion, a desire I felt easier living without.

Still, I missed her. I missed the flirtation, the attention, the chance to look down her shirt when she leaned just so. I missed her sense of humor, her friendship. But I knew it couldn't work, us just being friends. That's what made Adrienne so hot to me. There was a sense of urgency, of a need that could not be denied.

John was disappointed. He kept talking to me about her, and the fantasy grew more intense because I wasn't seeing Adrienne every day. John would work my cock with his hand while he told me, in excruciating detail, how Adrienne was jerking me off. It always got him totally hot.

Maybe John's suspicions and fetishes were encouraged by the fact that I only read straight porn, and sometimes got off reading hetero sex manuals like *The Sensuous Woman* and *Total Sex*. I don't know—it was weird—the thought of all those married straight people fucking like weasels in their suburban houses always got me going. So I probably knew as much about women's bodies as I did about men's, though I'd only been to bed with two women in my entire life, and those were fleeting romances.

I was quite happy in my relationship with John. But when I read about tits and clits and cunnilingus and hetero anal sex, I found myself invariably thinking of Adrienne.

I missed her, all right. I missed the possibilities, and the knowledge that I just might lose control of myself in the stockroom and tear Adrienne's clothes off and fuck her wildly amid stacks of *Love and Rockets* and *Sandman* and *Hothead Paisan*. And she might do the same to me.

John missed her, too. He missed what Adrienne did to me, how she made me feel. That's why he did what he did, the fucker.

*   *   *

When I arrived at John's place, I smelled the telltale scent of sandalwood incense. I knew something was going on. John was well aware that the smell of sandalwood made me desperately aroused. But he was also aware that I associated sandalwood quite intimately with Adrienne, who used to wear sandalwood body oil. Perhaps that's why I wasn't surprised when I found her on the futon, sitting cross-legged and smoking a clove cigarette. John was across from her in the big easy chair, the one he'd found at the thrift store. His legs were crossed and he smiled at me devilishly.

"Paul . . . we were wondering where you got to. Adrienne came by. Well, actually, I invited her. . . . "

Adrienne smiled at me sheepishly. "Hi, Paul," she said. She looked a little nervous. She was as cute as ever. She had on a pair of black jeans and a tight lace top, outlining her breasts and making the rings in her nipples oh-so-slightly visible. I sat down at the end of the futon, and we hugged awkwardly. The scent of her body made me very nervous. Plus, I knew something was up, John hadn't just "invited" Adrienne.

There was awkward small talk, as I tried to figure out what was going on. Then John decided to dispense with the pleasantries.

He was behind her smoothly, quickly, without missing a beat. Adrienne seemed to melt into his arms as he coaxed her head back, and she presented her lips for him. He kissed her, deeply, parting her lips and teasing out her tongue. Adrienne let out a little moan of abandon as John's arms came around her and one hand rested absently on her belly just below her breast.

John glanced up at me, but only for a second. I noticed a smirk as he went back to kissing Adrienne.

John had never kissed a girl before in his life. But he
seemed to be doing okay. I felt a momentary wave of
anger as I realized that he was doing this for my benefit.
Then, suddenly, there was nothing. I was freed from my
responsibility to fight off my desire for Adrienne. John
was giving her to me. She was the most succulent of
gifts, the willing one.

I moved closer to her as she and John kissed. Tentatively, I leaned forward, feeling the pressure of her body
against mine.

John released Adrienne, her lips slick with his spittle.
She turned to me, her eyes sparkling and terrified, her
face pale and ashen. Her lipstick was smeared. She took
my hand in hers and begged me with her eyes to kiss her.

As I did, I tasted her lipstick and felt the stud in the
center of her lower lip. The lipstick struck me as much
stranger than the piercing. It was the first time I'd tasted
lipstick in years. Adrienne's whimper was faint, distant,
as I descended upon her. John's hand closed around her
breast, and his tongue explored her left ear while I
kissed her. Her smell overwhelmed me: sandalwood and
roses. Her hand trailed invitingly up my throat, then her
fingertips cupped my face. John reached out and took
my wrist, holding me insistently. He placed my hand underneath Adrienne's shirt, and her eyes opened to me as
I felt her nipple harden. I slipped my other hand into her
hair, stroking her cheek with my thumb. John leaned
over Adrienne's shoulder and began to kiss me, his hot
tongue sliding deep into my mouth. Adrienne seemed
buried in ecstasy, snuggling deep between the two of us
and arching her back to press her breasts more fully into
my grasp. I stroked the slick metal rings, fascinated by
the way they felt. I had a boyfriend once who had rings

in his nipples, but they felt nothing like this. The im-
plied sense of bondage or submission was overwhelming. Then again, maybe it was the way that Adrienne
squirmed underneath us. John nipped at my lower lip,
biting gently, his breath coming sweet and hot as he
nuzzled closer and placed his lips against my ear. "She's
yours," he whispered, telling me what I wanted to hear.
John could enjoy our tryst, could be part of it. I would
even make sure he came—and that, John must have
known. But this fuck was for me, his gift to his lover. He
had brought her to me for the pleasure of watching me
have her.

The sandalwood incense had burned down; the three
of us went into the bedroom.

John and I began by undressing Adrienne. First came
her lace shirt, very goth, peeled away to reveal a matching bra. She had larger breasts than I had expected. The
bra opened in front. The rings in her nipples were thick
and stainless steel. I bent forward and took one in my
mouth as John removed Adrienne's shoes and socks.
The two of us helped her struggle out of her black jeans.
She didn't wear underpants, which I found somehow
fascinating. She stretched nude amid the tangled sheets
of the futon, her face buried in the sweat-scented fabric.
John came up behind her, his shirt gone, his arms finding their way around Adrienne's waist as I played with
her breasts. She breathed deep, as if the fragrance of
two male lovers was better than anything.

Naked between us, Adrienne watched wide-eyed as
John and I began to kiss again. As I ran my hand over
John's bare chest, Adrienne's breathing shortened; her
face grew bright red. She squirmed, unable to contain

herself. But she wasn't asking for attention. She wanted to watch us.

That excited me more, and so I relinquished my hold on John's lips and slipped my tongue into Adrienne's mouth. She put her arms around me and sank into my grasp as I kissed her, deep, toying with her tongue. I was fascinated by the feeling of that piercing against my mouth. Fascinated, too, by the feel of Adrienne's naked body between John's and my clothed bodies, rubbing against us, her bare thigh curving over my waist and pulling me closer, harder against her, her breasts pressed tight to my chest. She slid her hands under my shirt and ran them up my back, John had slid his hand between her ass cheeks and was touching her cunt. I guess she liked that. John looked down at her body, watching in amazement, exploring the ways his touch made her feel.

John looked up at me then, his eyes sparkling. He could tell I was enjoying myself, and that was enough for him. He bent forward and offered me a tender kiss.

His tongue tasted of Adrienne's lipstick. My hand, resting gently against Adrienne's hips, slid to meet his wrist. I felt the juices running along his fingers, and joined them. The two of us began to feel her up, toying with her lips, tormenting her clit. As we did, we continued kissing, and I felt Adrienne unfasten my belt.

Her hands circled my prick as John and I shared her sex. The curve of her thigh was so different from John's. Adrienne ran her black-nailed fingers up and down the length of my cock, rubbing her thumb on the underside of the head. John slipped his fingers out of Adrienne and lifted them to my face. He stared into my eyes as I licked his fingertips one by one, then slipped them into my mouth, tasting her sex. Adrienne leaned forward to touch my cock with her lips.

She licked up the shaft, and I moaned softly. John looked at me hungrily, and I knew what he wanted me to do. He wanted to see it, wanted to know the texture and the feel of having it done in his presence, but John wasn't going to do it. I began to struggle out of my pants, easing Adrienne back before she could take my cockhead in her mouth.

Adrienne slid further back onto the futon, relaxing into John's arms. He had quickly gotten his pants off, and now the two of them were naked against each other. His cock pressed up against her ass. Adrienne turned her head and the two of them began to kiss again, John's hand lazing gently over her breasts, playing with her nipple-rings. Now the three of us were naked. I lowered myself to Adrienne's belly, kissing her soft flesh and toying with her navel ring. Adrienne's body went taut against John's, her ass snuggling against him as I parted her thighs. Memories flooded back to me as I tasted her cunt. I licked slowly into the silky wetness, breathing her fragrance. I flickered my tongue across her lips and made my way to her clit. I closed my lips very gently around it and began to suckle. Adrienne choked, her mouth filled with John's tongue. I began to feed on her cunt, drinking the taste and smell of it, swallowing hungrily. I curved my hand under her ass and began playing with her asshole, almost before I realized what I was doing. Adrienne's body stiffened again, but then she relaxed as she gave herself over to the sensations. So I didn't stop. I wanted to explore the feel of a woman's asshole as opposed to a man's. John must have liked that; he could feel my hand at work, and between deep kisses with Adrienne, he looked down at me and smiled approvingly.

John reached out to the nightstand and handed me a rubber glove. Obediently, I put it on.

John next held out the bottle of lubricant, which he poured into my palm, I worked it over, getting my gloved hand slick with it. Then I slid one finger into Adrienne's cunt.

She whimpered approvingly, reaching behind herself to take John's cock in her hand. John slid out from beneath her, rolled an unlubricated condom over his prick and turned on his side so that Adrienne could take him into her mouth. She lay on her back, head turned to the side and propped up on a pillow, as John eased his hips back and forth, sliding his cock between her parted lips. Her hands tangled in the rumpled sheets. Adrienne's ass lifted off the futon, pressing her cunt hard against my hand. I gave her two fingers, moving them in and out slowly, and from the rhythmic fucking motions she made with her hips, she wanted more. I got three in, which was the most I'd ever shoved up John's ass. Her cunt felt tight, but somehow secure, inviting, hungry.

Guided by my memories of *The Joy of (Hetero) Sex,* I started pressing against Adrienne's clit with my thumb. Her hips began to rock faster. She was jerking John off while she sucked him, her lips closed tightly around the head of his cock. John was watching me as Adrienne went down on him. He looked like he was about ready to do it in her mouth. I had no idea the sight of me finger-fucking a woman would get him so hot. Adrienne was really into it, her whole body moving with the two of us. I had no way of knowing what I was really doing to her, but I could tell from the spasms and contractions of her cunt that she was coming. But she didn't lose her grip on John's cock for a moment.

When her hips slowed down, I was struck by a sensuous and perverse urge. I eased my hands out of her cunt, reaching awkwardly to get more lube from the nightstand. John knew what I was doing. He grabbed the lube and poured it for me as I held out my rubber-gloved hand.

Adrienne stiffened again as I parted her ass-cheeks and touched her tight hole. I could sort of guess from the way she moved that she'd never really been touched much back there. That was what turned me on. I'd spent so much of my adult life getting fucked in the ass that I couldn't let her go without, though I guessed it wouldn't feel the same for a woman as it did for a man. She continued sucking John's cock, making him sway and moan as he crouched over her. Adrienne once again relaxed into the sensations as I worked the lube into her crack and felt the gentle give of her asshole. I slowly pressed one finger in, being as tender as possible, imagining that I was with a virgin guy. Adrienne sucked her breath in sharply as the finger slipped into her. She seemed uncomfortable for a second, and then it was all right.

"Oh, fuck yeah," breathed John, watching me intently.

I went very slowly. By the time I had two fingers inside her ass, Adrienne was moaning and John was ready to come. He did so with a groan and a forward slump against Adrienne's body as I managed to squeeze a third finger into her ass. Adrienne writhed underneath him, her hand thrust up between his legs and playing with his ass, middle finger stroking the outside of his asshole, up and down in quick strokes. I knew from experience what she was feeling. The pulse of John's cock as it spurted his come into the condom. The warm feeling as the tip of the condom filled. The squeeze of his buns as the spasms went through him. The rush of terror at the warmth in her mouth and the feeling: what if the condom breaks. Then the wave of momentary regret, usually just for a half-second, and then, the delicious sensation as the thought flows through you, *So the fuck what* . . .

I eased my fingers out of Adrienne's ass, knowing she

was ready for something else. I managed to get the glove off and toss it into the garbage without splattering anyone. Adrienne looked spent, but I knew there was at least one indulgence she hadn't yet been granted.

She bent forward as John, panting and flushed, handed her a Trojan red unlubed. John reached out and took my shoulders, guiding me back onto the bed. I stretched out as Adrienne got the condom over the head of my prick and started licking down the shaft. She paused over my balls, licking them hungrily, taking each one into her mouth. John joined her, putting his mouth over the head of my cock and pushing the condom down. Then she and John began to kiss, sharing my prick. For a while they worked bottom to top, John at the balls while Adrienne swallowed me, then vice versa, then back again. Finally, John eased his body up against mine and started kissing me while I moaned and writhed. He stroked my chest and face, nibbling on my lips and sucking at my tongue as he squeezed and kneaded my nipples. All the while, Adrienne had her way with my cock.

She had swallowed me again, her fingers curved around the base of my cock. She then rubbed the latex over her face, smearing her cheeks with her saliva while she looked up at me. She stroked the cock between her tits, something I really didn't expect a chick to do anywhere outside a porn movie. But I had to admit it was pretty hot. Then she went back to sucking my cock. I could feel the ridge of the stud in her lower lip, pressing against the condom, smooth but somehow threatening, exciting.

She slipped her hand between my legs, sliding the fingers under my ass cheeks. I felt her finger going home, stroking my asshole, bringing on my climax. Adrienne knew how to make me come. I wondered if John had had a talk with her.

When I did come, it was like a lifelong need suddenly overwhelmed in an explosion of brilliance. Adrienne's mouth was hot around my cock as she worked my asshole and milked my prick.

Adrienne kept her lips closed on the softening knob of my cockhead for a long time. Tiny spasms went through me as she suckled on my soft cock. Every movement of her lips and tongue made my body twitch in agony / ecstasy. It was too much stimulation, but somehow I liked it. And Adrienne was enjoying herself pushing my limits.

After a while, she stopped sucking me, slipped the condom off, and tossed it into the trash.

John slipped away from me, running his hands through Adrienne's hair as the three of us curled up into a complicated ball. I faded in and out of consciousness, losing myself in the warmth of the two bodies surrounding me.

I slept deep and hard, exhausted. I dreamed hard, too, hot and deep like it was reality, the way you dream when you're horny as fuck. But I found myself awake, in the middle of the night, not sure at what point I'd dreamed of myself fucking Adrienne and at what point I'd actually done it. Not sure if the taste of her cunt and her asshole, the smell of my come as I smeared it over her body, was real or imagined. Adrienne's body was pressed against mine; every inch of our naked flesh seemed to touch. I was in a dazed stupor, hardly aware of what I was doing. Adrienne's legs were spread around my belly and she was rubbing herself hard against me while she kissed me violently.

I could hardly breathe, the excitement was so overwhelming. I had completely forgotten, for a moment, that Paul existed. I felt no guilt, no danger. Adrienne's body felt so good against mine, it never occurred to me to stop for a moment. Suddenly Adrienne, who must have been more awake than I was, got a condom open and over my cock. Then her thighs were spread around me, and she was sitting up over my body as she rubbed the head of my prick between her cunt lips. She worked the head into the notch of her cunt and sank down on me, her breath coming short. Her cunt felt tight, as if she hadn't been fucked for a while. Adrienne pressed her hips down, pushing my cock into her as deep as it would go so the head ground against her cervix. She bent down and began to kiss me, moaning softly. She started fucking her hips back and forth. I choked on her tongue and on the smell of her hair and body. My cock seemed alive inside her. She pulled on me hard, rolling me over on top of her—over the edge of the futon. The two of us fell the six inches from the futon to the floor and I came down hard on top of her, pushing my cock inside her, fucking her slow and deep. She dug her teeth into my throat, holding on to my ass. She started playing with my asshole as I fucked her. The sensations joined somewhere deep in my body, and it was almost like being fucked by her. I kept fucking her, holding back my orgasm, feeling Adrienne keep the muscles of her cunt tight around my shaft, milking my prick. I rested one hand on her breast, squeezing gently, teasing her nipple with my thumb.

"I'm going to come," she whispered, nuzzling my ear. "Don't come yet. Please don't come yet. Keep fucking me."

I held back, feeding her long, slow, hard strokes into her cunt, keeping the rhythm. Adrienne's thighs closed tighter around me with each thrust as she got closer and closer. She whispered again and again, "Please keep fucking me . . . keep fucking me . . . " and so on, letting me know that she was getting there slowly. Just knowing that she was about to come while I fucked her was enough to keep me working, pumping my hips up and down on Adrienne's supple, spread body, begging her with my cock to cream all over me.

Then she came, a silent exhalation—no moan, no scream, just a long, low breath and a spasm of her cunt on my prick. I started fucking her faster, trying to bring on my own orgasm. Adrienne, satisfied with her climax but wanting mine, started stroking my crack, feeling for my asshole, working me into a frenzy. I finally was able to let myself go, and I came inside her, kissing her hard.

I reached down, holding the filled condom as I pulled out of her cunt. It had been so different than fucking a guy's ass.

Adrienne and I squirmed back onto the futon. I was still half asleep. I realized in my stupor that John was lying there, awake, eyes wide. He had been watching us the whole time.

Adrienne got out of bed to go to the bathroom. John leaned over and started kissing me—deep, hard, possessive thrusts of his tongue as his hand drifted over my soft cock. He rubbed me down around the base, where my pubic hair was damp and matted with the juices of Adrienne's cunt. Then John rolled over. With his back to us, Adrienne and I slept entwined like straight people. But as he had turned, I had seen that there was a smirk on his face.

*   *   *

The three of us curled up and slept the rest of the night. I felt totally happy. When the sun broke through the sky, Adrienne was gone. She'd let herself out.

John and I fucked long and hard that Saturday morning, him sucking my cock while he played with my ass. As he did me, I smelled her on the sheets, a feminine scent mixed with ours; but strangely, her memory didn't overwhelm me the way it had. I was content to be with just John.

John spread my ass cheeks, entering me from behind and fucking me for as long as either of us could stand it before tossing the condom and letting himself go all over my back. He licked up his own come, smearing it into my smooth skin and whispering to me that he loved it when I played submissive. Which was par for the course.

Adrienne and I talked a few times on the phone over the next week. We were going to have lunch together, and soon. Eventually I asked her if she'd had fun that night.

"Of course," she told me, her voice dropping to a whisper. "Having sex with two guys—two queer guys. It was everything I'd ever wanted in the whole world."

I froze, unable to ask her the question that begged to be asked—whether she'd like to come back.

We sort of lost touch, calling each other every few weeks but never managing to get together. I figured she was afraid. I was, too.

John didn't mention her much, but one night he whispered to me, jokingly, that I didn't give head as well as Adrienne. I didn't pursue it, and I was really hurt. Just a little lost.

That was the way it went for a while. For many weeks.

The other day, Adrienne and I ran into each other on the street. We went and had coffee. She was as gorgeous as ever. She kept leaning toward me, her delicious smell drifting into my mind as I watched her, and a couple of times I really thought she was going to kiss me. But she didn't. We promised each other we would get together sometime soon, and as we parted, we hugged longer than we were supposed to. I had a hard-on on the bus later, thinking about Adrienne. It was good to see her. It was really fucking good to see her.

I felt a strange melancholy later, as I thought about what John and Adrienne and I had done that night. John and I had never really talked about it that much. I knew that John had enjoyed it as much as I had, maybe more. I was sure that blowjob he got from Adrienne wasn't exactly just a fringe benefit. It's taken me months after the actual event to understand it, but I knew that in bringing her home, he'd acknowledged an intense attraction for her as well an intense attraction for me. But even if what got him hot about Adrienne was what she, and her female body, did to me, by the very nature of the situation, it did something to him. That was why he did what he did, the fucker. And now every once in a while, I catch him slipping. He's not the faggot he's always pretended to be, though he still fucks me better than anyone. His brain and his balls are more complicated than anyone might have suspected. I'm only now starting to figure the fucker out, and he keeps throwing me curveballs. I even walked in on him reading my copy of *The Sensuous Woman* once, when he thought I was asleep in the other room. He had a hard-on.

SHE GETS HER ASS FUCKED GOOD

Rose White and Eric Albert

WHEN SHE WAKES up, he's in her ass again.

"Isn't this your second time tonight?"

"I'm not the only man who's taken another turn."

That accounts for the ache there, for the raw, tender, exhilaratingly sensitive feeling in her ass. It's so relaxed, his cock slides in and out easily, just like all the other cocks did. Her ass has been used for hours tonight, and she's loved it. Waking up, she pushes back against him, really grinds her ass into his crotch, makes sure his cock is up her as far as it can go. She's certainly sore, but she still loves feeling his hard cock in her, loves feeling it get harder while he thrusts, loves feeling his crotch hit her ass, and hit her again, his balls slapping against her gently even though the fucking is hard.

She's up on her hands and knees now, her ass tilted up to get the best of his cock, to get the most of it up her ass. She puts a hand between her legs and starts to play with her pussy. She fingers her clit and he moans, he

78

tells her how tight that makes her ass. She puts a finger in her cunt and feels his cock through the wall of her cunt. She presses against it and makes him moan again. She's getting really worked up and she loves to come with a cock up her. She loves feeling her ass contract around a hard cock. Just like all the other times tonight.

She can't count anymore how many times she's come, come just like this, with a man behind her, with his cock up her. She can't count anymore how many men. She's completely lost track, lying there on the bed, with the blindfold on. Sometimes she knows them, knows them by how they touch her, how they fuck, how they moan. When they're quiet, though, when they don't make noise and they don't touch her, she doesn't know them, she just knows their cocks. For long stretches tonight, that is all she has known.

She starts to get serious about coming. He's still thrusting, and that makes it easier for her. She fucks back against him as she fingers herself. First she just plays with her clit, touching and teasing it, feeling it rise. Then she starts in on it, pressing against it hard, rubbing it with her fingertips. She feels the warmth start to spread, so not just her clit, but her whole cunt feels hot and wet and ready.

"Put it in my pussy."

He pauses, then begins to move in her ass again.

"Why?"

"I need it there."

He fucks her some more, sliding in smooth and fast and banging her, hard, each time his cock hits bottom, taking her breath away, keeping her from doing anything but moaning. Finally he slows down.

"Why?"

"Because it's hard. Because it's dirty."

"You sure?"

"Yes. Yes, I'm sure. Fuck my pussy."

He pulls completely out of her and she feels his cock hard and straining in the cool night air behind her cunt.

"You sure?"

"Yes, yes, yes."

He slams back into her ass; there's no resistance as the head of his cock enters her, she's instantly full with him.

"Your asshole's so loose, might as well be your cunt."

"Please."

"Why?"

"I want your cock up my cunt. I want to feel your shitty prick filling my pussy. I want you to fuck my cunt then my ass then my cunt then my ass so I can't tell what you're fucking any more."

"You say that to all the guys."

She gasps.

"That right?"

She's shaking. His prick moves in her tender ass.

"You put your butt up in the air and wait and anyone comes along can stick his thing in your holes, that right?"

". . . that's right." She's whispering.

"Asshole, cunt, you don't care, long as someone's fucking you."

"Yes."

"Tell me."

"Anyone. Anyone can stick it in."

"Three guys, one after the other."

"Yes."

"Ten guys."

"Oh. Yes." Her clit jumps. She stops rubbing, starts tapping lightly, holding the orgasm back.

"Tell me."

"Ten hard pricks sound good to me. Ten guys using me."

He jerks out of her. She moans. He slaps her ass with his prick; she feels the sticky mark he leaves.

"Put it in my pussy. Please."

"Suck me clean first."

She opens her mouth without a thought. Behind the blindfold she sees herself: crouching, ass up, nipples hard, mouth open, everything open. *Bitch in heat*, she thinks.

He slips back up her ass.

"You'll do anything to get me in your cunt, won't you."

"Yes."

"Say it."

"I'll do anything you want. Uhh." He's rammed her. He pulls back out.

"Tell me."

"I'll take your prick down my throat."

"You do that anyway."

"You can hit me. Hard as you want."

"Don't feel like hitting you."

"Anything. You tell me what."

"You going to piss all over this bed?"

"Jesus." She yanks her hand off her clit, too close to coming. "Put it in. I'll soak your cock. I'll soak the sheets."

"Anything you won't do to get me in your pussy?"

"No."

"It make you hot, the idea of my dirty cock sliding into your sweet cunt?"

"Fuck, yes. You know I'm fucking burning up."

"Good. 'Cause I'm not going to do it."

And he's in her asshole again, fucking the shit out of

her, forcing her to the edge of coming. She gasps, she starts touching her clit again, she's losing it.

He's moving in her, light and quick, working her ass so sweetly she wants to scream. She's going to come. She stays there a while, riding the knowledge, her clit full and her cunt dripping and her ass on fire. It's so dark with the blindfold, and all she can think about is how good it will be when she comes, how good it will feel, how it doesn't matter about her ass being sore, how nothing at all matters but this come.

Suddenly, he reaches forward and grabs her breasts. He pinches the nipples, rubs them hard between his fingers, and that's it, that starts her coming. She's touching herself and he's fucking her and she's fucking back, rocking on his cock and he's pinching her. She's coming and it's the hardest she's come all night. She comes hard because he's the best fuck, he knows what she likes best and he gives it to her. She keeps coming and he's yelling at her. He stops pinching her and he's slapping her ass, yelling, "You can come harder than that, I know you can!"

"Well then fuck, you just keep fucking me, fuck me harder, fuck me, fuck me, fuck me!"

He stops slapping her, he stops touching her, he's kneeling straight up, connected only by his cock, fucking her ass as hard as he can, as hard as she's ever been fucked, as hard as any man can fuck. She's yelling. She's coming so hard she thinks she'll pass out. She knows it feels good to him, she knows he loves to fuck hard, and that turns her on even more. She feels him slow down a little. She feels his fucking get steadier and she knows this is it. She loves feeling him come, loves feeling his come shoot up her ass, his cock pulsing and his body shaking. He thrusts, and he thrusts, and when he thrusts again he moans just a little and he hesitates and then he buries himself in her and she feels him coming in her ass and she screams, she's so happy. He keeps fucking her, keeps coming for a little while and then he slows down. He fucks her a little more. He stops.

They collapse on the bed together, he covers her with his body pressed against her length. They roll onto their sides, spoon to spoon. Time disappears.

She takes off the blindfold, lets the world explode in the sudden brilliance of the bedroom light. Behind her, he pulls out, wincing from the long night's loving. Stars dance in her eyes as she reaches across the bed and twists the switch. Darkness covers them, they rest in peace, they fall asleep, his cock against her ass, where it belongs.

QUEER PUNK

Bob Vickery

I'M STILL HALF asleep, staring up at the ceiling and wondering whether or not I should get up. Part of me just wants to roll over and catch a few more z's, but I don't think my body can take the lumps in the couch anymore (Darlene told me she had found the couch in front of some apartment building a couple of blocks away during a trash pickup day). I can hear Darlene and her dickhead boyfriend, Buck, in the bedroom; it sounds like they're having a fight. I guess that's better than the times when I have to listen to them fuck, hearing Buck groan like he's got a bad case of the trots. I can't make out most of what they're saying, but every now and then I hear my name. Ol' Buck is probably ragging on Darlene again about how much longer her deadbeat little brother is going to be hangin' around. If it weren't for me, I don't think they'd have anything to talk about.

The bedroom door opens and Buck walks in, wearing nothing but his jockeys. He glances at me once, giving me the evil eye as he makes his way to the kitchen. I give him my best *Fuck you, too* look. A few seconds later he's back with a carton of orange juice in his hand. He takes a swig from it. "So, Jamie," he says. "How's the job hunt going?"

I shrug. "No luck yet, Buck," I say. I catch myself checking out his body again. It really pisses me off when I do that. Buck works out regularly with his weight set, and his body is tight and cut, but he's such an asshole. I'd cut off my dick before I had anything to do with him. Still, I can't help copping a look at him every now and then.

Buck takes another gulp of orange juice. "You know, they're looking for a busboy over at that Italian restaurant on Haight."

I turn my head and stare at the ceiling again. "Thanks. I'll check it out." *When monkeys fly out my ass,* I think.

I can feel Buck's eyes on me. "Another thing, Jamie," he says. "I don't want you using my weight set anymore. You never put the weights back right."

I ignore him, and he goes back into the bedroom. A little later he comes back out again, dressed for work (he runs a forklift at some K Mart in Daly City). We don't look at each other, and when he leaves he slams the front door. What a douchebag.

A few minutes later, Darlene walks in, wearing a bathrobe. "Good morning, Jamie," she says.

"Hi," I grunt.

Darlene scratches her head and yawns. "You want some breakfast?"

I shake my head. "Nah. Maybe a cup of coffee."

Sitting at the kitchen table with her, I can see that Darlene is trying to work herself up to say something. I decide to make it easy for her. "I *am* going to look for work today, Darlene," I say.

She looks apologetic. "I'm sorry about Buck."

I laugh. "So am I." I shake a cigarette out of the pack and light it. "What do you see in him, Darlene? He's such a loser."

"Yeah." Darlene snorts. "Unlike the parade of winners you've called boyfriends." She bums a cigarette from me and lights it, even though I know she's trying to quit. She breathes out a cloud of smoke. "Listen, Jamie," she says. "I got to go to work soon. How about you doing the laundry? Buck's been grousing about running out of clean shirts, and I just don't have time to do it myself today." I make a face, and Darlene's eyes shoot daggers at me. "Don't give me a hard time about this, Jamie," she says in a pissed tone of voice. "I've already had to deal with Buck's bullshit this morning, and I don't want any attitude from you."

I don't say anything. "Okay, fine," Darlene snaps. "I'll do the goddamn laundry myself when I get home from work today."

I push my chair out and get up. "Oh, chill out, Darlene. I'll do the fuckin' laundry."

Darlene still looks pissed; I guess I didn't agree *nicely* enough. She gets up and piles the dishes in the sink. When she leaves, the good-bye she throws over her shoulder at me is like a fuckin' icicle.

As soon as she's gone, I go to the bathroom and work out with Buck's weight set. I check myself out in the mirror as I do my curls. I look fuckin' *good*, my biceps pumped up nicely, my pecs hard and defined. I put the dumbbells down and pose, flexing my arms, checking out my definition. Hot stuff. I drop my shorts and stare at my reflection. My dick flops against my thigh, half hard, but under my gaze it stirs and stiffens, the head flaring out. I fuckin' love my cock, the *meatiness* of it, its redness and thickness, how the veins snake up the shaft. I wrap my hand around it and begin stroking, first slow 'n' easy, then picking up the tempo till my balls are a bouncing blur. I pull my dick down and let it slap against my belly, and then shake it at my reflection. "You want to suck on it?" I croon at the hot naked stud looking back at me. "You want me to fuck your face, ram this dick down your throat?" A sexy punk with too much attitude stares back, sneering, shaking *his* dick at me as well. I walk up to the mirror and start humping my reflection, my body pressed tight to the glass, my hands grabbing the corners of the closet door. The mirror feels smooth and cool on my skin as I thrust my cock up and down against it. It doesn't take long before I'm ready to shoot. Groaning, I squirt my load on the mirror and watch as it drips down over my reflection. I wipe my hand across the splattered jizz and lick my fingers clean. Then I clean off the rest of the load with my jockeys and get dressed.

I gather all the dirty laundry and take it to the laundromat just down the block. The place is empty, and as the clothes are washing, I sit out on the front step, soaking up rays and smoking the last cigarette in my pack. I think about my living situation. I gotta line up some kind of gig, get some money so I can get my own place. I've been in San Francisco about three weeks now, and it's pretty clear that I've just about milked dry the setup I got going with Darlene.

When the laundry's done, I toss it into one of the driers and walk down to Haight Street for more cigarettes. I pass the winos lined up by the supermarket, the panhandlers, runaways, and dopers on the street corners, and buy some Marlboros at the mom-and-pop over by the park. On my way back, I check out the neighborhood piercing studio. It would be bitching to get my nose pierced, or an eyebrow, but that shit costs more money than I can afford. I push the idea out of my head.

The first thing I see back at the laundromat is the open drier door. *Oh, shit!* I think. A quick check shows that everything's been cleaned out of the drier, not just Darlene's and Buck's stuff, but most of the clothes I own as well. The fucker didn't even leave any of my old ratty underwear behind. "Fuck!" I shout, kicking the drier door as hard as I can. It slams against the drier and bounces open again, and I kick it again, hard enough to put a crack in the window. I storm outside and cross the street without looking. A car screeches to a stop and the driver gives me a twenty-second blast on his horn. I spin around and kick one of his headlights out. The dude gets out of his car, and I just wait, with clenched fists. He has second thoughts, calls me an asshole, and drives off. I laugh, but I still feel like ripping someone's head off.

Darlene is the first to come home. Even before I open my mouth, I can see she's had a bad day and is not in the mood for any bullshit. When I tell her what happens, she freaks out.

"What a goddamn stupid thing to do, Jamie!" she shouts at me. "I can't believe you just left that stuff by itself for anybody to rip off!"

She goes on like this for a few more minutes. I smoke a cigarette, slouched in a chair, and pretend like I don't hear her. After a while, she storms off to the bedroom, but when she reaches the doorway, she turns around again and glares at me. "When Buck gets home, you can go ahead and tell him what happened," she snarls. "You tell him you lost his favorite shirt, the one he always goes bowling in." She slams the door. *Jesus Fuckin' Christ,* I think.

I'm not about to hang around to hear Buck piss and moan at me. I change into my one last T-shirt, the one that says QUEER PUNK, and head out to Haight Street. A few guys are jamming on one of the street corners, playing guitars and congas, and I hang loose there for a while, toking up whenever the joint they're circulating comes back to me again. Later, I grab a burrito somewhere and wash it down with a couple of beers, then wander up to Club DV8 to see what's happening. Some group called Hog Maw is playing tonight; even out here on the street their music is loud enough to pop an eardrum. The gateman sits on his stool by the door, cracking his knuckles and staring at the world with his fat biker's face. I wait till a group of people show up, pushing through the door, and I crowd in with them, slipping by without paying. By the time the gateman sees me, I'm already in. "Hey, you," he yells, but I dive into all the bodies crammed together on the dance floor and lose the fucker.

The band sucks, but I like the way the noise just sweeps over me, pushing everything else out of my head. I grab a beer at the bar and watch the dance floor, checking out the guys. There's some hot meat out there tonight, bodies pumping to the music, slick with sweat, ripe, smelly, pierced, tattooed. My eye suddenly snags on one of them, not because of his tight, muscular body (which *is* hot) but because of the T-shirt he's wearing, with THE BOOGERS written across it in black and red. I bought that shirt in a Chicago punk club last year; any doubt I might have that it's the same shirt goes out the window when I see the grease stain on the back that I got from changing the oil in my car. That's the fucker who ripped me off.

It looks like he's dancing by himself. I push through the crowd toward him, sometimes losing him in the crush of squirming bodies, but then catching sight of him again, closer each time. I finally squeeze through right behind him. His shaved head, his muscles, and the ring in his left ear makes him look like a punk Mr. Clean. Just then, the band stops playing. I put my hand on his shoulder and he turns to face me, his eyes narrowed. Along with his ear, he's got a ring through his nose, and another piercing his left eyebrow. I smile at him. "Hey, man," I say. "I like your shirt." Then I slug him as hard as I can.

The dude falls against the stage, but then comes back at me like a hound from hell. We start slugging it out on the dance floor. He gets a good one to my right eye but I connect flat on his nose; blood streams down over his nose ring and splatters my Boogers shirt. He tries a head-butt on me, but I jerk away in time and hit him with a body tackle. We're down on the floor now, sometimes me on top, sometimes him. The crowd around us is cheering us on. When I'm on top again, I pull my fist back to give him a pounding so hard his parents will die. Somebody grabs my arm before I get a chance and yanks me to my feet. It's the gateman. "Okay, you little shithead," he growls, "you've caused enough trouble for the night." He pins my arm behind my back and shoves me forward through the crowd. People are hooting and jeering on both sides of us. My upper lip is cut, and I can taste my blood as it flows into my mouth.

When we reach the door, the gateman gives me a final hard shove, and I go crashing into a parked car. A couple of seconds later, the other guy goes flying through the door as well. The gateman stands at the doorway, glowering at us with a face like raw ground chuck. "If I see you guys here again," he snarls, "I'll rip your fuckin' heads off." He points a fat finger at me. "That goes especially for you, asshole." He goes back inside the club.

I climb to my feet and spit the blood out of my mouth. The other guy has pulled off his (or rather my) T-shirt and is dabbing his bloody nose with it. His body is lean and muscular; his abs are cut like a six-pack, and his pecs are hard and ripped. Both his nipples are pierced, too. His arms are covered with tattoos; I can't make them out in this light, just a few scattered images: tits, skulls, knives with blood, that kind of shit.

"You want to give me my shirt back?" I growl.

He looks at me and then at the shirt in his hand. "Oh, is this yours?" he asks, his eyes wide. He blows his nose into it. "Here," he says, tossing it to me. I let it fall to my feet. We glare at each other.

His eyes flick down to my QUEER PUNK T-shirt and then back to my face again. "You queer?" he asks.

Okay, I think. *Here comes the bullshit.* It looks like we really *are* going to have to take up where we left off in the club. "Yeah," I say, squinting. "What of it?"

"Nothing." He shrugs. "Except I'm queer, too."

I didn't see that one coming. "So?" I finally say, after a couple of beats.

He grins, and for once it's not a fuck-you grin. "So, do you want to fuck?"

I laugh. "Are you for real?" But I start wondering what he looks like naked.

The dude shrugs. "Hey, it was just a thought." A few seconds go by. "We could keep on fighting if you want to do that instead," he adds. It's like we're on a date, trying to figure what movie to see.

I take in the muscles, the tattoos, the piercings. In the streetlight, his body shines with sweat, and I can see the meaty bulge in the crotch of his torn jeans. His lip is puffed up where I hit it, pushing his mouth into a permanent sneer. His dark eyes sneer too, looking hard at me, challenging me. I feel my dick growing hard. I haven't been laid since I moved to this city, and I'm getting real tired of fucking my fist. "Okay," I say slowly. "If I get to choose, then I choose fucking."

The dude laughs. "All right!" he says. He sticks out his hand. "I'm Crow."

I take his hand and shake it. "Jamie," I say.

Crow lives in a shotgun apartment on Fell Street, one long hallway with a whole bunch of rooms branching off it. He tells me he shares it with four other guys, but it feels as if half of fuckin' Haight Street is crammed into this place. A tape deck blasts from one of the rooms in the back, playing something from Smashing Pumpkins, and I hear laughter and loud voices. People wander in and out of the kitchen, mostly guys, but a few chicks too. The place smells of grass, incense, and ripe garbage. It makes Darlene and Buck's apartment look like Graceland.

Crow's room is nothing more than a storage closet with a mattress on the floor. There's no other furniture in it—no other furniture could *fit* in it—but there are piles of clothes stacked along the walls. I recognize some of my stuff, and damn if I don't see Buck's bowling shirt, a neon-blue polyester piece of shit that should be taken out somewhere and burned.

Crow sees me staring at the clothes. "You can have them back if you want," he says, grinning.

I don't say anything, I just pull him to me and pry open his mouth with my tongue. Crow wraps his powerful arms around me and starts grinding his crotch against mine; I can feel the bulge of his dick rub against mine, a slow, circular massage of cocks separated by blue denim. With a sudden jerk, he topples us both onto his mattress. He grabs my wrists and pins my arms down as he continues to dry-hump me nice and slow. His tongue pushes into my mouth and down my throat, almost deep enough to taste the burrito I had for dinner.

I bury my face in his armpit and lick the sweat from it, breathing in deep the rank smell. Crow's body squirms on top of mine and he bends his neck so that he can stick his tongue in my ear. I trace my own tongue across his firm pecs to his left nipple. It's huge, sticking

out sharp and erect like a little toy soldier, with the ring
in it gleaming in the light from the bulb overhead. I
place the metal hoop between my teeth and tug at it.
Crow reaches up to yank the string that turns out the
light, but I pull his arm away. "I want to see your
body," I tell him.

Crow's mouth curves up into a slow smile. "Okay,
man," he says, "if you want a show, I'll give you one."
He stands up at the foot of the mattress and kicks his
boots off. I lie back with my hands behind my head and
watch. He unzips his jeans and drops them, revealing a
pair of bright red bikini briefs. He looks fuckin' hotter
than hell in them.

"Nice briefs," I say. "You've been hitting some high-
class laundromats."

Crow just laughs. He slowly, teasingly pulls them
down, first showing his pubes, then the base of his dick
shaft, thick and promising. He stops there. "You want
to see more?" he asks, eyebrows arched.

I don't answer, but just reach over and yank his briefs
down; his half-hard dick swings heavily between his
legs. It's a beautiful dick, fat and meaty, with a dark red
head that flares out from the shaft. His foreskin is
pierced with a thin steel ring. I just about shoot a load
looking at it.

"Christ," I whisper. I never saw anything like it before.

Crow looks proud. "I had it done a couple of months
ago."

Under my eyes his dick slowly stiffens and gets
harder. "Check it out," Crow urges. "It won't bite."

I get up on my knees, but Crow holds me back at
arm's length for a second. "Get naked first," he orders
me. Only after I strip does Crow let me take his dick in
my hand. I work the foreskin back and forth over the
head, watching as the ring winks in and out of sight.

Crow's fat dick is fully stiff now, and the feel of his warm, hard meat inside my hand gets my own cock all stiff and juiced up. I squeeze his dick, and a drop of pre-come oozes out of the piss slit. I lick it up, whirling my tongue around the head, tasting the saltiness of the spermy pearl. I look up at Crow and grin. "My favorite flavor," I say.

"Yeah." Crow grins. "Rum raisin." We both laugh.

I work my lips down the length of Crow's shaft in small nibbles, until my nose is buried deep in his pubes. I inhale deeply, breathing in the musky, pungent stink of Crow's cock and balls. Crow begins pumping his hips, and his dick slides easily in and out of my mouth; I feel the ring scrape inside my cheek, and I run my tongue over it. I wrap my hand around Crow's balls; they have a solid heft to them that feels like they were made for my palm. I squeeze them as I twist my head from side to side, giving his dick the full treatment with my tongue. Crow groans loudly. He seizes my head with both hands and thrusts his dick deep down my throat, mashing his pubes into my face. Then he pulls back and continues fucking my face in long, steady strokes. My other hand plays over his body, kneading the muscles of his torso, feeling his hard ass, tugging his tit rings. With his dick still in my mouth, I look up past the cut abs, the muscle-packed torso, the bull shoulders, to his face staring down at me from what seems like miles. Crow grins. "You're a real pig for dick, aren't you?" he croons. "You just can't fuckin' get enough of it." And he's right. I'm a dickpig for sure, and I got my face buried in the trough tonight.

I take his cock out of his mouth and start flicking his balls with my tongue. They hang loose and heavy above my face, furred lightly, the left nut lower than the right. I suck them both into my mouth and slobber my tongue over them, drool running down my chin. Crow starts beating my face with his dick, slapping my cheeks, my nose, and my eyes with it.

My tongue blazes a wet trail down the hairy path to Crow's asshole. His ass cheeks are fleshy and muscular; I bury my face between them and then burrow in deep, probing his bunghole with my tongue. Crow goes apeshit, writhing around, grinding his ass into my face. I replace my tongue with my finger, working it slowly up his chute to the third knuckle and then corkscrewing it around.

Crow groans loud and deep. "How do you feel about fucking my ass?" he rasps.

"I feel just fine about it," I tell him.

He rummages under a pile of clothes and comes up with a jar of lube and a rubber. "Lie down on your back," he growls. He straddles my hips and wraps his greased hand around both our dicks, squeezing them together. I look down at the sight of it: our two cocks being stroked together, slipping and sliding against each other inside Crow's big, callused hand. Crow bends over and we kiss again.

I take the lube from him and grease up my hand as well. Reaching behind, I pry apart Crow's ass crack and slide my grease-slimed finger inside his bunghole again. Crow squeezes his asshole tight, and I feel the muscles clamp down around my finger. I slowly pull it out, wiggling it all the way, and then shove it hard back in. Crow's body squirms against mine, and I push a second finger in. Crow groans loudly. "Lie down on your back," he gasps.

I do so, holding my condomed dick up straight as Crow lowers himself onto it. It slides into his ass smoothly, and Crow eases onto it like he's sinking into a hot bath; he closes his eyes and sighs loudly, and the look of pleasure on his face is so intense I almost laugh. He begins riding my dick, pushing off my body and then sliding down again, and I pump my hips to meet him stroke for stroke. It's such a fuckin' hot sight, his pierced, tattooed, muscle-packed body sliding up and down my cock. I wrap my still-greasy hand around his dick and stroke it long and slow. With my other hand I tug on his nipple rings, first the right one, then the left, then back to the right again. Crow's eyes glaze with pleasure, and something close to a whimper comes out of his open mouth.

I pull his head down and kiss him hard, pushing my tongue deep down his throat as I pound his ass. Crow turns into a fuckin' maniac. He wraps his arms around me, and we roll around on the mattress, him snarling and howling like some goddamn animal. I feel like I'm in a segment from *Wild Kingdom*. I hear footsteps down the hallway outside and then a laugh. "Go, Crow!" someone yells out.

Crow's on his back now, and I shift to overdrive, roaring down his ass like he's just so many miles of bad road. Each pounding I give him seems to shove Crow deeper into the mattress. One hard thrust gets my dick in full to the balls; I grind my hips and slowly tear up his ass. Our eyes lock onto each other; Crow's are bright and sharp, not missing a thing. I see the challenge in them. He wraps his legs around me and clamps his ass muscles tight; my dick feels like it's gripped in soft velvet, and as I pull out and then thrust back in it, I feel like my whole fuckin' body is about to implode. Crow's lips are pulled back and his eyes laughing. The message in them is clear enough: *Don't even* think *you're running this show.* I pump my hips a few more times and Crow matches me thrust for thrust, drawing me to the edge with a skill that blows my mind. The things I could learn from this guy! I groan loudly, and Crow reaches down and pushes hard against my nuts. Sweet Jesus, I just explode in that boy's ass, my dick squirting what feels like a couple of quarts' worth of jizz into the condom.

Before the last spasm is over, Crow flips me on my back and sits on my chest. As he fucks his hand, I reach up and pull down hard on his tit rings. He gives a whimper that trails into a long groan. His balls are pulled up tight now, and his dick is as stiff as dicks get. He's going to blow any second. He begins to spasm, and then the first load of jizz squirts out of his dick, full in my face. Crow cries out as his wad rains down on me, sliming my face, dribbling down my chin and into my open mouth.

Crow collapses on top of me. Through the closed door I can hear Pearl Jam on the tape deck down the hall. After a few seconds Crow raises his head and starts licking his own pearl jam off my face. When he gets to my mouth, we kiss again, not like before, just nice and tender. I close my eyes and drift off to sleep, with Crow's naked body sprawled on top of mine.

The next morning Crow gives me back all the clothes he swiped. I catch him looking at Buck's butt-ugly bowl-ing shirt. I hand it over to him. "Here," I say. "Do you want it?"

Crow's happy to take it. He tells me that one of the guys is moving out in a couple of days, and if I'm look-ing for a place to crash, the room is mine. I say yes with-out looking at it.

The sun is just rising when I finally step out onto Haight Street. The winos and other homeless are just beginning to stir in the shop doorways. As I walk by, one of them sleepily asks if I have any spare change. I give him another one of Buck's shirts and then just head on toward home, grinning.

VIRTUE IS ITS OWN REWARD

Tsaurah Litzky

"DID YOU EVER do it before, Owen?" I asked him as I climbed on top.

"Oh, yeah, many times," he said but I did not believe him: the down on his face was as soft as a flower and his body hair was so sparse, just a feathery plume or two on his chest and no genital hair at all, but his rosy mouth excited me and his limp pink cock was thick, longer than my hand, and promised much pleasure if only I could get it to stand to attention. He shimmied beneath me like a nervous fish as I stroked his cock up and down with my wet slit.

Last night he told me I had lovely eyes, but he pronounced it "luuve-le" having come up from Louisiana to work in his brother's Cajun seafood restaurant, and lovely in my panties was what I thought he would be but now in my bed he was hesitant, tremulous, scared, a young cock who didn't know what to do with me. I should have known better but how I love my foolish pleasure. All the time he sat at the bar and sipped his Guinness his eyes played with my big, D-cup tits but with them hanging just above him he was too shy to touch them. I put my hands beneath their heaviness, hefted them, made them shake and dance a jig, I lowered a big, brown nipple to his face and brushed it back and forth across his rosebud lips as I kept so slowly stroking his cock up and down with my wet slit, he started to thrash and moan, "Oh, mother," he said, "Oh, mother," which was not what I wanted to hear but I was so hungry for it I would have fucked him if he called me Michael or Gregory, I lowered my head, covered my teeth with my lips so as not to bite, and sucked him hard, he smelled like talcum and bread and the more I sucked the more the juices simmered between my legs, after a while the sap rose up in him, his prick began to quiver and twist, I took a condom from the box beside the bed and peeled it out but when I turned to sheathe him, hop astride, and ride to paradise I saw his mouth was slack, his eyes were shut, his head lolled back on his neck, he was asleep. *No fool like an old fool* is what I thought, as I climbed off, went to the refrigerator, and selected a fat carrot from the stock I always keep there, I washed it and cased it in the Ramses-X-tra sensitive, X-tra thin I had opened for Owen, put a generous dollop of K-Y on the tip, went into the toilet, and, seated on the throne made myself come 3 times and then one more time as a prayer for a better-luck-next-time fuck. . . . When I got into bed I poked Owen several times in a nasty fashion, but he did not move; his snoring echoed through the room. I lay down beside him and tried to remember the names of all the lovers I had taken whom I had picked up in bars; I remembered 13 and then drifted off to sleep.

I was awakened by a flurry of soft kisses around my neck and on my shoulders; it was still dark outside; I turned to Owen, returned his kisses, and we cuddled together wrapped in the lap of night, reaching down I found him hard, I got another Ramses from the box, slid it on, kissed the latex-ed tip, rubbing it between my lips but not taking it further into my mouth, I teased him with my tongue until he cried out "Oh, oh, oh" and this time he did not call me mother, I turned over on my back and seizing hold of him pulled him on top of me, parting my legs to let him slide in, on the first attempt he got my pee-hole and I had to take him in hand to lead him home, he thrust wildly three or four times and then he came as fast as an exploding rocket and left me forlorn on the launching pad. Whatever virtue there might be in initiating a young inexperienced man, it seemed for me virtue would have to be its own reward for I certainly was not getting any other satisfaction from young Owen.

In the morning I made coffee; I set a steaming cup before him as he sat at my kitchen table. "I was your first, wasn't I?" I asked and I poured myself a cup of coffee and sat down naked across from him spreading my legs so he could get a good look at my thick bush and the pert, pink lips within. He blushed, averted his eyes and denied that he had been cherry. "Owen," I said, "you are not being truthful and I know you'll always remember me in a special way." He did not comment on that but started talking about his brother James's restaurant, I couldn't wait for him to finish his coffee and leave, which he did sooner than I expected because on the second sip he found a cockroach floating in it belly up and I didn't offer to pour him another cup. As soon as he was out the door I turned the shower on; I wanted to scour his ineffectual little chicken kisses off my skin; in the shower I started to write a song about a cock as hard as a rock that would fuck me through millenniums.

Then I drank 3 cups of Café Bustelo black with 4 sugars and got to work on my novel about a poet who works as a barmaid in a bar where they sell guns and cocaine, which they do not sell at Monty's, where I work, although Monty can get you a diamond or a VCR and if you are short on money he'll lend you some at 15% a week. Monty has 4 daughters and told me if a guy gets too fresh to always let him know; he calls me Bazooka Tits and I don't mind, he watches over me, pays me on time. He tells the customers Bazooka is a writer and one of these days she's gonna leave us when she wins the Nobel Prize.

When I go to work that night, Carlos the bouncer gives me what on his face passes for a grin which means he opens his mouth and salivates, he says, "Well, how was he?" and I lie and say, "Great," then I go into the bathroom and change into my work costume of black jeans, black leotard, and the padded push-up bra that makes my big tits look like watermelons; I rub some peach body oil into my cleavage and checking myself in the mirror, *Camille Paglia is right, if you've got it, use it.*

I am now ready for work and soon I am dancing up and down behind the bar pouring Absolut straight up and J. W. Black to secretaries with Joan Collins hairdos, red-tape brokers, water cooler jokers, and femmes fatales who work for the phone company.

Monty believes in pouring with the glad hand; business is good and soon they are lined up three deep at the bar and Monty has to step behind the bar to help me and when the phone rings he gets it, "It's for you, Bazooka," he says and hands it to me. When I say hello a squeaky male voice says,

"I was in half an hour ago and you poured me a Dewar's straight up, water back, please let me buy you breakfast when you get off." "No," I say. I don't know who it is but then I remember a guy with a big beard and horn-rims who left me a 5-dollar tip.

"But you smiled at me," he says. "No," I say again and hang up the phone.

I am happy to be going home alone that night, I shower, dry myself with my favorite pink towel, then, spreading the towel on the bed, lie down on it and coat myself all over with cocoa butter, I love to oil my breasts until my nipples thicken and grow hard, then I get out my hash pipe, fill it, light it, and a few puffs later I want to go to Africa, I want to ride a camel across the desert, I want to be penetrated by a Berber chieftain with my back pressed into the hot sands . . . I go to the refrigerator and get another carrot, it does not disappoint me.

I have the next three days off and work on my book without making much headway; mostly I fart around and ask myself why I am in this world. When I go back to work Carlos tells me someone has been looking for me; "Who?" I want to know; Carlos says, "I never saw him before;" "What does he look like?" I ask; "Looks like a model in a magazine," says Carlos. This doesn't sound like anyone I know. I change in the john and then Monty cashes me in.

"You look good Bazooka," he says, "rested." *Cocoa butter and carrots,* I think and say thank you.

My first customers are 2 Bass ales in flannel shirts, and then a couple comes in, she is very young and looks like Twiggy, he is much older, potbelly, dirty fingernails, he orders a shot of Jack for himself and then says, "Get my daughter a glass of white wine," I think I know their story but I could be wrong, I have been wrong before, but I don't have time to think about it because it is now after 6 and they are bellying up to the bar as if I am giving away holy water and maybe I am, I turn to go to the cash register and notice I am being watched by a man at the end of the bar. I wash a few glasses and observe the fine bones of his face, the broad shoulders beneath his expensive-looking black leather jacket. The big hands he has placed on the bar are manicured, well kept, no marriage ring but then the ring could be in his pocket, his blue eyes sparkle and he is smiling right at me, there is something familiar about him yet I can't place him. I remember what Carlos said about the guy who looks like a model and I think this must be the one. As I walk down the bar toward him his eyes are on my cleavage and I lean forward to give him a better view. He orders a Guinness; as I draw it from the tap I do this little trick of moving the glass under the spigot to form a sham-rock on the foam. When I set the glass in front of him he says,

"You've put a shamrock on my Guinness."

"Maybe this is your lucky day," I say.

"Maybe," he says, and smiles wider; he reaches inside his jacket and extracts a wallet made out of some strange leather I have not seen before.

"What kind of leather is that?" I say.

"Stingray." I wonder if this is some kind of exotic shark and sleek and sure of himself as a shark is what he is as he pulls out a 20 and pushes it toward me across the bar. "Keep the change, girl," he says. I tell him I haven't earned such a generous tip and that I don't want what I don't earn.

"Owen said you were a smart one," he said and then I knew why he looked familiar to me, he was Owen ten years older and ten times as tough, Owen's big brother James come to check me out.

I gave him half a smile and then took the bill and while I was ringing it into the register I sucked in my belly and opened my mouth to make hollows under my cheeks like Katharine Hepburn, then I brought him back his change and turned without looking at him as I moved down the bar, serving drinks, joking with customers, emptying ashtrays that were already empty. Maybe he fancied himself a shark and wanted to chew me up, and I just might let him.

As I set down his fourth Guinness, he said, "I want to thank you properly for what you did for my little brother."

"No thanks necessary," I said; I wonder what Owen had told him—that he had fucked me five times, that he had me down on all fours begging like a dog?—then the big brother said, "Well, then, I'd like to thank you for being so beautiful," which is when I asked him what he had in mind.

"Come back to my place after your shift and I'll cook for you."

"Will you put Guinness in the sauce?" I asked him.

"I put Guinness in all my sauces," he answered.

Later in the taxi, he was saucy all right: he put his tongue deep into my mouth when he kissed me and taking my hand placed it below his belt, the swelling was as thick as a Campbell's soup can and I hoped it wasn't a trick like some sort of inflatable prosthesis; he put his hand inside the waistband of my leggings and reached south until his fingers found my other mouth and fed me some sugar. The cabby was driving with one hand and the other was playing in his lap as he watched us through the rearview mirror.

"Say you want it, tell me how much you want it," James said as we were riding up in the elevator. He had one hand on the back of my neck, the other he held cupped over that big bulge beneath his belt.

"Tell me how much you want it," he repeated but I wanted to make him work for it, at least a little, and so I said nothing.

Still holding me by the neck, he walked me out of the elevator and down the hall, with one hand he unlocked the door and pushed it open to reveal a room with white walls, black-leather-and-steel furniture, a large thick white rug. He pushed me down on a big leather chair—only then did he take his hand off my neck—he pulled off my shoes, my leggings, and spread my legs, his tongue was hot and rough as he licked my slit, all the while he was holding my legs apart at the knees so I couldn't move. He found my clit and began to suck on it like a baby sucking on a tit but just as I was about to come, he stopped and stood up, leaving me wild and crazy for it. He unzipped and pulled out his cock, he had a lot to be proud of, he stood over me, pointing it at the moist pelt between my legs. "How do you like my big sword?" he said. "Say you want it," but I bit my lips and said nothing.

He started to touch me with it, pulling it like a hot blade across my face, pushing it between my breasts, tapping it against my belly; then he knelt between my legs and sucked my clit so hard I came twice in a minute.

"Tell me you want it, tell me you want it," he said again and I told him I was dying for it; then he got up from between my legs, his cheeks wet with my cunt juice.

"Good," he said, "good." He ripped off my sweater and bra with one swift motion. My fat tits fell out and he took one in each hand, pulling them, milking them. He led me by the nipples into the bedroom and pushed me face down on the bed. I felt a ripple beneath me; I was not surprised to find he had a water bed.

"Spread your ass for me," he said, "spread it," and I did not try to swim away, oh no, I put my hands on my cheeks and did what he asked; he must have liked what he saw there because he bent his head and started to rim my asshole with his tongue, he traced a circle around and around until I was squealing, yielding, and then he grabbed me by the hair and pulled my head back so I could watch him as he pulled on a giant love glove, then he pushed my head face down again, reached around, grabbed me tight by the nipples and rammed into my ready asshole fast and hard just like I like it and all the while I was coming I was thinking how virtue is its own reward.

BAJANDO LA LUNA

Ioana dp valencia

MIRA M'IJA, AUNQUE es cierto que la madre tierra es madre de toda la creación, es importante saber que no lo hizo sola. no, no m'ija—ella tenía un amante.

sí, es cierto.

¿que? ¿cómo se llamaba? mar. se llama mar.

si te fijas bien, te vas a dar cuenta que pasan TODO EL DIA besándose, lamiándose, agarrándose. son anhelistas esas mujeres—son adelitas pa' sus quereres.

acomódate bien y te voy a contar cómo nos crearon.

see, it used to be that mar pasaba todo el día aburrida. she didn't even make waves she was so bored. one night, there was a faint touch underneath her that tickled her *real* soft-like & made her reír de puro gusto. that's how ocean swells got started—they're mar's laugh-ripples.

anyhow, the tickling kept tickling her & in her joy, se levantó su falda & ¡discovered someone underneath her!

"*hasta* que," le dijo la madre tierra. "tengo días tras días ROGANDOTE que te levantaras tu falda. ayyy . . . que *bonita* espalda tienes."

well, that mar was tán sorprendida at realizin' that all this time she hadn't been alone that she threw her head back & exposed her erogenous zone without knowing it.

now, maté (that's short for madre tierra. ¿see how fast she got her love name?)—she knew an erogenous zone when she saw one, so she did what *any* mujer apasionada would do: SHE LICKED HER. she licked mar long & slow & left such a wet trail that mar didn't know where she ended & where that wetness began. this is how their lusty love/lovely lust affair began & how waves were born. see, waves are just mar reachin' for maté with her hands, y las espumas—¡híjole!—that's just concentrated lust con bubbles. and when those bubbles pop, you can hear the whispers of passion between them.

they fuck ALL DAY, esas mujeres. they grind on each other so *much* that their sand, water, heat, & air collide into each other and *make* things. check it out: maté would dig her hands into herself in the heat of the moment & actually tear a piece of herself out! then mar would say in her raspy voice into maté's ear "*dámelo mamita,*" and maté would hand over her chunks like nothing. they'd whip their tongues all around them makin' some parts smooth & leavin' some parts rough. . . . la mera verdad es que we were born out of two women's orgasms.

wait, kick back. there's more.

okay, so one night mar decided she wanted to sneak a peek at maté while they were kissing. she wanted to know: did maté keep her eyes closed too, ¿or what? that's when se dió cuenta que había OTRA MUJER mirándolas . . . ¡y masturbating even! yup, that otra mujer was none other than LA LUNA. that horny woman had

been watching 'em ever since mar & maté started ha-
ciendo cosas. at first, she watched all wide-eyed, but
sometimes she'd get scared of being busted so she'd
keep her eye ½ closed. or she'd just go off on her own
fantasy & close her big eye completely. that's what the
different phases of the moon are—they're just different
stages of luna bein' a peepin' tomasa.

¡i ain't shittin' you! ¡my abuelita told me! and my 'lita
ain't no mentirosa.

¿what?

¿what did mar & maté do about luna gettin' off on
'em?

shiiiiiit, ¿don't you get it? high tide is just those two
women reachin' with their wild arms to bring down the
moon.

THE CASE OF THE DEMON LOVER

Nancy Kilpatrick

"THE SON OF A bitch lives in the Quarter, I can feel it."

"When did you become a psychic?"

Adrian glared at Lionel. Her partner was a potbellied toad of a cop, who had peaked a dozen years ago and had evidently given up on the body beautiful. It was her bad luck to be assigned to work with this turd because she was the new kid on the block. How the hell she'd ended up in New Orleans was anybody's guess, because for Adrian, it was like some drunken blackout. The last thing she remembered was working for the police department in Philadelphia, being cited for outstanding service above and beyond, growing to hate all men, needing to get away. It was New Orleans or Miami. Maybe she just couldn't tear herself away from dangerous cities.

"He's here, all right. Stalking women, some kind of sexual pervert—"

"Pervert?" Lionel laughed. "You want perverts, missy, don't we have a city full?" He slurped his coffee loudly, as he did everything, and stuffed a beignet into his mouth. Powdered sugar spilled down the front of his shirt and pants.

Why were there no men left with style? What kind of woman would mate with the likes of Lionel? Better no sex than rutting with her piglike partner!

"This bastard's different. He's laughing at us," she said.

"Well, hell, I'm laughin' myself. None of 'em will press charges—"

"Oh, come on, Lionel! They're afraid."

"Bullshit! They can't even remember what he looks like. Tall, short, fat, thin—"

"Mind control."

"They don't act like it's their minds that were controlled—"

"What? You think they enjoyed being assaulted sexually?"

"None of 'em look the worse for wear. Hell, we find 'em without any panties on, bent over like they been fucked royally from behind . . ."

She shot her half empty Café du Monde coffee cup past his face and out the passenger window. It landed in the trash can sitting at the curb.

"Score!" Lionel shouted, in that southern drawl she had grown to loathe.

A black mood settled over her. She turned the key and the engine growled to life. The heat tonight was intense—she wished she'd worn cotton underwear, because this polyester shit made her crotch hotter than hell.

She pulled the cruiser away from the curb and did a U-turn on Decatur Street, narrowly missing the tail end of a horse-drawn carriage, and drove back toward Canal, then north to Bourbon. Bourbon Street was packed already, and it was barely midnight on a street where the show went on till dawn. They idled at the corner of Canal and Bourbon, in front of the Woolworth's where they'd found the last victim.

She was about Adrian's age, similar blond shade of hair, pretty, her butt raised over a toppled paper box, her behind bare, both orifices raw but moist. The fact that the twit had had a smile on her face made Adrian want to slap her. Whoever this sick son of a bitch was, he had raped a dozen females in the last two months alone.

The Captain pegged the perp—papers had taken to calling him the Demon Lover—for a druggie, but Adrian wasn't so sure. She had a gut feeling, nothing she could talk to any of her peers about, certainly not Lionel, that was for sure. Something wasn't right about this, though, with the women refusing to testify, differing descriptions of the perp, the fact that they all looked possessed. But the M.O. was the same—found just before dawn, bent over, bare-assed, fucked doggy style in the vagina and the ass until they were tender. . . . The women were old and young, black, white, Hispanic, college students, waitresses, and lawyers, locals and tourists. Nothing similar, except that all were single, intelligent, independent women, sans boyfriend. Why wouldn't they cooperate? They weren't in danger. She had a hunch that wouldn't quite manifest; she needed time to figure out what was bothering her about these cases.

Revelers stalking the ultimate good time rounded the corner wearing stupid hats and carrying strings of cheap beads in multicolors. The first block of Bourbon was dark—no streetlights—and no action either. It all started one block east, and sitting at Canal was a waste of time.

"I'm going around," Adrian said.

She drove up to North Rampart and turned. They passed the St. Louis Cemetery on the left—she'd never gotten used to the burial methods of this city—and turned up Orleans. The streets at the north end were dark *and* quiet, but as they neared Bourbon, the noise and crowds and lights exploded with a nuclear velocity.

At Bourbon, she parked the cruiser and Lionel got out. He hiked his pants up over his belly and took a cock-of-the-walk stance. He liked to sit on the hood and look important, was the way she saw it. Tonight he plopped only half his lard butt on the hood, so he could face east and watch the festivities from that direction.

Already the jocks had prime positions on the second-floor balconies, hooting and hollering and coaxing the prettiest women passing on the crowded streets to pay them attention. Everybody carried a plastic cup of something alcoholic, and half of that everybody was already shit-faced. The air reeked of fried seafood, stale booze, and sour vomit. Adrian stayed in the car, listening to the radio squawk codes, the most common for assaults and B & E's.

She watched a buxom beauty stagger through the intersection, where no vehicles except the horses and carriages had the nerve to push through. Large tits bounced mightily inside a tight red *Dumb and Dumber* T-shirt. Already she wore six strands of fake pearls—she'd been having herself a good time.

The yelling and screaming from the balconies increased when the guys spotted the party girl. She stopped, planted her bare feet wide apart for balance, and glanced up smiling and waving. That was enough to garner applause. People passing stopped to watch the show, and Lionel had a big grin pasted on his sloppy face. Miss Tits, as Adrian came to think of her, did a little bump and grind, greatly appreciated by the hordes. But they wanted more and dangled strands of neck jewelry enticingly, while shouting "Let's see 'em!" and "Knockers! We want hooters!" Eventually the message seeped through Miss Tits' soaked brain. She grabbed her peasant blouse by the hem and lifted it. White breasts—maybe 38Es—with big areolas and firm nipples hit the air. The bimbo jiggled them seriously, and ropes of pearls dropped down as rewards. How the hell could these women just do whatever these guys told them to do? Damn if Adrian didn't see Lionel secretly rub his crotch.

She got out of the cruiser. "I'm going for a walk," she said, but Lionel didn't seem to hear, and she'd be damned if she'd repeat herself.

She headed north for a block, then east. This part of the Quarter was where the quadroons and other racial fractions had lived back in the 1700s, shortly after the French Quarter had been built. Most had been freed slaves, women lured into being mistresses by rich white plantation owners who wanted exotic voodoo priestesses to screw through summer nights hot as this one. The street faces of the houses were plain, with high, narrow French doors, grillwork on the windows, and small balconies above; it had surprised her when she'd discovered the hidden alleyways that led to lush gardens at what was really the front of these houses. Gardens that cooled overheated bodies in the steaming Louisiana humidity. The farther she traveled away from Bourbon Street, the quieter it got.

Soon she reached North Rampart. Across the boulevard stood Louis Armstrong Park. It was dangerous to be here alone, although she had her handgun, nightstick, and radio. Not much traffic tonight. She crossed the eastbound lanes to the grassy meridian, then waited for a solitary car before crossing the lanes headed in the opposite direction. This park drew winos, junkies, and other assorted lowlifes like flies to honey. The station boys had even busted up a couple of modern-day voodoo ceremonies. The park was empty, the gates locked, and she didn't feel inclined to investigate. She strolled along the sidewalk. The only pedestrians were on the opposite side of the street, few at that, and all turning up toward the heart of the Quarter and the nightlife that lasted twenty-four hours a day.

Being here made her depressed, but the neon spectacle she'd just left was worse. At least here she could think. Why the *hell* had she moved back to the South? She was three when her parents divorced and her mother fled Louisiana—Adrian couldn't remember it—like her life depended on it and moved to Chicago. Adrian had never heard from her father, never cared to. She'd grown up fast, though, started college at the U. of C. at seventeen, dropped out at nineteen because it was way too easy, moved to Philadelphia to escape her mother, tried to have a life. But there was no life, just five years of work, which she excelled at, no matter what she tackled. She was offered a detective's shield after just two years on the Philly force, and the next day started looking for a new job. Whatever interest she'd had in the opposite sex vanished collar by collar. Men, she figured, were either Jell-O you could jostle easily, or macho slobs like Lionel, too repulsive to even fantasize about. And she had yet to feel any juices flow toward her own gender. What the hell was wrong with her? What was she running from? How did she end up in this sweltering hell? Was it some kind of twisted subconscious desire to suffer? There had been other cop-shop offers—well, a few anyway. Baton Rouge: she couldn't have stood it there, too claustrophobic. No use living in a place where you know everybody, and they think they know you. Miami—the city was big enough, and she'd debated a while. But the offer from New Orleans was better, or so she'd assured herself. The city was large enough that nobody gave a shit about her. She could be as anonymous as the tourists, whose faces changed every two days.

She stopped suddenly, aware that she was outside the front gates of the St. Louis Cemetery. This, the oldest graveyard in the city, gave her the creeps. Of course, the city was full of cemeteries—they loved their dead. Three graveyards had been built way up where Canal Street divided. And although some of those crypts there were as old as the ones in St. Louis, somehow the layouts had more symmetry, more order. Down here in the Quarter, where things crumbled to nothing on a daily basis, this necropolis had a spooky feel. If the dead could come to life, it would be here.

She shook her head at such stupid thoughts and turned, trying to convince herself to rejoin Lionel and the mad throngs. A noise stopped her. Damn if it wasn't coming from inside! She moved close to the wrought-iron gates. There was nothing to see but boxlike crypts in white and shades of gray. Was that another noise? Maybe laughter?

Shit! This was ridiculous. Likely black-clad Goth kids smoking grass or drinking rotgut. She should go and get Lionel if she wanted to check it out, and she wasn't sure she did. But she couldn't stomach the thought of Lionel, not this soon.

A kind of swishing sound, like fabric. She walked around the side street; the gate there was locked, too. Well, the walls were low enough, and kids usually climbed over easily. The cemetery wasn't safe—bodies had been found in here that weren't yet interred—but her adrenal glands were already pumping. It went against every police regulation she knew, but what the hell! The thought of Bourbon Street left her eager for any diversion.

She used her skeleton keys and opened the padlock, lifting the chain carefully so it wouldn't rattle too much. Adrenaline rode her muscles, and her hands felt slippery with sweat. The full moon made it easy enough to see clearly without a flashlight, although the spaces between some of these tombs might need illumination.

Adrian stared down the wide path. On each side rectangles bearing the recent dead, and the dead before them, had been crammed together, some only inches apart. It was eerie in here, like a playground for children, although why she thought that, she didn't know. The way they buried people in New Orleans unnerved her. It was because of the water table, just six feet deep in some places, so there was no room for graves. These aboveground tombs had been rented by the living to store the deceased for a year and a day. The summer heat rotted all but the bones. When the next family member departed as soon as three hundred and sixty-six days had passed after the previous burial, the tomb was opened, the ashes shoved to the back, and the new corpse loaded in. Many of the crypts had little chimneys, where the putrid gases had escaped before embalming became fashionable. She shivered at the thought.

She passed crypts with long lists of relatives who had used them as a temporary home, long enough to marinate, anyway. The thought of having your ashes mixed in with those of your kin made her feel sick—who wants to spend eternity with people you can't get along with in life?

A noise to the left! She jerked around in time to see someone dart between two tombs. Adrian followed, her holster unsnapped, her hand on the gun handle, her thumb on the safety. Was this heat or fear? She couldn't tell. Her armpits dripped sweat, and moisture made her uniform shirt stick to her chest. The undersides of her breasts were hot and sticky. Her crotch itched, and she wished she was home, having a shower, cooling down, instead of baking as she prowled an old graveyard full of moldering bones in the middle of the night.

She stopped at one of the so-called voodoo tombs, the ones that aren't marked with crosses or angels on the roof, or any of the other symbols of Christianity. This one was plain gray, the square door that pivots open gouged with many Xs, for favors asked, and far fewer Os, for favors granted. She tried to listen over the beat of her heart.

Breathing? Someone breathing. On the other side of the crypt. Her temples pounded with fear, and it was all she could do to soften the sound of air coming from her nose and mouth. She eased her gun from the holster and unsnapped the safety, which made a loud click. The breathing stopped, to be replaced by low laughter.

"You won't need that. You didn't stalk me to kill me."

The voice came from behind her, and she whirled. "Hands in the air, motherfucker!"

He held his hands palms facing her. "I'm unarmed, officer."

"I don't give a shit. I said, hands up!"

He lifted his hands into the air. Before her stood a man she could only describe as gorgeous. Tall, broad-shouldered, wearing tight crinkling gray leather and, well, gray everything. Despite the heat and the hide, he wasn't obviously sweating. His face was perfect, sculpted almost, as if it had been patterned after one of the marble angels. Silver hair, long at the back, short at the sides, slightly wavy; full lips that turned up at the corners; gray eyes. He was like some seductive night god who had slipped between two worlds. *Get a grip!* she told herself. *This guy's probably dangerous.*

"What are you doing in here?" she demanded.

"Waiting for you."

This she hadn't expected, and it unnerved her. "Listen, smart guy, put your hands against this crypt and spread your legs wide."

"Certainly." He complied immediately, his voice smooth as quicksilver.

She moved behind him cautiously and frisked him, down the sides of each leg, up the insides—accidentally her hand brushed his leather-clad genitals. He swung his head around and grinned at her.

She checked his jacket, his back, sides, front. He had no weapon, which made her—not relax, exactly, but at least she didn't get more tense. Until she felt along the back of her utility belt. Her handcuffs were missing!

In a second, she thought back over the night: She hadn't taken them off. They should be there. Where the hell were they? This was no time to worry about it.

She took several steps back, for safety. "All right. We're going to walk to the gate, nice and slow. You're going to put your hands behind your neck and keep them there. Understand?"

"I understand you, Adrian. Very well."

A tremor snaked the length of her spine. How the *hell* did he know her name? Her heart raced in real terror, and she saw the gun in her hands quiver. *Ignore him,* she told herself. *Just ignore him. It was a lucky guess. No, that can't be true.* Her name was unusual.

"How do you know my name?"

"You've been in the papers, haven't you, Adrian? You've been looking for me."

That made sense. She had been quoted a couple of times; maybe her picture had appeared. The press liked to get quotes from the female officers and the black cops; that way the illusion was maintained that the department was more integrated that it really was.

"Okay, so you can read. I'm impressed. Now, move it!"

He pushed away from the crypt slowly, like some goddamn animal biding its time. He turned his head and stared into her eyes; the moon glinted off his. All of a sudden she became aware of her breasts. The nipples tingled. They felt entrapped in the bra cups, and the heat of confinement almost overwhelmed her. She assumed her shooting stance, struggling to steady her arms, which trembled out of control.

"You don't really enjoy control," he said, and turned.

She should yell at him. Make him turn his back to her. Get moving. She should take charge! Why couldn't she speak? "I'm going to feed you my cock, Adrian. Until you're full." Her mouth felt desert dry, her cunt moist as a swamp. This creep! . . . This creep! . . . She wanted to think of him as a creep. But all she could see was a tall, sexy man, sophisticated, someone who wasn't afraid of her. She couldn't miss the bulge at his crotch, a reaction to her reaction to him. Or was it the other way around? Whatever; the sight of it triggered another response, one she had forgotten she could feel—longing.

He stepped close.

"Stay back!" she managed, wondering whose voice had just come out of her mouth, because it did not sound like her own.

"You need fucking, Adrian. Hard, long fucking, until you cry out, and then more, until you can't cry out anymore."

Hot and cold shivers alternated through her body. Her skin became clammy, then hotter than the air surrounding her. She wondered for a second if she was coming down with something. But this was no flu bug that had bitten her. She felt possessed, as if somebody had slipped her an aphrodisiac and she was under a spell.

He moved on her, and she could only watch him coming. He reminded her of a gray snake, sensuous, iridescent in the moonlight, the glinting eyes of a predator focusing on prey, ready to entice it into his mouth and swallow it whole. God help her, she wanted to be swallowed!

When he reached out, she was ready to hand him the gun, but he didn't take it. Instead, he pushed his arms up through hers and broke her arms apart. Then his hands went right for her breasts. Through the cotton shirt, she felt skin of fire, scorching her. The itch between her legs became unbearable, and heat shot along the crack of her behind, swelling the entire area with a burning sensation she reveled in yet could hardly tolerate.

It was as though she had become paralyzed and could only stand there, submitting to the sensations. She watched him undo the buttons of her shirt. His long, cool fingers pulled down the straps of her bra; her breasts felt liberated. The humid air on her nipples made them pulse. His thumbs rubbed the nipples in circles clockwise, then counterclockwise, then clockwise again. When he pinched them between his thumbs and forefingers, her head fell back and she arched her spine and moaned, unable to bear the heat, unable to stand the sensations coiling through her. She panted like a bitch in heat. The crotch of her panties and the uniform slacks were soaked. A vague thought passed through her stunned brain: *What the hell are you doing?* But he began unbuckling her heavy cop belt, unzipping her pants, and she let that thought melt down.

Hot ice froze her. Every erogenous zone of her body flamed. He slipped her slacks and panties down to her knees and the hot, moist air contacting her skin acted as a stimulant.

"Bend over and offer yourself to me," he said, his voice even, the demand subtle but unmistakable. She obeyed like a zombie, immediately, without question. The three steps of the tomb would do, and she knelt so that her hands—still clutching the gun—were on the highest, and her knees on the ground. Heat pressed in from all sides. Clotted, heavy air left her barely able to breathe.

She felt her shirttail lifted, exposing her ass and the fire down there. Her body trembled, out of control. In a minute he would enter her, somewhere, with something. Her vagina throbbed painfully in anticipation. Suddenly she was aware of having been empty for a long time, of needing to be filled. She would be raw when he finished, her pussy red and swollen, as well as her rectum, just like the other women he had taken in the dark and quiet corners of this city, but she didn't care. Right now she needed this, wanted it with all her being, and felt helpless to stop the process.

"I need a more serious offering, Adrian," he said, laughing at her.

Mortified, she obeyed by lowering her head to the ground and lifting her ass high.

"I'm not a rapist, Adrian. If you don't beg me to fuck you, I won't."

She felt ashamed of the need he saw in her, embarrassed by the wanton lust she recognized in herself. It was humiliating that he would force her to beg! Her dry mouth nearly kept her lips from forming the words. "Fuck me!" she whispered, her voice to her ears pleading, not for pity, but for penetration. "Please!" She had just asked a criminal to use her! Was she losing her mind? But these thoughts faded when hot hard flesh kissed the mouth of her cunt.

The contact sent a charge through her. Spontaneously her vagina spasmed, flooding her with slick, steaming liquid. She gasped, startled. The orgasm lasted a long time; it was too short.

Afterward, when her pussy had not quite cooled and his cock lingered at her opening, suddenly he entered her. His head was large and solid, probing between her labia like a tongue between lips, and she realized she wanted him to kiss her, to feel his mouth engulf hers, to feel him force his tongue down her throat and take possession of her, but she could not move, or speak.

He invaded her excruciatingly slowly, and had only gotten a little way in when she orgasmed again. Her cunt was so hungry. Could she eat enough in one night to fill her a lifetime? Is that what the other women had wondered? Was that why he fucked them so long and hard, until their openings resembled fresh, raw meat? *What stupid thoughts,* she told herself, but then the thoughts ended, and his cock plunged in deep. She cried out. Her eyes filled with tears of gratitude. She tightened around him automatically. He only needed to thrust twice and she came again.

Her mind turned to mush. She lifted her head to lay her cheek against the cool, rough, solid stone of the crypt while he thrust in and out of her cunt, rubbing the flesh until it swelled impossibly hot, painfully so, until she felt she might ignite. All she could do was take him in, respond and, when the pain turned to luscious sensation, come. Time passed. Her pussy cried tears of passion, then sobbed with pain. She felt helpless to move, to do anything but submit to his unspoken demands. She stopped counting when the orgasms reached thirteen, and the moon hung big and low over the cemetery, and the air surrounded them like a cocoon, encasing them in sultry passion.

This couldn't be happening. No man could fuck this long. She had never allowed herself to be a receptacle of pleasure. No wonder all his victims had looked sated. She could only mumble now and then, "Fuck me!" And he did.

As the sky turned gray, she heard birds, then traffic. They would be coming to unlock the cemetery soon. They would find her, ass bare, cunt swollen and raw, that smile on her face, just like all the others. Pain changed to pleasure again. Her pussy soaked his cock again. Another orgasm rocked her, leaving her limp and mindless. He withdrew.

She had never been penetrated anally. As his penis, slick with her juices, nudged her bottom hole, fear washed over her. He did not move slowly into this orifice, but with urgency, as if the imminent sunrise might turn him from a gray apparition to a pile of gray ash.

Pain seared her. His merciless cock filled her rectum until it felt stuffed to bursting. Cold sweat sprouted from the pores of her quaking body, but she soon discovered that she could relax into the sensation, which was like nothing she had ever experienced before. Even more than staking her vagina, this newly claimed territory left her feeling owned. She offered herself up to him in complete submission, and he accepted the offering as if it were his right to take her. As if she existed to be taken, which was how she felt. The orgasm that rocked her left her trembling, panting, lapping dirt, her vision blurred. Suddenly he exited, leaving a scream streaming from her lips at this new suffering, the pain of abandonment.

She was sore beyond what she would ever have imagined possible, and yet needy still. The need forced her to turn. She watched him zip his tight leather pants. Was he real or some ghost from this haunted city's past, resurrected at midnight from a voodoo tomb? Had this happened? Was she here kneeling, kissing the door of a crypt, a door that opened to ash and bone? Had she offered her cunt and ass to the Demon Lover? A criminal responsible for molesting so many women? Was she insane? The abandonment gave her energy. She pointed the gun at him, hands trembling. "Don't move!"

He paused. "Adrian, I gave you what you needed, what you asked for, just as I did with all the others. Is that a crime?" He turned and started walking away.

She staggered to her feet, lightheaded, pants slipping down to her ankles, her body stiff and sore, liquid slicking the insides of her thighs. "One more step and I'll shoot." He stopped and turned. The look on his face was of amusement, not fear, as though her resistance delighted or challenged him in some way that he had been waiting for. Finally he said, "I understand," in that smooth, firm voice. "You need more. Much more. When is your next night off?"

"Tomorrow."

"Tomorrow night you will go to the French Market at midnight. Wear a skirt, and no panties."

"Why the French Market?"

"Because I tell you to go there, Adrian. Because we do everything my way. From now on."

A shiver of desire ran through her, at his order, at the words "from now on." At the knowledge that this would not be easy, and she desperately wanted it not to be easy. He turned, and she watched him leave Saint Louis's. Just before he closed the gate, he glanced back, his steel eyes piercing in the light of dawn. "And Adrian, bring your handcuffs."

DAY OF ATONEMENT: CONFESSIONAL

Michael Lowenthal

For the sin we have committed before Thee by unchastity:
And for the sin we have committed before Thee with utterance of the lip:
And for the sin we have committed before Thee by deliberate lying:
For all these, O God of forgiveness, forgive us, pardon us, grant us remission.

It wasn't deliberate lying. Nothing passed through my lips that was specifically untrue. It's a distinction, okay? Omission and commission. I'm not living with a lover right now. So what if Randy's due back in three weeks? The kid didn't need to know.

I didn't lie to Randy, either. Not that I feel great about the phone call, because I don't. But he's the one who set his own trap. "Did you have sex last weekend?" Correct me if I'm wrong, but Sunday night is not the weekend. Sunday night is a school night. It's the first night of the week.

And that's the whole thing: it was just one night. Big deal. Who said we had to be monogamous while we were apart? I don't remember signing that piece of paper. Randy said it would make him more comfortable if we didn't sleep around, and I told him I wanted him to be comfortable. That's true. I don't like to see him upset. But I never said I wouldn't do it.

For the sin we have committed before Thee by impurity of the lips:

And for the sin we have committed before Thee by folly of the mouth:

And for the sin we have committed before Thee in meat and drink:

For all these, O God of forgiveness, forgive us, pardon us, grant us remission.

All right, I did promise Randy I wouldn't suck anybody without a rubber. But let's be real. The kid was only nineteen. He just came out a few months ago. *He's* going to be positive?

Besides, he dove right into my crotch before I could say anything. I would have told him about our ground rules, but he was already slurping away, darting his tongue into my hole, everything. After that, it would have been rude for me to say I couldn't do the same thing. I'm not into all that top and bottom crap. If he sucks me, I'm going to reciprocate.

I didn't abandon all of my senses. I would never have put it all the way in my mouth if there had been a lot of pre-come. But there was hardly any in the beginning. Maybe one drop at the tip. Usually, if people are leaky, you can tell from the start. He didn't start dripping until he was all the way down my throat.

In an ideal world? Sure, I might do it differently. It probably wasn't worth the risk. But do I believe for a second that Randy hasn't done the same thing? One little suck without a rubber?

For the sin we have committed before Thee by violence:

And for the sin we have committed before Thee in wronging our neighbor:

And for the sin we have committed before Thee by association with impurity:

For all these, O God of forgiveness, forgive us, pardon us, grant us remission.

First off, the kid *asked* me to be rough. I would never do that kind of stuff unless a guy asked me to. He kept begging me to do it harder, harder. "Make it hurt," he said, "I can't feel you." I'll admit I got off on it. Randy never lets himself go like that.

After a few minutes of really pounding him, I pulled it out as a tease, to make him want it even more. I love to see a guy's hole pouting in exasperation, like a baby's mouth when you take the pacifier away. That was when I saw the streaks of blood mixed with the smears of shit on the rubber. I would have stopped if he wanted me to. I don't want to kill anybody.

"What if there's blood?" I said. The kid got this intense, ecstatic look in his eyes, like a teenager hitting the bonus round on a video game, his eyes focused on the lights dancing across the screen. "Make it bleed," he said. "Make it all come out."

So I shoved it back in, even harder this time. I pulled his ankles tight around my neck and lifted him off the bed. Then I fucked him straight down, imagining my come flowing all the way into him, through his bowels, into his stomach, right up into his throat. I was filling him up all the way.

That's how I came, and it was one of those totally smooth orgasms, none of that shuddering and stuff. Which is how I could feel that the come wasn't pooling in the tip of the rubber the way it's supposed to. You can feel it when it does, that body-warm wetness on your skin, like pissing in a swimming pool. I hadn't seen the rip in the latex when I'd pulled out earlier. I guess the blood and shit had masked it with their messiness.

I had to tell him right away. That's some pretty heavy stuff. He looked at me strangely for a second before he spoke, and I actually knew then what he was about to say. "What do I care?" he said. "I'm already positive."

When I got home, somehow I forgot about it enough to sleep a few hours. But then I had to get dressed and rush here to the synagogue. I promised Zaydeh I'd stay with him while he prayed. I hadn't really planned to fast; I haven't done that in years. But I forgot to grab breakfast before I left, so I haven't had anything to eat. All day I've been tasting the traces of pre-come in my mouth, bitter and rancid, like pennies dipped in salt water.

I can feel the place on my cock where the rubber must have pinched too tight. There's a tiny blood blister that popped and is oozing stuff. I can't remember if it burst open during the sex or after. My throat is sore. It feels like the lymph nodes, but it could be just from chanting all the Hebrew with its harsh consonants. I'm dizzy, too. Is it the fasting, or the beginning of something much worse?

I just hope I make it through until they blow the shofar. Not that I really believe in this religious stuff, but it's kind of like an insurance policy. If I last until sundown, maybe that proves I mean it when I say I'm really sorry.

For the sins for which we are liable to the penalty of death by the hand of heaven:

For all these, O God of forgiveness, forgive us, pardon us, grant us remission.

BEHIND THE

MASK

Serena Moloch

1. Maid and Mistress

Sometimes it begins like this.

I follow my mistress as she makes her way through a crowded train station. I carry her bags for her. Her bags are very heavy, so heavy they dig into my hand, and later, when I look at it, there will be a rough red mark where the bag bit my hand with its toothless mouth. My mistress is dressed in a pale travel costume, the latest style, with billows and ruffles that come right down to her heels, and she is clean, so clean that I can track her even in this mass of people simply by following in the wake of her stupendous shining cleanliness. Her hair glows with it, her skin gleams with it, her clothes remark loudly on the absence of any disfiguring spot.

I, on the other hand, am dirty, so dirty that even in this filthy crowd I can feel people turning to stare at me. I am remarked upon. Perhaps, I imagine, someone will mistake me for a spitoon or a rubbish tip and absent-mindedly make me the receptacle for some choice piece of garbage. I feel the impulse to protest; it's not my fault, it's my duty that coats me in dirt. The servant's life: up at 5:30 to clean the grates and fill the coal scuttles, out on the steps at seven, bucket and soap and brush in hand, to wash the house clean, to kneel on their marble and try not to imagine how everyone who passes can look at my legs, will look up my skirts, insult me in language as foul as the chamber pots it is my duty to clean at nine.

Nine o'clock when I must attend my waking mistress, I bring up her breakfast tray, I sniff the aromatic chocolate steaming in the dainty, oh so dainty china cup, as thin as her calla-lily neck and just as easy to snap if one doesn't take the proper care. I carry the hot rolls and the linen napkins; gingerly, I bring her the chamber pot and watch her piss and shit into it and then I prepare to wash her clean. First she tosses off her sheets and grabs her chocolate, sucks it greedily down—there are times I've seen when I can tell you, she's no lady—and then she points at the tub. She isn't ready to speak, yet. I trudge up and down and up then down again to get enough hot water to satisfy her and then she undoes her night frock and I know my duty, I pick her up (like a stack of pillows, she's so light) and lower her gently into the tub, so gently she'd never suspect how easily I could crack her head against its edge.

Then I get to work, I know my task: with a bar of the best French soap I begin to clean every bit of her body, sliding the soap under her armpits, down along her back, by the sides of her neck, in between each one of her toes, skimming along her downy calves, up to her heavy breasts where I take special care, sliding the soap around and around, down to her belly, rubbing it up into a fine lather, until she shows how impatient she is with me by arching her back and thrusting her cunt toward my face. Because even she has a cunt, my mistress, though certainly it's pinker and pearlier than mine or any other one I've seen, and quite, quite clean, thanks to my daily labors.

So I begin, soaping her fleecy hair, rubbing my fingers between her lips, pulling up the hood of her little knob to clean beneath that, prodding her opening with the soap, cleaning her little brown hole until I feel it open beneath my fingers so that I can reach in and clean deep, deep inside. And if I dared to look up to her face, I know, I'd see her eyes hooded with mean enjoyment of the pleasure she feels when I kneel outside the tub and my hands swarm all over her and my fingers probe inside her and she wallows in the sweet hot water. And when the pleasure gets too strong, and I feel the heat in her asshole penetrating to my finger's very bones and the skin around her pearly little cunt goes taut and tense, I hear the voice that always comes: "What's the matter with you, you sluttish thing? Don't you know your work? Get this soap off me, now."

I do know my work. I lower my head and begin to lick her soapy cunt, lapping up the lather with my tongue, which is as strong and muscular as the rest of me, dipping my head into the water to spit out the soap and fill my mouth with fresh hot water so I can pour it out of my mouth and over her mound. My finger is still up her ass, I push her buttocks up so I can lick her cleaner and cleaner, and as I clean she thrusts herself toward me so that her lips smack into my teeth, oh, I've come to learn she likes it a bit rough, so I rasp my tongue harshly across her until she convulses, smothering the sides of my face with her greedy thighs, then pulls away from my fingers and my face so she can loll back in her bath and throw her washcloth at my still-bowed head so as to let me know that she wants me to fetch the towels and dry her off.

What I wish for more than anything during my mistress's bath is to take my hand, my soapy hand with the dirt well worked in under the nails, and ram it up her foaming cunt, my whole hand right up her, clean up to the top of her head, show her what a real going-over is, not these pretty little games with soap and water and scented oils, but she knows better than to give me a taste of her insides. The one time I tried to put my fingers in her cunt instead of her bum she slapped my hand hard and said, "Filthy thing. You know your hands are too dirty to go in there—and anyway, that's for master, not for you. I'm afraid we'll have to have words about this later."

Words from her always mean one thing, of course— me, kneeling on all fours with my face touching the floor and my hands tied together in front of me, my skirts lifted up and my knickers pulled down, being whipped by my mistress's pretty lash or hairbrush, or worse, one of master's belts, all to remind me of my place. Then I'm forced to gawk at my red and welted bum in the mirror behind me while I tell her how sincerely I repent of my sinful, soilful ways.

But I do know my place and when I've finished dutifully cleaning my mistress with my tongue I wrap her in clean white towels and help her to dress. And on days like today, when she is about to make a voyage, I pack her clothes and toilet things and I scurry around trying to finish my household tasks—washing, dusting, scrubbing, and oiling—so that I might at least snatch time to do up my hair and wash off my arms before I accompany her through the streets to the station. It's a race we run, she and I. I know she wants me to look as filthy as possible as I follow her through the streets, so that people will remark on us, my shameful grim lagging behind her haughty self, and it's a race she always wins.

And so here we are, as we began, in Victoria Station, waiting for the train to accept passengers. I stand by her luggage, my hands clasped before me and my head bowed low, while my mistress scornfully looks over the crowd and then prods the ground with the tip of her umbrella. I quiver and turn hot and cold when I feel people stop near me and whisper to each other. I can imagine the spectacle I must make for them, standing in the middle of the station, my face and hands streaked with coal marks and dust, greasy strands of hair flying about, my dress hopelessly soiled, my shoes caked in dirt, and as I imagine their eyes, some skimming over me and turning away in disgust, others staring in fascination at my impossible dirtiness, I hear my mistress hiss, "You hopeless wench! Look, look, *look* at that!"

I keep my head down but turn in the direction to which her umbrella points, at her feet, her boots, made of the finest kid leather with pointed toes and a high heel sharpened almost to a stiletto point. And what she points at are little specks of dirt, splattered on no doubt as we walked through the streets, but the umbrella points accusingly first at her feet, then toward me, as if to say—which she soon does—"Is this how you work for me?"

I know what comes next. I pick up my mistress's bags and follow her to the place we've always used in this situation, a retired part of the station where there is just enough danger of being seen and just enough certainty that we won't be. I gently place her bag on the floor and admire her endless spirit, the nobility and panache with which she pulls a handkerchief from inside her sleeve and drops it so that it flutters to the floor beside me. She lifts her skirts just above her ankles and says to me, "On your knees, and be quick about it. I want these shoes spotlessly clean before I board my train."

And so I kneel, and as I've always done, I pick up the handkerchief from the floor with my teeth and bring my head down so that I can move the cloth about her shoe with my mouth. But there is so little, little time that very quickly I let the cloth drop and simply go to work with my tongue, taking all the little spots off and working the soft leather into a respectable shine with my spit, all the time wondering how soon someone might come along and find us at our shameful game, so I work even faster, grabbing my mistress's leg just above the heel so that I can lick the bottom of her boots clean, as both she and I love, feeling the bits of grit work down my throat, and then the moment of supreme bliss for us both as I suck her heel into my mouth and gently, so gently, she slides it in and out of my slippery hungry mouth, and as I think of how useful and obedient I am, how I would do anything for my mistress, even take her dirty boot proudly into my mouth, I feel my cunt contracting, its slimy juices squirting out of me as I come and come and come, so hard I don't even notice how brusquely my mistress's foot has been jerked from my mouth.

Then I hear the voice. It's what we've always dreaded—the educated and indignant voice of a young man come to interrupt our seedy pleasures with his outrage and his testimonials. A poorer man we could bribe; an older rich man would be charmed and in any case hardly shocked, old rich men being what they are; a woman would merely scurry away—or stay to join us. But this man, I can see, will not be nearly as simple to handle, as I stand up and smooth down my dress. His sandy mustache is quivering with conceited pleasure at having someone to save, and that someone is me.

"What do you mean, my good woman, performing such an abominable act in the middle of Victoria Station?"

"My dear sir, I would hardly call this the middle of the station and any act I may be performing is certainly no concern of yours."

"I should think it is," he said. "I'm an active member of the Domestic Reform League and this past month we've been particularly concerned with the abuse of servants. Why, I've been on the committee that's been drafting a bill to present to Parliament on this very question. And I won't stand by and see this poor woman abused without interceding." He turned to me. "Can I help you, my dear?"

Before I could answer, my mistress laughed and said, "I would love to draw you out more on the subject of servant abuse, but I really must run to catch my train. Do stay here with Hannah and rescue her, by all means, if you see fit. I wish you all the best in the endeavor. Good-bye, Hannah dear." And with that, she leaned over, kissed me full on the mouth, picked up her heavy bags, and teetered away unsteadily. I wiped my mouth and turned to my sputtering savior.

"It's unspeakable," he said. "Unthinkable. Never have I seen such a thing. Most of our young women's troubles are with the masters of the house, not the mistresses. But such, such . . . perversion is simply unheard-of. My dear young woman," he said to me forcefully, each word a wedge, "you must let me help you. Follow me to my club, and perhaps from there I can find new accommodations for you."

And having nothing better to amuse myself with, since my lover, my playmate, my pretend mistress, my beloved partner in crime had fled, follow him I did.

II. The Offending Member

For the third time that day—though by now it was night—I was kneeling, this time inside a tub rather than outside one, and the person I was cleaning was none other than myself. Some strange circumstance had dictated that my rescuer's club was closed for the evening, though he had a key and let himself in. He had led me to the basement, to a marvelous tiled bathroom, the latest in sanitary reform and engineering feats, he assured me, with hot water and cold water both running out of taps into a deep and delicious tub that drained into pipes laid underground.

It had been a pleasure to wash myself, once he left me to my own devices, with a bar of scented soap and some rough cloths. I watched dirty water run down the lustrous copper drain and clean, hot water fill the tub up again; I felt my skin begin to pucker up and the room fill with aromatic steam. I cleaned beneath my nails, scrubbed under my arms, washed my hair, soaped my breasts carefully, tended to every hidden fold. And then he knocked, my crusading hero. I snatched up a towel and tied it around my breasts to cover them, then called to him to enter.

He came and sat in a chair, an enormous stuffed chair, by the tub.

"Do you have everything you need?" he asked solicitously.

"It's wonderful." I sighed. "Delicious. Luxurious. Absolutely continental."

"Continental?" He looked startled but avoided looking at me directly. Under cover of his bashfulness, I stared at him hard. He seemed transformed from the earnest prig at the station to something more dissolute, looser about the mouth. Had he been drinking?

"Missus always says her bath makes her think of France and such, sir."

"Your mistress," he said, "seems to be all too familiar with the sorts of viciousness that we know tend to insinuate themselves into this country from abroad. Particularly from France." He rose from his chair and knelt by the tub. How pleasant it was to float in the water while someone lowered himself before me.

He took my hands, keeping his eyes averted from my face. "May I?" he asked.

"Lord, whatever for?" I tried to pull them away. He held fast.

"You can tell so much about a person from their hands," he murmured, a touch maliciously it seemed to me. "Their future . . . their past." He turned my hands palm up and began to trace lines on them with his finger. "Here is the path of love, and here is the path of life. I can see that you've loved loyally up until now, that your line of life is curiously . . . ruffled. I can see a difficult past . . . a troubled future . . . and here," he said, suddenly raising his eyes to mine and digging his nails into my hand, "here we have the unmistakable sign of the deceiver. Because these," he said, shoving them away from himself, "these are not the hands of a servant. These hands are not callused, these hands are not hard, these hands are not marked with years of labor. These are the hands of a lady. A lady given to strange amusements and curious pleasure."

"This is correct," I said, leaning forward in the water, "and very penetrating of you. And now," I said, undoing the damp towel I had knotted about my breasts, dropping it along with all pretense of modesty, "if you permit me, I will demonstrate how very amusing those pleasures can be." And while his eyes were riveted on my now-exposed breasts, I pressed on his mouth a hot and very hungry kiss. I climbed out of the tub, pushed him onto the capacious chair, and straddled him, water streaming down my body onto his, raising a musty but not unappealing odor from his suit.

"You're fascinated by these, aren't you," I murmured, bringing his hands to my breasts and to the rings that pierced my nipples. "You're staring at them. Go on, touch them. Pull on them." Tentatively, he tugged at the golden hoops. "Hard," I ordered before bruising his mouth again, sucking his tongue between my lips, gently biting him, running my hands under his jacket, loosening his tie, unbuttoning his shirt. I pulled away from him to better feel the strain on my breasts. A tense thrill ate me up. I ran my hands over his face as he put his hands flat up against my breasts. He grasped the nipple rings and pulled, as though guiding a horse by a bridle, I opened my legs so that I could rub my cunt and clit against his trousered thigh. I let my weight fall on him. Now I was riding him; my breasts led his body. I shoved his head against my tits and forced him first to suck one ringed nipple, then the other. I grunted with pleasure, grunted because he didn't deserve to hear me moan or cry out. When his licking, pinching, and pulling had excited me as far as they could, I roughly opened his trousers and took out his cock. It was hard enough for me to be able to push it inside me, and so I did. Then I began to ride him in earnest, diving up and down on his prick, one hand grasping his shoulder, the other busy working my clit into a frenzy, until, almost too quickly, I came in resisting spasms. I pushed his mouth and hands away from me then, and got off him though he tried to keep me in place. I rose and stood before him and watched while he wrapped his own hand around his cock and frantically pulled a climax out of it.

I reached into the tub and pulled the stopper to let the water drain. There is nothing I detest more than a tub filled with cooling, dirty water.

"Take off your clothes," I told him. "I would like some company in my nudity."

He stood up and wrestled out of his costume. Then he pulled me to him and back down on the chair, in a parody of a domestic embrace. He stroked my hair and planted a kiss on the top of my head.

"I too, have a confession to make," he murmured.

"I have made no confession for you to add to," I haughtily corrected him. "You made a surmise which I have as yet done nothing to confirm. But by all means, do confess."

"I am not a reformer. I am a scoundrel. I did not bring you here to rescue you."

"How refreshing." I smiled, trying to duck out from under the hand that held my head down.

"In fact, I brought you here on a wager."

I stiffened beneath the increasingly strong pressure of his hand.

"You see, every week the chaps, the members, bet on whether one of us can lure a woman into the club and have our way with her. That's why it's shut. To leave the field clear. Not everyone wins, but I always have. Though this time my trophy is of extraordinarily unusual—shall I say quality? Interest? What word would you use, Miss . . . ?"

I snapped my head away from his heavy hand. "Wouldn't you rather have to say that it is I who have had my way with you?" I looked coldly into his face.

"Ultimately, it's immaterial. Evidence, ocular evidence, is what counts, and in the end, that evidence never reveals who took whom. My fellow members are not particularly imaginative men, my dear Miss—shall I call you Hannah? Such an unsuitably plebeian name for one so perniciously refined. And when my fellow members see you impaled to the hilt on my stalwart tool, they certainly won't hesitate to hail me as the conqueror."

"And what is this ocular evidence to which you refer, pray tell? Do you have spies hidden in the next room? Trick mirrors on the walls?"

"Oh, nothing so primitive." he said. "The club has a camera, the latest thing, doesn't require that one stay still for nearly so long as those old daguerrotypes did. Almost instant. And you're going to pose for some pictures. With those lovely rings of yours. I'd heard they were all the rage among society women lately, but this is the first time I've had the pleasure. Tell me, did it hurt? How and where did you get it done?"

Hoping to disarm him, I said, "The woman you saw me with at the station is my lover. You caught us, I'm afraid, playing one of our favorite games—maid and mistress. But when we're not at play, we're New Women. I take courses in political economy at the University of London, and my friend studies medicine. She is also the daughter of an eminent surgeon, whom she often assists in his operations. She obtained the necessary instruments and anesthetics and performed the piercing herself."

"Capital," he said, rubbing his hands, "absolutely capital. I knew right away you were no serving girl. A veritable decadent, that's what you are. Tell me, did she use ether? I've heard women become the absolute devil when they're under the influence of ether."

My swain was beginning to reveal a most annoying incorrigible disposition.

"Aren't you," I asked, taking his hand, "going to show me your picture camera?"

The photographic apparatus was in a miniature laboratory, filled with flasks, retorts, acrid vapors, heaps of papers, scraps of material, mineral specimens and odd fleshy objects floating about in jars like last season's pickles. I had wrapped myself in a robe that had been lying about in the bathroom, and stood by while my hero, now metamorphosed into a young man eager to prove himself to someone more advanced than he in the school of corruption, rustled about looking for old photographs to show me. He pounced on a pile in a corner. "Here they are!" He waved a sheaf of thick paper at me. "Come look."

I stood by him while he flipped through an apparently endless series of pathetic portraits, each girl looking more embarrassed and put out than the last; breasts flapping to one side, legs awkwardly parted to reveal a hairy slit, one arm stretched before a face in a wretched attempt at anonymity, the other arm stretched forward toward the camera as though to balance an eminently precarious act.

"That's Helen," he said enthusiastically. "She was a virgin and we paid her mother ten pounds to have her. She lost her virginity twenty times in that one night! And each time screamed as though it hadn't just happened before. By the time I had her, the jism was pouring out of her. Fred, he's the president of the club, he wanted to etherize her like they do in the specialty brothels, but we couldn't get hold of any. Maybe *you* could get us some," he mused. "And that's Kitty. You see the stripes on her legs? That was Harold, he likes to whip them. Has a special cat-o'-nine-tails for it. That's what comes of too many beatings at Eton. He's a regular devil. But Kitty was a sport, she was always happy to suck on one gentleman's member while getting fucked by another. She brought a friend along, too, where's her picture"—more furious flipping—"there, Phoebe, I think her name was. Phoebe was terribly fond of Greek love, if I remember rightly. Had three or four of the member's cocks up her asshole that night. You see," he said, "on the outside we call this the Sportsmen's Club, but amongst ourselves we're the Randy Bohemians. Most nights it's a collective proposition, but Wednesdays, as I told you, it's more of an individualistic endeavor. Are you ready for your pose, Lady Hannah?"

"Soon," I said, leaning into him. "Show me some more so I have an idea of how to arrange myself."

"Of course," he obliged. "Lovely of you to be so agreeable. Most girls put up a horrible fight, we usually have to threaten to turn them in to the police for prostitution. Well, that's if they're working girls. In your case I suppose blackmail would be more the trick."

"Won't be necessary, dear," I answered breezily. "Do show us some more."

He returned, engrossed, to his pretty pictures. "There's an awfully good one of an old hag named Hermione. She seemed pleased to have someone taking such an interest." As he searched, I undid my robe, working loose the belt that tied it. I wrapped each end tightly around my hand and stood poised, ready to seize my moment.

When it came, I had the belt tied around him quicker than even I could apprehend, and soon I had his arms completely immobilized, pinned tight against his sides. A pained expression overtook his features.

"I say, this isn't very sportsmanlike of you."

"Well, darling—what did you say your name was?"

"Arthur," he pouted.

"Dear Arthur," I hissed, pulling some rope from a mound of odds and ends, turning him around to secure each of his legs to the handles of the drawers behind him, "I am many things, but I am not a sportsman and have never claimed to be one." I took the pictures off the table and dropped them in front of his feet. "And neither, by the looks of *these,* are you." A match came easily to hand and I used it to set the pile aflame. "I'm afraid these have to go. And you'd better not move to save them, or you'll get a nasty burn."

"The work of years," he moaned, "years and years of planning, research . . ."

"They're easily replaced, Arthur."

"They are not."

"Oh, yes, they are," I said, "by some stunning portraits of you, a martyr to your own lust and your too, too trusting nature. Do maintain that look of agony, and strain at your bonds a little bit more." I picked up his camera and stood at the requisite distance, fiddling with the various knobs and buttons. Emma had attended the Ladies' Photographic school for a bit to learn about medical pictures, and she'd told me some of what she'd learned. How amused she'd be when I showed these to her and told her everything that had happened after she left me at the station. "If you'd arch your back and turn your head to the left, you'd look very much like that delightful Spanish oil of Saint Sebastian in the National Gallery. With the fire blazing at your feet it's really quite wonderful." I shot and shot until the flames went out. Then I stepped through the ashes and delicately took hold of Arthur's prick.

"Why, here it is," I said, clasping his limp cock. "The offending member." I tugged at it a bit. "You really should be more careful, Arthur, whom you pick up in Victoria Station. I could be anybody. I could be that mad Ripper who keeps cutting people open. Of course, he's only been cutting women open till now, but one can never be sure. . . . Perhaps that's all been a ploy to make fools like you feel safe." I wanted him to tremble. Instead, of course, I only made his cock swell and rise up in my hand. I dropped it in disgust, then began to slap it from side to side. "You see, Arthur, you're terribly unaware of your true nature. You think you want to come between women, to conquer and capture them as trophies and possess them for all eternity, but really what you've always wanted is just this, to be tied up with some female bullying you about"—I slapped harder—"holding the power of life and death over you." My robe had opened and my breasts brushed against his shirt front. I grabbed his cock and squeezed it hard. "Don't you love the helplessness, the danger?" Silence. I squeezed harder. "Don't you?"

"Yes," he gasped. "It hurts."

"Good," I said. "I like that. And so do you, don't you?"

"Yes," he choked, "yes, please."

I relaxed my grip. "Such a good boy. So obedient. Perhaps you're not really a boy at all." His cock got harder than ever in response to these taunts. "Perhaps you're a girl. Perhaps you'd like me to perform a little operation on you to help you be a girl." I pressed against him so that his cock was smashed between us. "Would you like that, Arthur? Would you like me to cut off that offending member?" I gestured toward the preserved specimens. "We could put it in a jar for you to look at from time to time." I felt his hips straining as he writhed against me. I let him. I even helped him along. "Take it out to play with now and then. And you'd be free to be the girl you really are, wouldn't you?" He was pushing faster, and whimpering. "Why, if you weren't so dirty and I weren't so nice and clean, I'd turn you around and fuck you right now, just to get you in the habit, Arthur." I pulled away and his cock bobbed helplessly up and down. "But I must go now, Arthur. I'm sure some trustworthy club member will find you here tomorrow and set you free. And an evening spent in bondage is an invaluable lesson in submission. You'll only thank me later. And you'll think of me every time you look at our photographs of tonight, which I promise to send to you here." I leaned over and kissed him on the forehead. "You will remember me, Arthur?"

"Yes," he gasped.

"Yes, ma'am."

"Yes, ma'am."

"And you won't interfere anymore when you see girls playing out of doors?"

"No, ma'am."

"Well," I said, gathering my robe regally about me and sweeping out the door, "good night then."

And I descended once again to the basement, where I found and donned my clothes. I assumed a grand gray mantle pillaged from the cloakroom and stepped out through the club's ornate and narrow doors. I stood poised for a moment on its marble steps, then made my way into the waiting city square, radiant in the misty, il-luminated night.

WHAT?

Marcy Sheiner

He CAME TO ME fresh from a relationship that had drained him dry, sucked him up, and spat him out, so he was now fairly useless. Before we even knew we'd be lovers he informed me of his psychic condition. When we moved into the preliminaries, he reiterated his disclaimers, clearly stating he was not what has come to be called "relationship material."

While this was typical male behavior—heading me off at the pass, as it were—he was far from your typical fortysomething divorced American male.

He called himself Rob, Robbie, or Robert, depending on his audience; when we met, Rob slipped off his tongue, and henceforth it would be impossible for me to call him anything else. Only later did I learn that he hadn't really settled on a permanent name to go with his permanent change. Still later he asked me to call him Robert, saying it was time for him to grow up; after all, he told me with an increasing air of self-importance, "That's what this is all about." Naturally, his therapist and his men's group supported him in the use of "Robert," thinking my adherence to Rob was, respectively, infantilizing and castrating.

He had been born Robin Joann Lanigan. By age five

he was known as Robbie, and by junior high had slashed Joann to a "J." Two years ago he'd begun the process that was supposed to transform Robin into Robert, the process that would match exterior to interior: hormones, surgery, therapy, support groups. Now here was Robert, unmistakably male, calling himself Rob.

I was, of course, fascinated by his story. For five hours I sat utterly transfixed, as Rob delivered a crash course in transexualism, something I'd previously thought of as being only within the province of Renée Richards, i.e., men becoming women. At first I didn't believe Rob—he was too masculine for his story to be credible. But as he continued to answer my barrage of questions, I caught glimpses, in his facial expressions and gestures, of the woman who still lived inside the man. The effect of these flashes upon my psyche was almost electrical: I could actually feel my brain cells straining to process the bombardment of bi-gendered signals.

I am forthright to the point of bluntness—some might even say rudeness—so I minced no words in obtaining the essential details. In response to the question everyone ponders but very few articulate—the one about anatomy—Rob explained that he'd had a genitoplasty, a procedure in which the clitoris, enlarged from testosterone, is reshaped into a one-inch penis, and the outer labia fashioned into a scrotum.

Naturally, I wondered about performance. Rob confessed that, although he'd done solo exploration, he hadn't yet had partnered sex.

The next morning I awoke feeling positively charged. If my brain cells had been dancing the previous evening, they were now absolutely rioting—for it had occurred to me that I could be a first for Rob. I had discovered a person whom I thought of as a "virgin stud"—someone with sexual experience, yet who had never been with a woman while in a male persona. Even more astounding was that I had stumbled upon a human being who seemed to be of a third gender, one of maybe 5,000 on the planet. This is something very few people can reasonably expect to encounter in their lifetimes.

I pondered the sexual possibilities. Obviously, a one-inch penis wasn't going to do much in the way of penetration. But there were dildos, fingers, mouths. Mouths. I imagined mine on his tiny cock. I was not, to be honest, excited in the traditional sense; rather, I was enormously curious. It's a gut instinct I have—my nose almost twitches when I'm hot on the trail of an adventure that's going to lead me into heightened learning experiences. Usually—not always, but usually—it's sex that triggers this instinct. If I followed my nose, I knew, I'd inevitably gather new and useful information. Oh, sure, like most single people in their forties I was also half hoping for a lover to save me from a lonely old age—but I'd mostly stopped expecting to find that in this lifetime.

What I had not expected was that I would dissolve in the wake of his touch. I had not expected that by allowing my façade to soften I would crack entirely, and that the molecules of my body would become drastically rearranged. It turned out to be an exhausting process that left me dizzy with need.

My own transformation was apparently necessary: I became another vital element in his process, as essential as medical intervention. He needed testosterone to induce facial hair, and to thicken his once graceful shoulders. He needed surgery to flatten his chest and to reshape his genitals. He needed my femaleness to elicit his maleness.

For this to occur, I had to abdicate my strength, at least temporarily. I would lie beneath him, open my thighs, and prepare to surrender. His fingers entered me with the slow steady crawl of a snake and rooted deep within while I grew weaker and weaker, sometimes losing all sense of personhood. In this way I enabled him to take what he needed. He extracted my essence and used it to make himself larger, stronger, more powerful.

I chose to give him what he needed, though he would probably have taken it regardless. There was no struggle; he took what he needed as his due.

What he needed I had been hoarding for centuries. What he needed was all I had become through my complicated history. What he needed had been waiting for the right moment, place, person to claim it. What he needed had mellowed and aged like fine wine.

Drink, my arched neck offered, beckoning him to suck. *Feed yourself,* my breast called to his mouth. *And, oh, yes, force your way in,* screamed my cunt, until his fingers filled my aching need with thrusts and poundings. *Melt me down, make me flow like a river into your hands, cup your palms to receive the holy wine, slake your lifelong thirst. Shape your blossoming muscles with every thrust of you arm, feel your cock swell and grow to meet my need.*

It was as if his whole body became one giant cock, and I became simply cunt, opening up to receive the energy. I had never experienced anything quite like this in my life. Ironically, I felt more female with Rob than I had ever felt with a genetic male. Maybe it was because I was more trusting of a he-who-had-been-she, and could therefore drop my survival skills, allowing myself to become pure, primeval woman. It felt liberating—for a while. Eventually, of course, there was a price to pay.

*　　*　　*

At first Rob's reasons for sleeping with me were primarily sexual. He saw in me a capable adult woman who would abdicate not one inch of her hard-won independence, someone with whom he could explore his newfound maleness, or, to be more precise, his old maleness in a new and more direct way. At the time, this was not an entirely false image. But once he placed his hand on my naked breast, years of resistance melted away. I sighed a sigh, the kind that is quite familiar to genetic men, a sigh that said I'd been waiting all my life to be taken over. This was not what he had expected.

He had expected a few orgasms, a little fun, some pithy conversation with an intelligent peer. What he got were hysterical phone calls at seven A.M., accusations, confrontations, and demands. What he got were hungry hands roving his body, restless eyes questioning his, frantic fingers tracing every line on his face, a mouth as greedy as a nursing infant.

He had naively expected me to remain as I'd been on that first night, sitting across from him with an easy peaceful grace, my eyes flashing with interest as he told me about his transformative process. He had not expected that simply because he had placed his hand between my legs, I too would be transformed. He did not understand the power in his hand. He did not expect it to be an agent of change.

I hated the insatiable creature that turned to him with swollen eyes and humiliating hunger. Hated her, yet felt strangely justified by the thoroughly predictable script, one inscribed, most likely, on the Dead Sea Scrolls. I had expected to give him the self I'd been cultivating for decades; instead I gave him one that had been formed prehistorically.

When he advised me against falling in love with him, I pretended to hear, but my heart secretly whispered, "He'll fall in love with me too."

And he did. How could he not? He had never fucked such an insatiable cunt, a cunt that never seemed to quit. I wanted more and more, and he took pride in his ability to give it to me. He'd roll me onto my belly and fill me with his fingers—two, three, four. I'd ram my butt back and forth in a frenzy, getting fucked deeper and harder than I'd ever been fucked by a penis. When I came, I would open even more and Rob would fuck me even harder. "Fuck me till I die," I once murmured, and meant it.

I learned how to suck his cock until it stood hard and straight, reaching maybe two inches, then with a few well-timed flicks of my tongue, I'd cause him to twitch and shudder in orgasmic release. Unlike many genetic men, he never assumed that this signaled the end of our lovemaking, but in a few minutes was ready to fuck me some more.

So, yes, he fell in love with me. He loved fucking me so much he would put up with almost anything.

Three months into our relationship I went on my annual pilgrimage to Florida, where my mother and seven other relatives now reside. Naturally, I brought along snapshot of my new boyfriend. My mother, who had previously endured—or, rather, ignored—twenty years worth of longhaired androgynous hippies, struggling black musicians, and one or two women, proclaimed Rob the most presentable man I'd ever brought forth for her scrutiny. He did, after all, cut a fine figure in suit and tie, and his photo was triumphantly circulated among my relatives as evidence that I'd rejoined civilization. I fed them a personality profile to accompany the picture, omitting, of course, the custom-made genitalia. The only spicy tidbit I offered them which bordered on truth, was the fact of his "ex-wife's" lesbianism, a detail they digested, thanks to Oprah and Phil, as a common contemporary occurrence.

I'm not much of a liar, and was surprised to find that I never once slipped up: all too easily, I passed off Rob—and myself—as thoroughly ordinary. I was equally surprised by my family's unquestioning faith in my story: they readily accepted that I'd fallen in love with a white middle-class corporate executive who seemingly had no aberrations other than a kinky ex-wife. This gave me pause: perhaps that was indeed whom I had fallen in love with.

Familial approval was entirely foreign to my experience. I found myself feeling more and more detached from Rob with each day spent under the Florida sun. The more I spoke of his child (neglecting to mention she'd been conceived by donor insemination) or his refreshing communicativeness (neglecting to mention the female conditioning that had nourished it), the more alien Rob seemed to become. It was as if I'd handed a precious gift over to my family; it was no longer mine.

Five days later I staggered off the airplane and into Rob's arms, full of apprehension. Suddenly I was aware of what people all around us were seeing: a woman reuniting with her boyfriend, or, for all they knew, her husband. I could have been a wife, something I had not been or wanted to be for twenty years.

That night, when Rob's hand dove deep inside me, I saw only the man I'd paraded before my family. I remembered my mother joking as I'd left about how I was short on sleep and probably wouldn't get much at home. It was the first time she'd ever acknowledged me as a sexual being. Suddenly Rob's hand seemed an extension of the one that rocked the cradle, and I was repulsed.

"I don't like my mother approving of my sex life," I said, trying to pull away from him. Rob laughed, and kept right on fucking me.

"Don't you understand?" I insisted. "It's like my mother is here with us. I can't have sex with her around."

Rob grinned his best Dennis Quaid grin. "Sure, I understand. You can just lie there—you don't have to be sexual. I'll do it all."

I was angry. I wanted to sit up and discuss, analyze, this extraordinarily revelation. "This is important, goddammit!" Even as I protested, though, my juices were dripping over his unyielding fingers.

"I know it's important," he said, "and we can talk about it later. Right now I wanna fuck you."

I felt myself weakening, but managed to say feebly, "That's just like a man."

"That's right," he said unapologetically, leaning forward to kiss me. I tried to resist, but it was futile; I'd gone under, to a place where there was no reality beyond the steady motion of his strong arm relentlessly driving his fingers into my cunt, probing around to extract all the wetness, withdrawing every so often to smear it over my erect clitoris. His hand moved back and forth in a long slow motion from clit to cunt, until I was thrashing and moaning helplessly.

He lifted my pelvis onto his leg, rooting around inside me. I watched his head bowed over my breast, his mouth fastened to the nipple, and perceived him as a woman, beautiful and strong. Then I glimpsed the hair on his flat chest and soared into new heights of ecstasy, transported by the dissolution of gender distinctions.

I rolled over and pressed my own hand to my clit while Rob, not missing a beat, followed my movements, his arm like a piston maintaining a steady rhythm, fucking me long and hard until I came, my cunt tightening and loosening repeatedly around his knuckles, my voice moaning his name in an exorcism of my mother and outworn childhood inhibitions.

What he needs to take is what I need to give. Sexual power flows from my cunt and into him and back again in an ever-widening circle, until we are both transformed into something far greater than we ever dreamed possible.

"What?"

He asks me this often, usually when we're lying together and I'm staring at him with, I am sure, glittering eyes.

"What?"

Sometimes I just shake my head and say, "Nothing." Sometimes I parade my list of concerns: when you get to know me better you won't like me, I won't like you, you're going to leave me, I'm going to leave you. Sometimes I think of fabricating something more interesting, but I don't.

He stood before his closet trying to select a shirt. I thought about the method I have devised to avoid making this daily decision: I wear whatever's in the front, returning it to the back later. If he knew about this habit he would think me eccentric, to say the least. In my defense I must add that I learned this trick from my best friend; still, it is but one of many obsessions I would rather die than reveal. He has no idea, for instance, that I'm a compulsive list-maker: I hide my lists whenever he comes over. He is oblivious to the fact that his presence disrupts my usual morning rituals, leaving me disoriented for the entire day.

"What?" he asks, finally pulling a shirt off the hanger.

"There's so much we don't know about each other," I wail, implying disaster on the order of famine or earthquake.

He laughs, that wonderful deep-throated sound I have learned in a few short months to elicit. He thinks my worrying is "charming." Does he think my habit of eating food from my plate in a precise left-to-right pattern, so ingrained I do it automatically, similarly charming? So far he hasn't seemed to notice. There are many things he does not seem to notice about me, for he is too enchanted with himself, with the self I have helped bring into being. He is sailing on an ocean of self-love.

He runs his fingers through my hair and across my breasts. My nipple kisses his hand and my eyes gaze into his.

"What?" he asks.

I shake my head dumbly. *I am yours,* I want to say, *I belong to you utterly, do with me what you will.* How can I say this to a man I've never even seen brushing his teeth?

I brushed my teeth in front of him one morning. I did it on purpose. He didn't seem to take any notice. Could I floss in front of him? Would he notice I have a precise system even for this?

Sometimes I feel like a character in a Dostoevsky novel, with my lists, systems, and rituals, one who must necessarily be alone to carry on these routines, without which my world might crumble. Then I think, *This will never work.* The next time he asks, "What?" I tell him: "This will never work."

He smiles and runs his hand along my torso, supple and yielding to his touch.

"What?" he asks again.

I part my thighs.

SPANISH MOSS

Stephen Spotte

I ENTERED SAVANNAH in a city of that name at eleven-thirty-eight, give or take. Savannah's legs, like Savannah's oaks, had a pleasing reach and fetch.

Your convergent canopy reminds me of Spanish moss, I remarked.

I know, she replied. I meant to dye it red like the rest but with Ricky taking sick and the hall light burning out and me without a ladder, one thing led to another. Her voice trailed off.

Savannah is a very sensuous city, I said. Spanish moss hangs in feminine tresses from the tree branches or nestles as shyly as pubic hair where the branches form a crotch. It's similar to the pineapple, did you hear?

More like sausage, I'd say, she replied. Straightened andouille or (Oh, my god!) kielbasa frozen stiff. But very definitely, sausage, not pineapple.

Spanish moss is a bromeliad and so are pineapples, was my reply.

I didn't know, she said apologetically. I only eat canned pineapple. Have you tried it with whipped cream and a maraschino cherry? Spoon whipped cream around the hole (pineapples are hollow in the center, I'm sure you've noticed), then gently insert a cherry minus its stem. No utensils allowed. The fun is extracting the cherry without getting whipped cream on your face. It's really quite, uh, excuse me, ooooh, *delicious*.

Forgive me, I interrupted, but the job at hand requires intense concentration. The trick is to think about other things. Maybe I can continue at this pace while still keeping to the subject. Spanish moss is epiphytic, not parasitic (or so the experts say), and goes by the name *Tillandsia usneoides*.

Oh, god! Don't do that!

Don't do what? I asked, slightly alarmed.

Start talking to me in Spanish: Spanish rice, fly, moss, men. Spanish tile. Everything Spanish is soooo sexy. Just the sound of the word *Span*-ish. She closed her eyes and grinned.

It's Latin, I said.

Yes, Latin men are the best, absolutely—their dark eyes. Are you and your pineapple Latin?

I myself hail from Minneapolis.

Is it wet outside? she asked.

Sometimes it has a pungent odor when wet, I answered.

I'm sorry, she said, her face reddening. I realize that we've only just met. Are you offended?

Not at all, I said. Those tangled gray-green mats of epiphytic vegetation simply remind me of pubic hair.

Even if the color is different from my hair?

Ah, certainly. Oooops. Slow down, please. Slow *down*.

Sorry. You don't have to shout. Is there a speed limit or something? Is there a law saying a girl has to travel at this or that miles per hour? She squeezed her lips into a pout.

No, ah, forgive me. Yes, that's it, yes. No, back off, that's a little fast, just a *lit-tle* fast, but everything's going to be A-okay. I can handle the occasional speed bump but not sustained acceleration. I'm trying to picture Spanish moss quivering in a light breeze, but it doesn't seem to be working. We're fine, however. This is quite restful.

Don't fall asleep, she admonished. I don't smoke during the ride, and don't you sleep.

It flowers, you know. It has little white flowers and spreads its seed far and wide.

I've never seen one with flowers, she said, suddenly interested. What kind of flowers? You mean a tattoo? What other sort of flowers could there be? I knew about the seed, of course. Everyone knows about the seed. It's even in the Bible.

Oh my goodness! Oh, *sí, señor!* she cried. Mercy me, sorry to step on the accelerator. Then Savannah yelled in my ear, I bet you never fucked a city before!

No, I yelled in hers, but I once fucked a state named Georgia (and possibly a Virginia too)! I felt myself pitched this way and that as if adrift on a violent sea. With a scream, I abandoned the slippery deck.

And then, what was that? It sounded like a bell. Of course. I remembered reading about a bell formerly in the tower of the Savannah Cotton Exchange. Must be noon, I said.

They don't ring that bell anymore, said Savannah.

Well, somebody just rang something, I replied.

A PUJA TO GANESHA

Simon Sheppard

THE END OF THE grimy corridor, right next to the unspeakable toilet. I wrestled open the heavy sliding door. Most compartments on these old railway cars accommodated "six seated, four sleeping," but the grotesquely misspelled reservation list placed me in a "coupé," a two-passenger compartment. The single bench seat was already occupied by a man in his forties, prosperously overweight in the manner of the Indian middle classes. He sat cross-legged, waving a stick of burning incense, chanting softly to himself. As I slid the door shut, he opened his eyes and smiled. "I have been making a *puja* to Ganesha." Praying, that is, to the elephant-headed son of Lord Shiva, supreme god of destruction and re-creation. Shiva thought his son was screwing his wife, Parvati, and cut off Ganesha's head. Repentant, Shiva swore to restore his son with the head of the next creature he saw. An elephant walked by, and the great Remover of Obstacles took on his present form. A better story, surely, than the tale of the Virgin Birth.

The Poorva Express started with a lurch. I wiped the dirt from the gray plastic seat cover and sat down. Outside the filthy window, the station platform went by. Impoverished families squatting by cloth-wrapped bundles of everything they owned. Two handsome soldiers asleep on a bench, one's head on the other's shoulder. An old man cooking his dinner over a kerosene stove. Tea sellers' cries of "Chai! Chai!" receded into the distance as the train left the wretched hutments on the edge of town. I resisted my compartment-mate's attempts at conversation—"From which country are you coming?"—and watched village India go by. The sway of the train and clacking of the tracks. The vastnesses of Uttar Pradesh. In clay-red fields, farmers guiding buffalo-drawn plows finished the day's work. Egrets flew into the evening sky. Peasants, dhotis drawn up above their waists, squatted by the tracks to take a dump.

A month after landing in Bombay, I was more confused than ever by these juxtapositions of loveliness and squalor. India, land of the impossible, the unspeakable, the unbearable. When Chas was dying, I resolved to make this trip, a journey we'd long dreamed of. We'd been planning the itinerary when the first lesions had appeared. Losing Chas had left an emptiness in me, an emptiness I thought could never be filled.

Usually, Westerners who end up in India are on a spiritual quest of one sort or another, looking for something to fill a void in their lives. And, like every Westerner, I'd gotten more than I'd bargained for, my expectations confounded at every turn. Nothing I'd studied about Hinduism back at Berkeley could have prepared me for India's tumultuous assault, its filth, its endless petty annoyances. Reading Ramakrishna in the comfort of a dorm room is nothing like watching peasant women smear clarified butter over a stone lingam, the stylized dick that symbolizes Shiva, Lord of Death.

"Veg or non-veg, sir?" My reveries were interrupted

by the porter delivering dinner. Indian Railways' vegetarian dinners were nothing special, but the scrawny
chicken legs provided for carnivores were even worse.
"Veg." The porter, stunningly good-looking with
sparkling dark eyes, smiled broadly as he handed me the
tray. I could have taken this as a mild flirtation if I chose
to. I chose to. As he left the compartment, his thin,
stained trousers rode up the crack of his ass.

My seatmate and I unwrapped the foil from our
metal trays. I said a silent prayer that the meal would
leave my bowels in peace, and dug into searingly spicy
vegetarian cutlets, watery yogurt, and a warm bottle of
Campa Cola. Ashok's transistor radio provided dinner
music, *filmi* songs from Bombay movies. Women sang
with a maddening little-girl whine, as though they'd
been inhaling helium.

Small talk over the cutlets revealed that Ashok was a
businessman from Calcutta who'd been in Delhi for the
funeral of his aunt. "She was wishing to die in Varanasi,
but it was not to be," he said in the melodic rhythms of
Indian English. "As you may know, old chap, Varanasi
is the city of Shiva, the place where all Hindus are wishing to breathe their last." He popped an after-dinner
paan, a leaf-wrapped packet of betel nut, into his mouth
and started to chew. Now he was headed home to his
wife and two sons, whom he loved immoderately.

"But you must tell me all about America. A cousin of
mine now is living in San José." As he spoke, he laid a
pudgy hand on my knee. I'd become semi-accustomed
to the subcontinent's "different standards of personal
space" (i.e., the way people were always getting in my
face). But Ashok's hand, with its showy gold rings, was
not just lying there; as he spoke, it slowly but inex-
orably crept up my thigh. He stared down at my crotch.

I'm not one of those guys whose Third World vaca-

tions include fucking exotic brown-skinned boys. That
sort of behavior always smacked of sexual imperialism
to me. And let's face it, my compartment-mate, with his
greasy hair and quivering jowls, was nobody's ideal sex
object. Still, a come-on is a come-on, and I hadn't had
sex since . . . since Chas died. Despite my better judg-
ment, my dick was starting to swell. Ashok smiled
lewdly, fussy black mustache curling above teeth red-
stained from betel.

There was a knock at the compartment door. I started
to draw back, but Ashok kept his hand firmly mid-
thigh. It was the gorgeous young porter. "Finish?" he
asked with an insinuating grin, then vanished with our
trays and bottles. Nice ass. Exotic brown-skinned boy.

"And would my new friend from America perhaps be
wanting to smoke opium?" Ashok asked. I was taken
aback. Opium was still available at government-run
stores in a few towns, particularly pilgrimage sites.
After all, Lord Shiva Himself was known to take an occasional hit. But dope was supposedly sold for sacra-
mental use only, and was otherwise not particularly
legal. I'd been around India long enough to realize that
even the most generous offer probably came with a
hook attached. Not a pleasant thought, but true. Was
this a shakedown?

"No, thank you, Ashok."

"Then would you be minding if a had a small smoke?"

I guessed not.

We'd come to stop at a station. Tundla Junction.
Crowds wandered up and down the platform, someone
occasionally pausing to stare into our compartment.
Ashok reached across me to pull down the metal window shutter, his knuckles gently brushing my hard-on.
He stood to get his luggage down from the rack. He was
hard, too. A drop of wetness seeped through his poly-

ester pants. He locked the industrial-strength latches of the compartment door, reached into his luggage, and removed a small cloth bag. From the bag he took out a clay pipe, a lighter, some resinous opium wrapped in plastic. He filled and heated the pipe.

The black blob in the pipe bowl sizzled. Ashok inhaled deeply, then put the pipe's mouthpiece to my lips. As he heated the underside of the bowl, I took a gulp of the sweetish smoke.

Several minutes and a few lungfuls later, I was flat on my back, watching the grimy ceiling fans lazily stirring eddies of opiated smoke. Ashok had repacked his paraphernalia. "You are feeling good then, my friend." He leered as he flicked the light switches, leaving the compartment awash in the watery blue of the night light. "I, too, am feeling veryvery good." The train whistle hooted mournfully.

Ashok turned up the radio's volume to distortion level. Humming to himself, he began to dance. His lewd winks and clumsy gestures were appalling, but my dick was still hard. I closed my eyes. The whine and drone of the radio's music was translated into crystalline designs on the inside of my eyelids. I felt a little queasy.

When I opened my eyes again, Ashok had become Lord Shiva. Long, matted hair swirled around His naked shoulders as He swayed to the music. His third eye gleamed. "Now it is time," He said.

He put two of His hands to my face, stroked my chest, my belly. My shirt was unbuttoned. His hands found my nipples as He bent to kiss my lips. His breath tasted of cardamom. Beneath Shiva's touch, my dick had become rock hard, white hot. I was naked, a god's hands prying my thighs apart. Beneath His leopardskin loincloth, the great heft of Shiva's lingam made itself known.

He pulled back, and began a graceful dance. With a flourish, the loincloth was gone. The god danced naked before me, the eternal dance of death and rebirth. I was on my knees on the dirty floor, looking up at Him standing above me, legs spread. Reaching up, I stroked His broad chest, his muscular belly, pressed His god-dick to my face. I ran my tongue from His balls up the underside of His hard lingam. His skin tasted of clarified butter.

His dick had grown enormous. I wrapped my arms around it, worshipped its rock-hard beauty, clung to it for dear life. We were naked in the Indian night. The air hung heavy with the smell of the evening's buffalo-dung fires, a smell that makes it seem the whole country is burning. Flames leaped up around Lord Shiva; His dark body gleamed.

"Come here." Two of His hands were working my nipples, tweaking them so hard I squirmed, while His other two hands reached around me, kneading my ass. He spread apart the cheeks, played with my hole until I moaned. His butter-slick fingers pushed into me. As Shiva held me in a many-armed embrace, I wrapped my legs around His waist, lowered myself onto His enormous lingam. No way that I could take it. I was being split apart, but pain soon melted into overwhelming pleasure. I had been empty. Now I was being filled. With every thrust, a jolt of electric energy shot up my spine, bursting into stars at the top of my head.

As I stared into Shiva's three eyes, His face softened and shifted, turned into the face of my dead lover. I was being fucked by Chas, I was being fucked by Shiva, I was being fucked by India. I was being fucked by a fat businessman and it was all right and it was what I needed. Tears welled up in my eyes. Four hands stroked my face. The god lifted me off His dick and gently set me kneeling on the ground. As He straddled me, I gazed up at His tremendous body looming against the starry sky. I tried to say, "I am yours, my Lord," but it came out as one long moan of desire.

I bent to kiss His feet, lick His toes, ran my tongue up His legs, up to the crack of His ass. I kissed His asshole, the flower of flesh, probing deep with my tongue. The taste of Shiva, of buffalo dung, of decay, of secret death and the cycle of life after life. I spread His ass wide, going even deeper. Inside Him, worshipping His most hidden parts.

With spasms that racked my body, I came. Came hard. I was enveloped by fire, fell into blackness. . . .

At 5:20 my alarm went off. I woozily slid down from the upper berth. Ashok was fast asleep in the lower, snoring away, a stream of drool trickling from the corner of his mouth. On his heavy chest lay a bright garland of marigolds. I grabbed my travel pack and swung it over my shoulders as the train, miraculously on time, ground to a stop at Varanasi Station. I leaned down and kissed Ashok gently on the lips. He snorted.

The station platform, still filled with sleeping people, smelled of piss and dirt. The chai seller poured thick brown tea from his kettle into a small clay cup. Steaming chai woke me to the start of another morning in India. In Varanasi, city of Shiva. I whispered thanks to Ganesha, then tossed the empty cup onto the tracks. It shattered. I ordered another two-rupee cup of chai. Down by the Ganges, even at this early hour, corpses were on fire. The sweet, milky tea poured like syrup down my throat.

Tumors & Humors

Joe Maynard

THE GIRL I'M SEEING has a brain tumor & the meanest dog in the world. She has beautiful eyes, never smiles, and has a dark, domed mole one inch above her long, Mediterranean nose. I think her dad was a mobster or something. I'm not sure. She always seems to have money, and when she visits me she arrives in a Lincoln Town Car. Otherwise, she spends most of her days laboring over dark, angst-ridden charcoal drawings, listening to John Cage–inspired noise.

I can't get to her apartment. Her dog has me cornered in the hall. She thinks her dog is cute. I try to think so, too. I lilt, "Hi, Bruno." I extend a hand, but am met with gnashing teeth, spit flying. Bruno's snarl begins with a bone-chilling deep, low growl, followed by a hideous sucking noise. He opens his mouth as if to bark, but only thick mucusy sounds escape. Teeth like a saw blade. Eyes like Satan. Neck fat enough to swallow a human leg. "Janice!" I yell from my corner. "Janice!"

The door to her apartment is at the top of a four-step platform in an industrial building. She opens her door in a tight Mr. Bubble T-shirt and nothing else. I smile at the sight of her slim belly with shimmering black bush beneath that extends its frilly arms from hip to hip. Above she is smaller than an A-cup but wonderfully spherical, legs skinny and long with childishly knobby knees. Her T-shirt is balled up into her armpits, her little nipples fitting into the crevices of fabric radiating from her armpits. She's either been writhing on the sofa masturbating, or she's just completed a psychotic fit. My guess is that she was masturbating, since Bruno is in the hall. But who knows?

"Hello," she said, her long, feline toes wiggling over the edge of the steps.

Bruno is excited that the door is open, and lumbers up the stairs into her apartment.

"Coming in?" she asks.

"Okay."

The smell of brown rice and steamed vegetables fills her apartment. She is very healthy for someone with a brain tumor. Mostly, she denies it exists. She won't have it removed or endure chemo or whatever you're supposed to do. She doesn't want to be damaged. Some kind of all-or-nothing way of thinking. She is captain of her body and willing to sink with the ship.

The kitchen is near the windows that face the East River. It's actually an island with a stove and refrigerator. Her apartment is a loft-style room, approximately the size of a basketball court. Her tortured drawings, at various stages of completion, are pinned up across a pressboard wall that runs the length of her space—her bed at the far end away from the windows. In the middle of the room, a Saran Wrap cocoon is spun from the rafters to the floor, a couple of feet wide at the top, brimming to ten feet wide at the bottom. I call it her "living womb." "Living Womb" keeps her warm with a space heater, sofa, TV, and stereo inside, warm and happy while the video lights break into marbleized rainbows on the clear plastic sheath. Two videos this week: *Breakfast at Tiffany's* and *Midnight Cowboy*. A fairly romantic view of New York considering she grew up here. She turns off the TV as we pass, and I follow her to the kitchen. She throws her books away once read, but I see today she's been reading Djuna Barnes and Richard Brautigan & fleetingly wonder if she'll give them to me when she's done.

I sit at the table by the window, imagining her sipping tea and watching the ships pass during the day. If I were her, that is what I'd do. The dog pants somewhere in the middle of the apartment. Did I say how sexy she is? For being so gloomy, she actually makes me happy. She could be a model if it weren't for her mole and the fact that she rarely wears makeup or combs her hair. She has that "bee-stung" look, and red cheeks. She streaked her hair recently. It was an impulse decision that she said made her look too bourgeois.

I, too, am Italian. But I am somewhat fat and dark, with a harelip. People like me because sometimes I am funny, but usually they just identify me as the guy who plays bass in that band & they're glad to have me around. Our band, I gather, is now "cool." We were never cool until about a year ago. I can't say why, but after five years it just happened that way. I am not cool, but somehow people think even that is cool. Ambiguities aside, I don't mind being someone people want to hang around with.

Janice is having a hard time getting the lid off the tea tin. She slams it on the stove, and her face wrinkles tightly until a tear escapes. I get up, brush her hair back with my palm and kiss her mole.

"Can you get this?" she asks, trying to maintain distance without offending me. I think she has been drinking coffee today. Her doctor told her not to, but she still does it and it makes her anxious when she does. I've quit smoking pot around her. It's out of the question.

My mother would tell me I should be seeing a happy, vibrant, confident, good-looking-in-some-vague-way woman who always goes out with winners like me. But of course, that means I would be a happy, confident, good-looking winner who meets my girlfriend for tennis at the crack of dawn and sips Campari all summer. I would be perpetually bored talking about my career, and have kids to keep from dozing off.

Fortunately, I have flaws. How lucky I am that this beauty, Janice, is cursed with a mole on her forehead, cancer, and a severely melodramatic outlook on life. Of course, I take back the cancer thing. I really, really wish she didn't have it. God, I don't actually believe in You, but just in case, please make her not have cancer. I wonder, if she didn't have it, would she still go out with someone like me? If she were healed, would she leave me? Go out with that guy my mother thinks I should be? Either way, I'm bound to lose her. I often think she's about to dump me anyway.

Bruno is now in the kitchen panting over his bowl. I am making tea. Janice opens a cabinet, takes a scoop of dog cereal, drops it in Bruno's bowl, then reaches around my back, twists my nipples, and bites my shoulder blade. She rarely gives me a peck on the cheek. In fact, she rarely kisses lip to lip. She's just an all-or-nothing kind of girl. Then she pours Bruno a bowl of water, walks to the sofa-cocoon, and sits with one knee up fingering her twat. I smile at her. She pats the space on the sofa next to her, signaling, with a rare smile, for me to sit next to her.

I bring the tea, set it on the coffee table, pour for her. We look at each other. I force my tongue down her throat. She likes it. She wraps her legs around me and reaches to unbuckle my belt, unzip my jeans. I let go, reach for poured tea, hand her a cup. We sip.

"I have to pee," she says, and I watch liquid squirt from her spread thighs onto the sofa. At first I put my cup there, but then decide to dive over her leaky bush and swallow as much of her as I can. It tastes like sea salt and penicillin, I guess. It's one of many firsts for me that I've done with her. When she is finished, I continue giving her head. She leans back. I kneel on the floor, licking and sucking. Quickly, she gets to a point where I think she will come, but she doesn't. She sits up, kisses my forehead just below my receding hairline, and walks to the kitchen. I hear dishes rattle.

She brings back a tray with two large covered bowls, two small bowls, chopsticks, tamari, and napkins. Very neat. She uncovers the bowls. Steam is everywhere. As usual, vegetables and brown rice. She serves me an appropriate portion, more than what she serves herself. Steam and tamari taste similar to her. She draws her knees up while she eats. I kiss her knee. She eats. I eat.

"You wanna watch a movie?" I ask.

She shakes her head no; we eat quietly.

When she finishes her bowl she kneels in front of me, pulls my jeans down around my boots, and sucks me slowly and methodically, tickling with her tongue, deep-throating down to my balls, licking underneath my asshole, et cetera. She does this for a long time before I pull her back on the sofa to "69." I spread her small thighs and hold on to her writhing buttocks. She's sucking and untying my boots. She's sucking and pulling off my jeans. She's very strong. Her arms twist around my legs. Pressure mounts in me. She digs her fingernails into my butt, and bucks hard three or four times into my face. I push her head all the way down to my scrotum and shoot semen deep into her throat. She bucks against my teeth and tongue. She moans. I suck. She bucks. She comes, but I'm not sure how big an orgasm it was. I can't get more inside of her. I run my hands over her smooth legs and squeeze them around my ears. When I release, I hear Bruno licking himself in another part of the room.

We sleep for a while, clutching each other's lower extremities, when she says, "I have something to tell you."

"You're pregnant," I say, half asleep.

"No."

"You're seeing someone else."

"Yes."

The dog awakens, makes mucusy noises, licks himself again. I look at the vegetables. They lack steam. They are beginning to get crusty. I don't feel sad, I feel corny. Why must I make such poignant observations during moments like these?

"What's he like?" I ask, as if *I* owe *her* sympathy.

"He's got one leg."

I laugh. "One leg?"

"He was in the army."

I look across her body to her eyes. She's squinting again like she's holding back tears, but instead she laughs.

I feel I must elaborate. "I meant, Why did you sleep with him?"

"He told me a joke."

"So?"

"We were at a party, he made me laugh, I sucked him off in a closet."

"I meant, What's the joke?"

Now she starts to cry. Her nose is running, tears dropping on my ankles. Her sobs are high and squeaky.

"What's the difference between the Rolling Stones and a Scottish shepherd," she snifts.

"Is this an amputee joke?"

"No."

"Then I don't know."

"The Rolling Stones," she says, struggling to withhold tears, "say, 'Hey you, get off of my cloud,' and the Scottish shepherd says, 'Hey McCloud, get off of my ewe.'"

My heart sinks. I chuckle, but it hurts. I squeeze her hips against my chest.

"I love you," I say, kissing her knees.

"I know." She sighs. "I love you, too."

REAL

Bill Brent

PORN STAR

Huge Dick

Very expensive. Worth it.

Mean 31, 6'1, 180, blond,

gorgeous. Farmboy looks,

dungeon attitude. For real.

And you?

So I was born lucky and raised arrogant.

It's possibly my best ad yet, good enough to ensure a lucrative month. If I don't want a job, or if a client has a particular need that isn't my specialty, I just refer him to a colleague. I don't take a cut for referrals; they're good for business. My friends and I trade clients a lot. It's pretty common. Ever since Governor Achtenberg decriminalized prostitution back in '11, industry standards have steadily increased. There's hardly a call boy in all of North Carolina who can't earn a decent living these days, provided he has good business sense and doesn't snort it up his nose. All in all, the Hedonism Decriminalization Act has been a real boon to the new state's tourism industry.

I got a sinking feeling in the pit of my stomach when my video pager went off. I can often intuit a heavy scene before I even pick up, and this one was a five-alarmer. It was deceptively simple, even typical: an older guy calls, needing to see me immediately because he's built up this intense fantasy of me based on my ad. By the time he actually makes the call, he's afraid that if we can't get together right away, he'll lose his nerve. These guys tend to be a lot of work, but treat them well, and they often turn into devoted regulars—the sweetest, most appreciative guys of all, and generous to a fault.

I saw his scan. "Hello." A handsome, well-built man, about fifty-five.

"Uh, hi. I saw your ad, and . . ." He trailed off.

"How can I help?" That phrase usually puts the timid ones at ease.

"Do you own a black leather trench coat?"

"Well, sure." Aha. A noir fetishist. The constant recycling of past decades through the culture had achieved its ultimate realization around the turn of the century: era fetish.

I subtly shifted into my best Bogart. "Not only that, my playspace is VR-outfitted, state of the art, and I have the latest discs. Everything from medieval dungeon to New York subway tearoom. Also got a Sony-Phillips phase-shifter, so if you wanna combine, say *Key Largo* and urban construction site—"

"No. Nothing virtual, please. I want the scene to be completely real. You and me and our passions merged. Nothing more."

"Except my trench coat." I smirked. I had a real poet on the line. "Okay, Dante. Tell me more. What merges your passions with mine?"

"Well, I'm into jockstraps, and heavy tit torture, I like verbal abuse . . . and I'd like to be your cock slave."

Embarrassed pause. "Actually, I've been thinking about calling you for months, but I didn't have the nerve."

"Sounds good to me." I was right; this one had been saving it up. "How much S/M have you done, anyway?"

"I've been doing S/M privately for about fifteen years."

I asked him about his limits, turn-offs, and so forth. He sounded insatiable. I would have to remember to pace myself so I didn't burn out before he did.

"Usually, I offer a two-hour session; sounds like we can skip the massage—"

"That was the next thing. I'd like to do an all-nighter, if you're available."

Wow, this guy was serious. "I'd love to, as long as you can pay my rate. That's a thousand in, with a two-hundred-dollar deposit up front, nonrefundable in the event of cancellation or a no-show."

"That's fine."

I keep all the deposits in my retirement account. I tapped the kitchen screen to call it up. "I've opened my deposit-accept screen. You can drop in the two hundred by pressing pound-one, star-37, and entering the amount plus pound."

I heard a series of beeps, and my screen rescrolled to acknowledge receipt of a $1,200 deposit. "I think you made a mistake—"

"No mistake. I fully intend to keep this appointment."

"But what about the extra—"

"Oh, I'm sure you'll earn it."

"Wait a minute, here. Why are you pulling my chain? I don't even know you, and here you are, giving me a twenty percent tip *before* the session, all of it up front; you want an all-nighter before we've even met—I mean, I guess you've seen my flicks, but still, that's unusual.

And you completely write off my VR playspace, one of the best in San Francisco. What's really going on here?"

"There's something more to this. I suppose I should explain—"

"You suppose. Yes, you should explain, and I didn't hear a 'Sir' at the end of that. If you're paying full-tilt, we might as well start right now."

The caller groaned appreciatively. "That's it. That's exactly what I want. That's exactly how I need to be treated. I want to feel something real, I want to be pushed around. I run one of the largest banks in town, I'm totally out in my public and private lives, and still everyone treats me like I'm going to break them in two. They fear my power. No one treats me like a real person."

"Are you hard right now?"

"God, yes, stiff as a board."

"Good. I want you to stay that way. Don't touch your cock until you arrive."

"No, Sir."

"Where does the noir fetish fit in? The black trench coat?"

"Well, I do like the old black-and-whites, but what really turns me on about a trench coat is a sense of mystery. And the revealing of that mystery, what's really behind the curtain. That's what a trench coat symbolizes to me."

Finally I noticed something strange. "You don't have your video on, do you?"

"No, I don't." Pause. "Uh, would you mind if I called you 'Mister' instead of 'Sir'?"

I grinned. "More mysterious, huh?" I was beginning to get into this guy's headspace. "Have you ever seen one of my flicks?" Almost every queen in town owned at least one dub of my gay ones.

"No, I hate video porn."

It figured.

"Okay. Be at my place at six o'clock sharp. My address is One South Park. Ring the penthouse."

The doorbell rang exactly at six. I had decided to see him in the library, though we could have used the dungeon. But, as he would soon learn, the library's leather furniture was strategically designed for more than just sitting and reading.

I saw him on the closed-circuit TV. "Hi. I'm going to buzz you in. Take the elevator to the top. Stop just outside the door and wait for further instruction."

I stood in the doorway in nothing but the trench coat and a pair of skintight boots. I did not introduce myself, just took the black leather cap from his head and placed it on mine. The look on his face was priceless, and I swear it made his dick jump. The moment when another guy feels me take control of him is still one of my favorite experiences. I indicated the library. "Go in there. Take off your clothes and leave them on the floor at the foot of the desk. Folded."

I followed him into the library. When he had complied, I stood over him in the center of the room and said, "Hang up my clothes." He sported a rock-hard boner that would have been the pride of a man half his age. He also kept himself in stupendous shape. Shit, I would have played with him for free if I'd seen him out cruising. This was going to be fun.

"Wait a moment." I took two chrome-plated clothespins (okay, bill holders) from the desk and attached them behind his nipples. "That looks much better." He groaned. "Thank you, Sir."

"I did *not* say you could speak!" I slapped his cock with a leather glove. His cock throbbed. I kicked over his pile of clothes with my boot. "You are nothing, understand?" He nodded quickly. "You are nothing but what I say you are. And I think you are a pig. All that remains to be seen is whether you're a stupid pig or a smart pig. I hope for the sake of your worthless nuts that you're a smart one." I saw a large drop of pre-come reaching critical mass. I pointed at his dick. "Okay, pig. Take your finger and scoop your pre-come into your mouth. Show me how much you love to suck. And keep checking yourself. I don't want your pig-drool on my boots or on my floor."

His dick jumped again when he stroked his tip with his finger. "Ummm," he breathed, sucking the salty wetness into his mouth.

"Down on the floor, pig, where you belong." He hit the deck. "I thought about collaring you, but I've decided you'll have to earn that privilege. He looked up at me. "Damn, but you're a stupid pig! Do not look at me, do not speak to me, do not do anything unless I tell you." I kicked him in the nuts with my boot tip, and he groaned loudly. "Shut up!" I snarled. "You were trying to look up my trench coat, weren't you?" He started to protest, then thought better of it. "You will have to learn a lot before you get to look under there. Here, put this on," I commanded, handing him one of my jock-straps. His dick jumped at that, but he caught the glistening drop of pre-come before it fell. He was learning. "When you're done, get on the bench, face down," I ordered, indicating a leather-covered bench perpendicular to the large window. Once he was in position, I bound his wrists and ankles with leather cuffs. Then I covered his head with a hood, making sure his eyes were covered. I pushed a button on the wall panel, and as the bench started to rise, I could tell he was startled. When I had him at a 45-degree angle, I stopped.

"Now the first thing to teach a stupid pig is obedience. One way I do that is to flog the crap out of you."

I took a soft deerskin flogger from the rack that hung behind me. "We'll start easy, and work up to rough as quickly as I think you can manage it."

We progressed rapidly through a series of heavier and heavier floggers, which I used happily on his beautiful back. I used all the technique I could muster. Once he was warmed up, I mixed up sharp and soft strokes at random, playing with his mind so he never knew how the next stroke would feel; then, hypnotically, I alternated sharp and soft strokes. Then cross-handed flogging, where I used two floggers at a time, circling each one in figure eights; after that, some really solid whacks with my heaviest buffalo flogger. I didn't have to tell him to breathe or give me his back; he responded beautifully to my ministrations and obviously drew great pleasure from the pain. There were quite a few raised, red areas crisscrossing his back when I stopped.

"You've done this a lot, obviously."

He didn't respond.

"You can speak, now. I grant you permission to reply."

Still no response. He was still tranced out from the flogging. Unseen by him, I took a glass of ice water from a pitcher and poured it down his back. He hollered.

"Hey, pig! I said, you've done this a lot, haven't you?"

"Yes, Sir, sorry, Sir. My lover for several years was quite into flogging."

"You have a beautiful back. Most guys can't take the last flogger.

"We're going to work your ass next, pig."

He brightened. "I'd love it, Sir."

I sneered. "Of course you would. You asked for it, remember?"

I slipped my hands into a pair of form-fitting Sleeveskins, which allow far more sensitivity than those cheap latex gloves (strictly for doctor scenes these days). I put him back on the bench and started playing with his hole. He sort of gurgled and arched his back, and I watched as his sphincter quickly expanded to swallow two, then three, then four of my fingers. He clearly spent a lot of time playing with his hole. Either that, or he was just naturally voracious; just like being born with a big dick, some guys just seem to be blessed with wide-open holes. After five to ten minutes, I pressed my luck a bit, as it were, added more lube, and soon found myself wrist-deep in his hot, undulating flesh.

I had an idea. "I know how much you like authenticity," I said, "but let's try something new." He still wore the hood and had no idea what I was going to do. I took a large, vinyl-sleeved dildo and slid it into place, securing it with a harness. I switched it on with a remote control, and he started thrashing his head back and forth in ecstasy. Then I adjusted the bench so that his ass was higher than his head and positioned a padded chair in front of his head. I poured some water into the glass and made myself comfortable in the chair.

I ran the dildo through its full repertoire of sensations, watching in delight as he reacted to each change. Finally I switched off the dildo. "Hold still, now," I told him, "I'm going to take you down." A couple minutes later, I had the dildo out of his butt and unstrapped him from the bench. I lowered a bar from the ceiling and told him to hold onto it no matter what I did. Once he was holding on, I yanked the steel pins off his nipples. He screamed and started swinging on the bar. I halted him and started slapping his nipples very hard with my open palms. Once he realized he was going to live, I stopped and removed his blindfold. He had that disoriented look that bottoms usually get when they've had their sight removed for an extended length of time. "Go to the bathroom and clean yourself up. Come back here when you're done."

When he returned, I was seated in the large leather recliner. "Let's get you out of that hood. Come here." I had him kneel so I could remove it. "Good boy. Now come around the front and put your head in my lap." I stroked his hair. "How's your ass?" I asked. "It feels great, Sir," he said. "I wouldn't mind some more ass-play, if it would please you." "Oh, good," I replied. "I thought I'd reward you for being such a hot bottom." I reached for the hugest dildo I owned, as thick as a forearm with a wide base that could sit on the floor. His eyes widened hungrily. "This is Mr. Jesus. Now squat so I can work him into place."

After a bit of effort, I had him squatting on the floor in front of me with about a third of Mr. Jesus up his enormous ass-cunt. "You really are such a good little pig. Now put your snout under my trench coat and see what you can find."

Of course, I had a jockstrap on. "Oh, Sir," he murmured, and nosed hungrily around my bulging pouch, inhaling in a possessed fashion. He began chewing on the jock. I took my low-hangers out of the pouch and fed them to him.

"Yeah, good pig, *that's it, yeah,* suck my balls, you hungry cockslave. Hot little pig-slut, *slurp* 'em, that's right," I moaned. He was good with his mouth, too. "Yeah, I want to hear some slurping sounds. Oh, yeah, noisy little pig, suck 'em good. And ride that big rubber dick.

"Hot little pig almost never gets enough dick, does he? Bet you love crawling around on your knees, don't you, pig? Go to a sex club and suck off all the dick you can find. Spend hours on your knees taking dick in your mouth, up the butt, through the glory holes, everywhere you can . . ." He groaned around my hard-on. "Suck my balls, yeah, clean 'em off real good." I took a leather crop—called, appropriately enough, a pig slapper—and started to slap him with one hand while I took my cramped cock out of its confinement and finally started to jack off with the other. The sound crackled through the air. He sank his butt further onto Mr. Jesus and sucked a bit harder on my nuts. It felt great. "Slobber on my hand, pig, yeah, give me some jack-off juice." After a while, I put down the slapper and started jacking in earnest with both hands. He had me so turned on, though, that I was worried I'd shoot too quickly. Finally, I started slapping my rigid monster against his lips and slowly fed it down his waiting throat.

I played with my nipples while he sucked me; my dick felt like stone. "Oh, yesss, cock slave; suck me, suck my hard fucking meat." I held his head and fucked his mouth. "This big dick's gonna fill your throat; yeah, gonna pump your mouth full of cock. Got a big deposit here for Mr. Bank Executive!" I raised my booted feet above his head and rested them, crossed, on his back. His groans told me that he loved it. "Yeah, Mr. Bank Executive, look at you now, down on your knees, sucking some whore's cock like he's your master, huh? Well, looks like he is. Guess it takes a whore to put you in your place, don't it?" The muscles in his back rippled from the triple effort of bobbing his neck up and down on my shaft and sustaining the weight of my boots as he continued to shove larger and larger amounts of Mr. Jesus up his butt.

I had to stop him. Reluctantly I pulled out of his throat and stood above him. "Take out your dick, pigslut," I growled. It was more as though he unstuck it; threads of stickiness clung to it as he wrenched it from the jock. "Now beat it off, with that huge dick up your butt. I want to see that entire thing up your hole, and then I want to see you shoot an enormous load on the floor in front of me."

I pulled on his nipples as he tugged on his slimy cock. Then I turned around and let him sniff my crack as I squatted over him and pulled on my own juicing dick. That sent him over the edge, and I doubled my efforts as he bit down on one cheek, then the other, and he hollered in joy and pain. I turned around to see his ass swallow what little remained of Mr. Jesus, as he shot an enormous, scalding load of come onto the floor, where it was joined a moment later by my own cataclysmic torrent.

We both squatted there, facing each other and trembling, for about three minutes until he grimaced and raised himself off Mr. Jesus. He sat again on the floor, where we were still separated by a small lake of mutual jism.

Standing, I threw a small towel on the floor and smiled. "Wipe that up, and then come over to the couch." I wiped myself dry, creakily moved to the library's small refrigerator and took out a platter of goodies, then sat on the huge leather sofa. A moment later, his head was in my lap and I was idly stroking his hair.

Some time later, I awoke with a start and realized we'd drifted off. I nudged my client awake. He stirred sleepily, then, realizing where he was, sat up, startled. I grinned at him. "Let's go to bed and get comfortable." And with that, I picked him up in my arms and carried him down the hall.

I figured I'd have him sleep curled up on the floor, attached to the foot of the bed by a chain just long enough to reach the toilet.

Fuck that.

I placed him on the bed and jumped in, pulling the covers over our shoulders. I ran my hands dreamily over his taut body and pulled him close to me so that we were resting on our sides, spoon-style, with his back hugged tight to my chest.

It was a position we would repeat often in the months ahead. Maybe money *can* buy love. At least, a little bit, for a little while. We'll see.

FEEDING FRENZY

Ted Blumberg

I FUCK WITH MY FACE, my nose and mouth being my dominant conduits of arousal, my cock an exhaust valve, a pipe that spews satiation's detritus. So when she—she, whom I would have made Faustian bargains to eat, braving like a pudendal mailman sleet or snow and certainly dark of night, yeast infections, chlamydia, dysmenorrhea, eating her in any number of circumstances and conditions (after a three-day hike, a step class, a long, wide piss, a D & C, even after sex with her lover)—when she said, during one of our casual, friendly, titillating after-dinner discussions about sex, over *grappa,* that she loved to be eaten and that her lover, Patrick, found pussy-licking demeaning, not fitting work for a man, I was stopped, stunned.

(I picture Patrick, her big *goyishe* lover—who of course would have a name like Patrick; find me a full Jew named Patrick—as a rabbit-toothed, eager-beaver blond boy full of beer lust and tips on cross-country skiing, Mr. Slalom, thick-cocked and ready to spurt, nothing special in the sack but genetically well-muscled and athletic and, once you get past the smug playing-field-cum-locker-room mode of behavior—the constant optimism, the thrusting energy of the speech, the high-

testosterone Rah! rah!ness of the whole demeanor—
lifeless. And there is the difference between the average
WASP and the average Jew, if we can still talk about
averages, if we can still make ethnic generalizations
without violating every precept of political politesse,
without unwittingly alluding to master races and final
solutions: The WASP's identity is based on sports, on
not making it to the major leagues—literally—and so
everything is a declension, an allusion to the ability that
was present, insufficient, but respectable: the erect
stance, the bouncing on the balls of the feet, the relish-
ing of any chance to throw something, anything—to
someone or at a trash can; the pushed, unwavering optimism, the chronic, bright-eyed aggressivity. The average
Jew relates like a man who's failed at the mysteries of
books and is consigned now to the marketplace, mer-
chants' row; slow or quick of speech, there is always the
struggle to overcome the doubt, the sense of inadequacy
at not being able to crack the Mishnah, to make use of
the Cabbala, the persona an allusion not to the playing
field but to the bazaar or the library. As lifeless, as bourgeois, as sexually obsessed as the WASP, but less
equipped for seduction, usually, and therefore more
prone to the perverse.)

"Did you ever think what it would be like to have a
lover you could do anything with? I mean absolutely
anything?" she asked.

"I can't imagine—I mean, it would be—can you
imagine how great that would be, if you did have a
lover you could do anything at all with—I mean anything. No rules, no balking, no looks of disgust or weird
judgments, just a pact, an agreement to say no to nothing? I mean, you could confect a Magic Kingdom of unnatural acts and playlets. You could create your own
attractions like at Disney World. You could have Fella-

tio Land, Ass Lickers of the Caribbean, the Haunted Condom . . ."

"You aren't thinking about it seriously," she said.

"I am thinking about it seriously," I said. "I am so serious I am making you the offer to form that partnership. Now. Let's be sex partners. No emotional stuff, no commitments except to the agreement—to the premise. Anything goes."

"But we're not lovers," she said.

"Perfect! No baggage," I said. "No bullshit. A clean slate. We could meet once a month or so in a hotel room or wherever and just *go*. I'm seriously making the offer. Think about it. Like in *Last Tango,* only mutual, like a fucking Disney World—like a *fucking* Disney World."

She liked that idea. Of course she liked that idea. She's from Orlando.

Six months later, we finished our second, conclusive set of HIV tests—Rebecca, then Hart (our third, indispensable for her first fantasy—she got to go first, having called "heads"—no pun intended but clearly unavoidable—and he had been patient and receptive, quite handsome, quite German, cheerfully bisexual), and myself, sitting in the clinic studying the result slips certifying us as noncarriers. A proud moment for me; I have never before kept a project afloat for six consecutive months.

The suites at the Four Seasons are smallish—at least, ours was—with white walls, a small bedroom, and a small sitting room, deliberately stark, in contrast with the sumptuous, old-fashioned, inside-of-a-wedding-cake look of houses like the Plaza.

Rebecca ordered two bottles of Pellegrino and a Riesling from room service while Hart and I installed a portable chinning bar in the sitting room doorway, hung a trapeze bar from it, and adjusted the seat to the right height, and Rebecca, in accordance with Step One, Fantasy One, sat nude on the bar while Hart and I knelt in front of and behind her. As she swung toward me I got a quick lick at her cunt and then Hart got a quick lick at her ass, bracing ourselves for impact, trying not to get whiplash or be knocked back on our heels, and after a dozen or so licks I started feeling like a dog being teased with cold cuts.

The three of us were laughing but none were hard or wet so we stopped and got onto the bed, Hart climbing immediately on top of her.

I burrowed under their legs, working my hands under her ass, his sac on my head, and started eating her pussy. She had her period, which seasoned the taste of her cunt, giving me feeding frenzy and making me realize that sharks and other predators aren't frenetic during the kill because of an intrinsic toughness or hunger—it's the blood. Once you get past the squeamishness, taking it in, that life right there on your lips and down your throat flushes you full of power and mania; that's why you see sharks and wild dogs ripping and tearing, wriggling and capering, jerking their heads to and fro—they're inflamed, wired from blood-rush as much as in a hurry to eat before others take their share.

With a truly strong (really impressive, if I say so myself) curling movement, I hoisted both their hips, both sets of pelvises up, Rebecca's cheeks in my palms. Hart on top of her until he lost his balance and fell. I was at her pussy when I felt my ass cheeks being spread and my asshole getting licked. As I eased back I wondered whether there was some blackness being perpetrated, some moral horror that would make me suffer later like a string of unleashed bad luck. Rebecca's murmuring brought me back home, to her lovely black-brown fur and pinkish island of slit. I kept lapping at the brassy-bloody taste, the hours-later, morning-after, V-8-from-a-can aftertaste, supping until she bucked, screamed, beat her pillow with the back of her head, screamed and tried to climb up the bed away from my tongue. My tongue and jaw were afire, my face pained with her smell, lips outlined in splotchy blotches of maroon, like a clown who'd napped in his makeup.

Hart was masturbating next to us and Rebecca started sucking him, sucking his uncut cock like it had layers you could dissolve to find a prize, and he started thrusting his nineteen-year-old hips, throwing his head back, flinging his long Stuttgart hair around his shoulders.

Rebecca rolled off the clammy patch of bedding, the striped mattress ticking showing through the translucent patch of linen, rolled to the center of the bed, pulled Hart down by his erection and eased him inside her. I walked to the edge of the bed and started shrimping, sucking her toes, licking and sucking her soles too, and gnawing at a thin shell of callus near the ball of one foot, watching Hart's narrow, lightly furred ass bob as he fucked her.

He turned from a sweet, longhaired German boy into a rude, snarling assailant, smacking the sides of her ass, slamming his pelvis forward, throwing his head up, arching his back like he was doing some kind of power yoga.

She seemed fine, though, and said she wanted him to come on her, on her tits and belly and pussy, and she started flicking her tongue against his lips, licking his lips and saying, "Come all over my tits, I want to see you shoot, all over me. I want to see it spurt, come on me . . ."

And he did, heaving himself back and out of her, the muscles of his thighs striating, the thin skin of his legs straining in support of his weight as he crouched, balancing on the balls of his feet in a low squat, grabbing himself and pulling. The three of us watched his cock, full of suspense, wondering exactly how his ejaculate would look, how far it would shoot—would it shoot or dribble?—what degree of whiteness and consistency?

His cock answered with a short-range, birdshot formation of come that formed a diamond-shaped pattern of drops on her ribs and tits followed by another burst, a stream long and white as waxed twine firing from his cock, arcing at an angle over the top of her head, soiling the pillowcase and headboard. The rest of the spurts he aimed, sort of, flinging his come across her tits like a drunken pastry chef, empearling her, making discs, sickle cells, Dali clocks and broken lines on her chest and throat, her tits, her ribs and belly, her chin too, wiping the late-coming dregs onto her lips and the tip of her gingerly offered tongue.

She lay back and looked proud, arms out to the sides, a performance art piece, *Woman With Come,* some Karen Finleyesque human sculpture.

She said, "Lick it."

She was looking at me so I said, "What?"

"Lick his come up."

I said, "Wait, I—"

"You said anything," she said. "That was our deal. *Anything.* You're breaking our agreement if you don't lick it up."

So I did, starting with the splatters on her bush, up the line of fuzz from the top of her mound to her navel, lapping up the little pool there, the smell of weeping willows, of pollen, in my nose, the stickiness getting onto my cheeks, my chin, the salt-and-baking-powder taste on my tongue, and I started wondering at the number of—millions, probably—sperm, German sperm, I thought, amusing myself with the rhyme, swimming in my saliva, wriggling on my tongue, feeling tricked as they swam down my throat to discover no eggs, just a huge pool of acid to die in.

I felt hardness against my ass and tensed.

"This won't really hurt," he said.

"Wet it," Rebecca said. "Here." She rubbed her fingers on her pussy, putting a coating of her fluids on the head and shaft, and then lay back, pulled me close, kissed my neck, my ear, sucked my tongue, and bit my lower lip hard—bit into it and drew blood. Hart thrust in at the moment I howled from the pain in my lip, like it was prearranged, a doctor-and-nurse team using misdirection to give a difficult injection, my belly feeling flame swirling up to it, and feeling his hands on my ribs, noticing I was shoved forward and back in someone else's rhythm. I thought of how at nineteen you can get hard so fast so often, how at thirty I have to wait, of the pain in my balls from not having come, of thirst, of wanting water, of the Pellegrino bottle on the nightstand. My cock slid into Rebecca, her cunt like a sea thing, like a toothless, warm sponge, a tight toothless guppy around me, gripping me, coaxing the come out of me, and the pain of Hart's cock in my ass, shoving at my prostate, pushing fluids up my cock and into Rebecca's pussy, various vas deferens fluids from the prostate blitz. The pain combined with the sucking glove of her cunt, the smell of her armpits, their wetness and smell as I rolled my face around in them, rubbing my nose and chin and mouth and hair against the dale of smell and sweat like a dog at carrion. Hart was grunting and dancing behind me, pulsing little shivers, tremors of muscle and quiver and I knew he was making me his cunt, and felt the rumble and gather in the space under my balls, felt the roar up my cock and into Rebecca, buttering her pussy, greasing her, making her loose and slippery. And then there was stillness, the three of us an exhausted Twister team stacked on one another, thoughtless, breathing, rolling onto our sides, still attached, blank and sated, breathing, catching our breath, heaving in air, murmuring sighs, wordless, wondering what happens next.

REAL BLOOD

Lucy Taylor

MEN SHED REAL blood all the time—women don't," said Jake the Snake Esposito, his full brown lips twisting in a beautiful sneer.

We were sitting in a dingy booth at the rear of the Campesino Bar in Tampa's Ybor City, the old Cuban part of town where grizzled old men still roll Havanas in dank workshops that reek of tobacco and sweat, and jet-haired, poppy-lipped girls slink among the tables in nightclubs, speaking Spanish and proffering sex and cigars.

Smoke swirled around Jake's hair like a halo on the head of a demon. He touched his massive right hand to mine. A hand that just a week ago, at the Ybor City Sportatorium, had beaten a man named Cory Bogdanovich lifeless.

Jake squeezed my fingertips. I felt a deep internal shimmy, my private muscles tightening like a set of Chinese handcuffs. I wondered how long I'd have to listen to him prattle before I got to fuck him. Not much longer, I hoped. The inches he had in his pants were a whole lot more interesting to me than the opinions he had in his head.

"Bullshit with this 'Women don't bleed' stuff," I said, making my voice cute and coy. "I shed blood just the other day, see? I cut myself slicing potatoes."

I held up the middle finger of my right hand, which was thickly taped at the second joint.

"Yeah, that's what I mean," said Jake, barely looking. "You had a kitchen accident. Big fucking deal. That's not what I mean by real blood. Real blood is blood shed in a fistfight or a knife fight or a boxing match. Real blood proves you got it."

"It? What's *it?*"

He groped for the explanation. I could tell that communication, if it didn't involve fist to flesh or dick to pussy, was not his strong suit.

"*It*—you know—guts, cojones, balls."

"Ah, those," I said, thinking: *Macho-speak.*

I lifted his huge hand up, palm outward, and swirled my tongue across the calluses and gritty flesh. His skin smelled of smoke and of Scotch. *I Want You.* I wrote in his palm with my tongue.

He slid a finger between my lips. I gave him a preview of what my tongue and throat could do. I saw him swallow.

I took his hand and slid it deep into my cleavage, let him caress the curve of flesh and pinch the thimbled nipple. He kept the same expression on his ruggedly asymmetrical face, but I could feel his blood rush like an undammed river spilling over rapids.

"I want you to tell me how it feels to kill a man in the ring," I said. "Every detail, every punch."

"I already told you, darlin'."

"Tell me again," I said. "While you fuck me."

His eyes narrowed and heated. We'd only met a few hours before, when I'd picked him up in this very bar.

Even for champion middleweight Jake Esposito, pussy just didn't come this easily. "What?" he said, looking comically incredulous. "When?"

"Right now, if you're ready."

He looked affronted. "I'm always ready. Where?"

"I'll tell you while we walk there."

"Being fucked in a boxing ring is a fantasy of mine," I explained to him for the third or fourth time. We'd left the Campesino, slightly tipsy, to meander along the cobbled walkways and past the graffiti-scrawled walls of Ybor City. "Violence, especially deadly violence, excites me. That's why I had to meet you after I saw you kill Bogdanovich. Sometimes when I go to the matches, I fantasize what it would be like to lie naked in the middle of the ring while the winner of the match takes off his trunks and fucks me senseless. They're so similar, I think, the thrill of sex and of power.

"Tell me the truth," I said, rubbing my breasts into his arm, "don't you think the real reason—I mean way back in Neanderthal days—to knock out your opponent in a fight was so you could flip him over on his stomach and spread his legs and fuck him?"

Jake stopped walking, gripped my hand until it hurt. "You are one filthy-minded broad."

I laughed and slipped my arm through his.

"I get off on bloodshed," I said. "I used to go to the wrestling matches. I saw all the great ones, Buddy Rogers and Antonino Rocca and Freddie Blassie. I thought what they did was real."

Jake hooted. "You gotta be kidding—everybody knows that stuff's a work."

"Of course it's a work," I said, growing irritated with his condescension, "but when the wrestlers bled, I used to think it was because they were really badly hurt, split open. Then a wrestler I was dating told me it's a trick. They cut their own foreheads real sneakylike while the match is going on. Then they 'juice' and the fans think they're hurt real bad."

"Not fans"—Jake sneered—"marks. Only marks are dumb enough to think the blood is real."

"Of course it's real," I corrected him, "it's human blood, not chicken blood held in a capsule or something."

"I mean, the way they spill it isn't real. You said it yourself, it's a trick."

I wet my lips and watched him follow the pink tip of my tongue along the edge of my crimson-painted lips. I decided to bait him a little, make him squirm. "What about menstrual blood?" I said. "Is that what you call real blood?"

"'Course not," he said, "it's . . . somethin' else. I mean, it's blood all right, but not like blood that's spilled in a fight or on the battlefield or somethin'." He looked at me. "Hey, you ain't on the rag or nothin'?"

"No way."

We kept walking. We were close to the Sportatorium now, the place where Bogdanovich had been beaten into a coma from which he never emerged. His jaw had been broken, his lip smashed. I'd seen it all from the front row. Some of his blood had spattered onto my dress, and I hadn't washed it yet. I probably never would. That was *real* blood—shed by a dying man.

"So how about it?" I said to Jake.

"How about what?"

"You gonna fuck me in the boxing ring like I asked you to or what?"

"Hon, I can't take you in there. What if someone found out I'd been boinking a chick in the ring, they'd—"

"They'd be jealous," I said, "but don't worry, no one will know. It's dark, and no one saw us leave the bar. And you said you had a key, didn't you?" I rubbed my breast against his biceps; the two mounds of flesh were about the same size but so different in firmness, my breast soft and yielding where it mashed against his concretelike arm. "It's the only place I'll let you fuck me," I added, and I caressed the bulge at his groin very lightly, a tiny promise of pleasures to come. "Unless you lied . . . unless you aren't really *ready?*"

"Fuck this," Jake muttered, "I'm horny." He dug a key out of his pants pocket and unlocked the green metal door. The smell of stale smoke and sweat and liniment wafted out on a pungent wave. The smell of blood, too. Or maybe I just imagined it.

We went in. It was black as a burial chamber until Jake finally found a light switch and flicked it on. Then everything—the boxing ring, the folding chairs set up around it, Jake's skin and mine—was bathed in a ghastly hue of sickbeds and yellow chalk.

I stared at the ring. Less than a week ago, a man had died here, beaten to death by Jake's merciless one-two.

Jake, the man who was about to fuck me.

"Did you get a hard-on when you killed him?" I asked.

Jake climbed up into the ring and glowered down at me. "What the fuck do you think I am, some kinda fairy?"

"I heard sometimes men get hard-ons when they kill—on the battlefield, in a fight."

"Only thing I get a hard-on for better have tits and a pussy," said Jake. He was angry now, impatient. Suddenly he reached down and half-lifted, half-dragged me under the bottom rope and up into the ring. My high-heeled pumps fell off. My skirt, blouse, bra, and panties required help and Jake gave it, stripping me nude with no hint of gentleness. He didn't even bother to take off his own clothes. Just opened up his fly and let his dick spring forth like a policeman's truncheon ready to administer a beating.

Then I was flat on my back, legs up and spread over Jake's massive shoulders, getting speared by his cock, his big fists braced on either side of my shoulders. I could feel the rough canvas abrading my back; I was getting a helluva ring burn.

I shut my eyes and imagined Jake's fists pounding into me, imagined my consciousness extinguished, my life dimming out in a final convulsion of battered synapses and neurons. I moaned and thrust my hips to meet Jake's. He slammed me harder.

Jake, who had shed real blood in this very ring, who had battered a man to death before my eyes, was now pounding me to orgasm.

He could kill me anytime he wanted to, I thought. A couple of good rights should do the trick and maybe a final uppercut, just to make sure the concussion was a permanent one and my battered brain never woke up.

Suddenly I wanted Jake so wildly I could hardly breathe. I wanted him and, at the same time, I wanted to *be* him. Wanted to know how it had felt when he watched Bogdanovich die. Because I didn't really believe what he'd said about not getting a hard-on. I thought he'd been hard as a steel rod when he threw that last, deadly punch.

Maybe he could read my mind. "Cocky bitch," he snarled, pounding into me.

I came and I screamed simultaneously.

Then I sat up as if to throw my arms around Jake's manly neck, but by now I'd coaxed the bit of razor

blade free from underneath the tape around my finger—
a trick the wrestlers use when they want to "juice" for
the marks—and I unzipped Jake's throat, left to right
and then back again, right to left. His neck gaped like a
strawberry pie with a big wedge carved out of it.

He gasped and made a glub-glub sound: fish-speak.

Then he fell back and twitched there on the canvas
and bled.

I watched him.

The same way I'd watched Bogdanovich die the other
week, a sense of horror mingled with a giddy, almost obscene excitement. Now added to that thrill was
a sense of satisfaction, rightness, of personal achieve-
ment.

Not just because I'd taken out the man who killed my
lover. After all, Bogdanovich was only one of many
fighters that I fucked.

But because I'd proved the SOB Esposito was wrong.

That garbage talk about women not shedding real
blood.

I could shed real blood, all right, and plenty of it.

His.

DICTATION

E. R. Stewart

THE WIZARD HAD his dick out again.

When he does that, I usually lie low, because there's no telling what'll happen when it goes off. See, he doesn't so much ejaculate as explode. Oh, and the dick itself is, well, strange. It's not entirely of this world, for one thing. For another, it has a mind of its own. A brain, little eyes, everything. Apparently the wizard can see through those little eyes, which means he can fuck a wench from the village and actually see what she looks like inside.

Not that village girls volunteer for such scrutiny.

Shutting the door behind me, I sidled past the bookshelf and set the steaming cup of palewort tea on the nearest flat surface, the skull table. Glints of light glittered in some of those skulls, as if intelligence lingered where no brains or eyes remained.

"Sir, your tea," I said, in as neutral and disinterested a voice as possible.

Heaving back, his head lolling, the wizard grunted, but his dick twitched and glanced at me. I shuddered as it wiggled back and forth hard enough to flap the wizard's open robes. "Leave," the wizard grunted.

I left, one last glimpse showing the wizard's dick shrinking back from the size of a man to the size of a man's.

From six feet to six inches in one easy splatter of ectoplasmic semen—which I'd have to clean up later, naturally. Where he splashed the walls it ate away at the stone, and it wasn't unusual to go through three or four new mops before getting the stuff up. And it crawled, too, but luckily it crawled slowly, sort of oozed like an amoeba.

What manner of protoplasmic life that semen of his might regenerate was something I didn't really want to know, but for sure the village girls he ravished would never know, because they usually went up in a burst of cold green flame about ten minutes after he schtupped them. It was a stylish way to go, but who wants to go in the first place?

I got a third of the way down the spiral stairs when the wizard bellowed for me again. Back up the tower staircase I climbed, panting.

He was out of breath, too, from having masturbated. "Clean that up, would you?" he asked, sipping the pale-wort tea and letting his beard and whiskers ripple like seaweed, which meant he liked the taste.

"Yes, sir," I said, slumping to the closet. When I yanked the wood door open, I saw only pitch blackness, a void so total that my head wanted to lean forward and fall into it. I squinted, looked sideways at the infinity closet, and stuck in my arm. A mop grabbed me, and I pulled it out. As soon as it was out of the infinity closet, it let me grab it, and became inanimate, a dead thing of this world.

Trying not to think about a world in which mops swam like squids, I started cleaning up the steamy mess the wizard's dick had made.

"Well," he said after a while, "how about we go wenching tonight?"

If there had been any doubt of his otherworldly horniness, it vanished exactly as I shrugged and said,

"Sure, boss. But maybe we ought to find another village. Elmbridge is getting kind of pissed off."

He grinned. His white beard, mustache, and fluffy eyebrows all rippled around his sunburned, wrinkled face. He raised gnarled hands and made a slight, slick gesture. "To the mirrors with them," he said. "The Elmbridge women are the sexiest."

I nodded and stowed the mop, feeling it jump from my grasp as I eased it into the closet. "They're the sexiest because of that spell of yours. Couldn't you cast that same spell on another place?"

He slammed down his teacup. Skulls rattled, and several of them floated upward, as if experiencing less gravity. "Did they put you up to this?"

"Who?"

"The Elmbridge elders?"

What could I say. Hell, yes, they'd asked me, begged me in fact, to try to get the wizard to pick on the young women of another village, at least for a while, but to admit it might cost me considerably more than my scrawny hide, considering his shifty moods, so I said, "I overheard their complaints when I went down the hill for supplies."

A sadness crossed his face. "Yes, I can see how they'd complain. The ghosts I send back aren't the same as flesh-and-blood daughters, I suppose. If ghosts sufficed, I'd fuck them instead. But what am I to do, Sauer?"

When he called me by my last name, Sauer, I knew he really wanted my opinion, so I said, "Why not go get your normal dick back?"

"Or die trying," he said, still not throwing a lightning-bolt fit, but actually considering my advice. "Would you come with me?"

As if I had any choice about it. "Of course," I said. My throat hasn't been that dry since the time he locked

me in the desert room for spilling the last vial of
dragon's blood.

I packed. Seven crates, each one stuffed with a different kind of herb, elixir, potion, or distillation. When I
was done, I let him know, and the wizard came down
(in a flash of black sparks; he who never uses stairs) and
waved his hands over the crates. Each one glowed
bright orange, and then faded away. "Travel light," he
said.

I didn't know if he meant the glow or the weight, and
didn't ask. All I knew was that the crates would now accompany us wherever we went.

It was quite a journey, too. The witch who switched
dicks on the wizard lives on an obsidian mountain that
jabs out of the Duendonian jungles. Normally the wizard just disappears one place and appears elsewhere,
but because he needed all the magic stuff with him, we
had to walk. Well, I walked. The wizard sat on a two-
wheeled cart pulled by our little wyvern, which is nine
feet long and looks like a flying snake, except that it
kind of swims through the air.

My nerves were shot by the time we got to the foot
of Mount Yagos, where the bad witch Aur lived, or
dwelled, or manifested, or whatever that kind of being
does when appearing to more mortal types.

Looking up, I shaded my eyes from the purple-hot
sun and said, "Sheer cliffs, smooth as glass."

"There are reflections, though," the wizard pointed
out. It was true. The entire black mountain, shaped like
a broken-off elephant's tusk, jagged side up, gleamed
black and shiny, so it reflected the trackless jungles, the
sky, the glare of sun, and even us.

Well, it reflected the wyvern and me, but the wizard
appeared in the gloss in negative. You could see his
bones. They weren't human. And you could see the crim-

son glint of his dick's eyes; it was hovering just inside his robes, tiny now but, with erection, big enough to throw him around as it thrashed in otherworldly ecstasy.

Muttering spells and fetching things from this or that crate, the wizard caused our reflections to stretch upward. Before I knew what had happened, I was looking not at the mountain but at the jungle around it. My awareness had gone into the reflections, which were stretching upward, ever higher.

The view grew spectacular. I could see silver rivers, white falls, dark stones, brown boulders, and multigreen vegetation covering gently rolling land clear to the horizon. And then clouds obscured the view.

My perspective flipped again, and I was suddenly freezing cold. We stood on an escarpment high above the world, on Mount Yagos. Icy winds slashed at us. Snow and ice blew.

"Boss," I said, shivering, "we've got to find shelter."

"Nonsense," he said, not bothered by the temperature. He could sit in a campfire and bathe in Arctic waters; nothing fazed him when it came to this world's creature comforts.

He waved his arms and yelled challenges to the witch. That went on for some time. Then a crack in the stone before us appeared, and we rushed in.

There was precious little heat coming from the single coal brazier hanging from the ceiling, but at least we were out of the wind. Our wyvern squealed the way they do and coiled in a corner for some temporary hibernation. I stood hugging myself, wishing I'd brought another cloak or three, and the wizard stalked around the big empty room.

We stood on an obsidian floor polished smooth as a mirror. Our reflections were distorted, and moved whether we did or not. The air was full of light from a source I could not locate. Rough walls surrounded us, and the ceiling was carved into grotesque faces, some human, most not.

"You know what I'm here to reclaim," the wizard said.

A woman's voice chuckled, low and throaty. "I can guess," the witch said, even as a form appeared before us, just suddenly there. Neither male nor female, the witch had pea-green skin; its hair was dark blue and the nails on its seven-digit hands glinted bright yellow. Snaggled ocher teeth pushed lips aside. A forked tongue flicked. Vertical pupils split the eyes. "Darling," the witch said. "I knew you'd come back."

The wizard gave me a look that warned me to back off. I did, right into the arms of a naked woman twice my height, who whispered with a three-part voice, "And you're mine."

She turned me around and peeled my clothes off. It was both exhilarating and humiliating, but I could do nothing to resist her; she was not only twice my size, but muscular and quick and apparently used to manhandling. Once I was stripped, she rubbed me up and down on her as if I were nothing but an oversized dildo. Her pubic thatch rasped me up and scraped me down from chin to knees.

She set me on the floor. I gazed up at her. She was, believe it or not, kind of attractive: a regular face, full lips, narrow nose, green eyes. Her blond hair was shoulder length but bound in a single big braid. Her shoulders were more than twice as wide as mine, and they rippled with muscle. Her breasts, each one the size of my head, stood proud, if not arrogant. A single nipple filled my mouth, which I discovered when I moved forward and stretched up to suckle a bit, hoping to appease her. The last thing I needed was this woman feeling scorned.

"Uh," she said, closing her eyes in pleasure as I worked on her boobs, and her labia parted then, releasing musk that affected me like a jolt of sexual electricity. My boner popped up harder and bigger than it had ever been before, and suddenly I genuinely wanted this Amazon flat on the floor under me.

"Lie down," I told her, and she did, quick, so quick that I fell onto her and bounced a couple times.

My weiner was too small. Oh, it felt marvelous to me, in a way, but I thrust into her and she lay with an expectant look, as if waiting for the kidding to be over. I knew I had to do something, so I, well, I jumped in head first, so to speak.

Her clit almost gagged me. It was the size of my hand, and moved under my oral ministrations as if trying to escape me. Knowing this might not satisfy her, I gently eased my entire left arm into her slick vaginal depths, hoping that, when orgasm came, her contracting muscles wouldn't snap my bones like kindling.

While I was occupied with pleasing my Amazon captor, I heard strange grunts, shrieks, and sloshing sounds from the center of the floor, directly under the brazier of hot coals. Risking a glance, I was disappointed. I'd expected to see the wizard and the witch in each other's grasp, at each other's throats, tearing each other to bits for dominance, but instead all I saw was the wizard, standing stock-still, staring at me.

Well, it was embarrassing, but I looked away from his eerie gaze and got on with my job of pleasing the giantess.

My arm was sore already, so I switched, all the while licking, sucking, nibbling, and at times choking on her clitoris. As I pleasured her, I thought to myself, "This is how the wizard's dick must feel," and that's when I got kind of excited myself. The emotions carried me away. I pulled my arm free of her inner spasms. With a gulp of air, I pushed my face downward from her clit, until her labia split for me, until my face began entering her. I had no idea if my head would fit or not, but I wanted to try; right then it was the most exciting idea I'd ever had with a woman, and when would I ever get another chance to try it?

Kissing her deep, tasting nectar as intoxicating and thrilling as any potion or spell, I let my entire body make love with her, become her object of slippery, sexy joy.

My ears slipped in, and things got quiet. I forced my eyes open, but could see only a dim pink glow surrounding me. I heard her moans, filtered through the length of her. I felt her inner tensions around me, and I pushed all the harder, wanting only to fill her, fulfill her, please her beyond her wildest dreams.

I don't know when I lost control of the thrusting. First, I realized I was being pulled back. I felt no grasp on my ankles or anything, but without my consent and against my will, I was being pulled backward. It felt really good, though. Her squeezing caught me under the chin and on my cheeks, and as I was pulled through that grip tingles shot all through me, bringing my entire body closer to an overpowering orgasm.

And then, just as I started enjoying my forced withdrawal, I was shoved forward again. The tempo increased.

My eyes adjusted, and I could see the clenching tunnel in which I moved. I watched ripples of enjoyment flutter the sugarwalls around me, and the fact that I was the cause of such wonderful feelings made me want to gush, to pour myself forth, to spew my own secrets into her.

And that's just what happened, only it wasn't like vomiting, it was like coming harder and longer and better than ever before. I got light-headed and my senses swirled. I watched the stuff come from me, soaking her pink recesses, filling cavities sought but not quite found. And as I gushed, she orgasmed around me, clenching harder than I thought I could stand.

Breathing never entered my mind until I was pulled out of her. That's when I realized that I hadn't been breathing for some time.

Funny thing, though. I felt no urge to breathe. And that's when I realized something even weirder, even worse.

As I was pulled back from inside her pussy, I watched her fall away from me at an alarming rate. Perspectives shifted and depth perception stretched. She looked huge now, feet to my inches. The whole room seemed as big as a valley.

That's when I noticed that hand, the wizard's hand, slightly larger than I was, come down from above to grab and fold me. I was doubled over, and crammed back into a close, smelly place.

Yep, joke of jokes, I was back in the wizard's pants, where I'd originally come from. In more ways than one, I felt like such a dick for having fallen for such a trick. After all, in the original encounter, I, the wizard's dick, had failed to please the sexless, mirthless witch, so she had removed me. I got to stay with the wizard, but only as a servant. And in my place, the witch placed, what else, itself. That way, the witch could torture the wizard with horniness, and punish anyone who fucked him out of his frustration.

But now, because I'd pleased the Amazon aspect of the witch, the witch had switched us back, and while the wizard was now out a servant, he had gained a regular hose, one to which the girls of Elmbridge would not object. They could fuck the wizard a zillion times now, and not burst into cold green flame once.

"Thanks," the wizard said, snapping his fingers at the wyvern to rouse it for more pulling.

Aur the Witch raised a hand in farewell and said, "Come again soon," and then burst into gale-force laughter that stumbled, rolled, and otherwise pushed us, the wizard and me, out of the room. We descended Mount Yagos and returned to our castle above Elmbridge, and although I miss being able to run around loose, I must say there are compensations.

By the way, I'm writing this between orgasms. We've impregnated seven village girls tonight already, and I'm raring to ram a few more, but I thought I should chronicle my return to service.

And no, I'm not holding a pen in my tiny little vertical mouth: number seven's writing this. I'm just dictating.

THE BUTCH'S NEW CLOTHES

Isobel Bird

SARA GLANCED QUICKLY at the photograph lying on the table in front of her, just long enough for her mind to comprehend what was happening in the shot. Her eyes cut back to the pile of scrambled eggs on her plate. A streak of ketchup slashed across the pale yellow softness. Suddenly the smell of the fried potatoes made her feel sick.

"See," said Jen, "I told you she was fucking around." There was triumph in her voice. It was wrapped carefully in the consoling tones of the smugly confident, but Sara felt the sting nonetheless. Jen loved to be right, and this time she had hit the jackpot. She pushed the photo toward Sara and leaned back in the booth, forcing Sara to pick it up.

According to Jen, the photo had been taken at a recent sex party of the sort that seemed suddenly to be the rage for a certain segment of the lesbian world. It clearly showed a very stern, very butch woman fucking another woman, a delicate redhead, from behind. The photographer had captured the scene at a moment when the butch was entering her femme, her body moving forward as she shoved her cock deep inside. The butch's mouth was set in a satisfied smile, and her hand was caught in mid-swing as she brought it down onto the pale moon of her girl's ass.

The butch was—or had been until the moment the photo had hit the table—Alex, Sara's girlfriend of nine months. The redhead's face, covered by her flying hair, was obscured.

"Pretty," said Sara. "Who is she?"

"I don't know," Jen answered. "She came with Alex. They looked like they'd spent a lot of time together, though. All I know about her is her name—Alice. I thought maybe you'd know."

"No," said Sara. "But it looks like there are a lot of things I didn't know."

Jen pulled on her cigarette, blowing the smoke out in a hazy cloud that settled over the table like smog. For once, Sara was too preoccupied to tell her to blow it somewhere else. "What are you going to do?" Jen asked.

Sara looked at the photo for a minute. Her mind raced with various ideas, none of which were either realistic or legal. She looked at Alex's face, and remembered how she'd told Sara she was going out to play pool with the guys.

"I think I have an idea." She looked up and smiled at Jen over the cold breakfast.

"I have your dick," she said simply. "And if you want it back, you're going to play by my rules."

There was dead silence on the other end of the line. Sara could tell by the faint rustling sounds that Alex was searching the box next to her bed and finding it empty. She could hear muttering as Alex barked a string of obscenities. Then she was back, her voice trembling with rage. "You fucking bitch. Who the fuck do you think you are?"

"I think you've got that wrong, sweetheart," Sara said evenly. "Who the fuck do you think *you* are? *You're* the one who took the randy-husband bit a little too far."

It was two days after the morning on which Jen had presented Sara with the evidence of Alex's unfaithfulness. Sara had gone to Alex's apartment the night before, where she had managed to act as though nothing at all were unusual. She and Alex had made dinner, watched a movie, and even had passable sex, during which Sara had clawed Alex's skin perhaps a little too enthusiastically. In the morning, when Alex left for work, Sara had slipped her wandering daddy's dildo and harness into her purse and left.

Now she sat comfortably in her favorite armchair, holding Alex's dick in her hand and feeling quite good about the whole thing. She threw her legs over the arm of the chair, nestled the cock beneath her chin, and listened to Alex rant. "You'd better bring that right back this goddamn minute," she was saying, her butch patter flowing like a stream after too much rain. Sara let her go on until she paused for breath, then cut in.

"Look." She took a sip of tea. "This is very simple. You want your precious manhood back, you do what I say. Otherwise I turn it into a scratching post for Simon." Hearing his name spoken, Simon looked up from where he was curled into a tight ball on the sofa. He blinked his blue eyes, yawned so that his tongue curled out in a graceful dip, and then went back to sleep.

Alex began to scream again. *Jesus Christ,* thought Sara, *all this fuss over a silly dick.* "You'd have made a great straight guy," she said into the phone, then giggled as Alex erupted in another fit or rage. The sounds of the Indigo Girls floated through the room, and she hummed along until she was bored with listening to Alex. "Be here tomorrow at nine," she said. "And there's just one little thing I want you to do first. . . ."

The next night, precisely at nine, the doorbell rang. *At least she's prompt,* thought Sara, straightening her dress as she walked to the door and opened it. Alex stood there, not looking at Sara. She was wearing her usual outfit: black jeans, white T-shirt, black leather jacket, and boots. Her short dark hair was slicked back. She brushed past Sara and stormed into the living room.

"Did you do what I told you?" Sara asked, shutting the door.

"Yeah. Now where's my fucking piece?" Alex was trembling with anger as she stood in the living room.

"Not so fast." Sara settled onto the couch. "This is still my game, remember? Your dick is someplace safe. If you're a good little girl, you'll get it back."

"What the hell do you want from me?" Alex demanded.

Sara smiled, pushing her long hair out of her eyes. "Nothing much," she said," Just a chance to show you the other side. Now, why don't you strip for me and show me what you bought today."

Alex turned her back to Sara and started to unbuckle her belt. "Not so fast," Sara said. "Turn around. I want to look at you."

Alex turned. Her face was red with rage, but she didn't say a word as she undid the buttons on her jeans and let them fall to the floor. As she pushed them down her legs, a pair of pink panties was revealed. She stood, arms across her chest, staring defiantly at Sara, who looked her up and down for a minute or two before standing up and walking over to where Alex stood.

"Very nice." She ran her hand over Alex's satin-clad ass and gave it a little pat. "These look much better than those boring old boxers you usually wear. Very feminine. I assume you have the receipt?"

"It's in my wallet," Alex said, her teeth clenched. Sara reached down and fished the battered wallet from the back pocket of Alex's jeans. She opened it and pulled out a folded slip, which she read. "Victoria's Secret," she said. "Good girl."

Alex bristled at the name. "I'm not your girl," she said.

Sara paused in front of her. She ran a finger along the waistband of the delicate panties. "But tonight you are," she said. "That is, if you want your cock back."

"That wasn't part of this fucking deal!" Alex shouted. "All I agreed to was wearing these fucking panties. Nothing else."

"Deals change," Sara shot back, her voice harsh. "You want out, then get the fuck out. But I get to keep your dick. The choice is yours."

She watched Alex's face as her mind weighed the options before her. Sara had been on the receiving end of Alex's similar ultimatums many times. She knew which choice Alex would make.

"All right," Alex said.

"Good," said Sara. "Now, if I remember correctly, I told you to buy a bra that matched those panties. May I see it?"

Alex looked down at her feet. "I didn't get it," she said.

"Excuse me?"

"I said I didn't get it."

Sara drew in her breath. "That's too bad. I really like my girls to be all dolled up. But not to worry. I have some things you can wear. Follow me."

She walked into her bedroom, with Alex shuffling behind her, pants still around her ankles. "Take your clothes off—everything except the panties."

Alex removed her boots and slipped off her pants. Then she pulled her T-shirt over her head. She stood, hands on hips, looking at Sara as if daring her to do anything else. Her large, muscular body was what had attracted Sara to her in the first place. Now, as she gazed at her ex standing before her wearing the daintiest of women's panties, she felt a thrill of power run through her. She went to her chest and brought out a bag she had prepared earlier in the day.

"Since tonight we're just two girls getting together," she said as she emptied the contents of the bag onto the bed, "I thought we'd do some girl things." She held up a lacy pink bra. "Let's start with dress-up."

She walked over to Alex, the bra swinging from her fingers. Alex looked at the garment in disgust, but lifted her arms when told to, and Sara slipped it on. She snapped the clap closed, adjusted the straps, and inspected Alex's chest. "My, my, my," she said, cupping Alex's breasts in her hands. "Seems those Wonderbras *do* perform miracles. You look like you just stepped out of a lingerie catalog."

"This shit is fucked up!" Alex growled.

Sara smiled. "But sweetie, you always told me you loved how a girl looked all wrapped up in silk and satin. Just like a Christmas present, I believe you said."

Sara ran her hand through Alex's military-short hair. "Oh, this won't do at all," she said. "Just a minute."

She returned to the bed and snatched a long red wig from the bag. It resembled very closely the hair of the girl in the photo that had been the cause of the evening's activities. Sara had been quite pleased with herself when she found it. Now, as she walked toward Alex with it, she thoroughly enjoyed the disgust she saw in the butch's eyes.

"I'm not wearing that thing!" Alex swore.

Sara pretended to be shocked. "But why not? You always said you liked your femmes to have long hair, right? Besides, if I recall correctly, you have a real thing for redheads."

Alex sneered. "Just give it to me!" She grabbed it out of Sara's hands. "Let's get this little game over with so I can go do something a little more my style, if you know what I mean."

Like fuck Alice is what you mean, Sara thought. She watched as Alex smashed the wig onto her head. It sat crookedly, the bangs falling unevenly into her face. Sara tried not to laugh as she straightened the wig and arranged the dark red curls over Alex's broad shoulders. "Mmmmmmmmmm," she purred. "Beautiful. You're a right little looker, girlie."

"I look like that bitch who dances on MTV," said Alex.

"Oh, not quite yet, you don't." Sara went to her dresser and returned with her cosmetics bag. "But you will in a few minutes."

In a matter of fifteen minutes, she had painted Alex's face up in a perfect parody of high femme glamour. Alex's lips gleamed in fire-engine-red gloss. Her eyes were rainbowed with the brightest blue, and her cheeks fairly glowed with pink blusher. Sara even managed to affix a pair of the longest lashes she could find at the drugstore.

"And now for the finishing touch," she said, pulling out a box of Lee Press-On Nails in brightest red. She took Alex's hands and quickly attached the impossibly long plastic nails to the carefully clipped fingernails.

Throughout the ordeal, Sara could feel Alex's anger and rage trembling through her body. She had spent her whole life running from this very image, although she was drawn to it sexually like a magnet to steel. Sara knew that this was more torturous to her than any of her S/M tricks had ever been to Sara, and she was loving it, because she knew that whatever happened, Alex would never break. She wondered, too, if the rush she was feeling was anything like the rush Alex got when one of her blows landed home.

When she was finished, she looked Alex up and down. She was by no means a pretty femme: there was just no hiding the butch daddy beneath the girlie costume. "Go lie down on the bed," she said simply.

Alex stomped over to the bed, her muscular thighs and heavy step incongruous with her getup, making it all the more amusing for Sara to watch her. Alex lay down, and Sara went to the bedside table. She pulled open the drawer and removed the familiar wrist cuffs that Alex had used on her so many times before.

"Uh-uh." Alex shook her head. "None of that."

"No play, no dick," Sara said quietly.

After a brief stare-down, Alex presented her wrists, which Sara wrapped tightly in the leather cuffs, securing them to the headboard. "Now wait here," she whispered in Alex's ear. "Daddy will be back in a minute." Alex bristled at the "daddy" reference, but kept her mouth shut.

Sara went into the bathroom and shut the door. After what she knew was a long enough time for Alex to have gotten good and angry again, she came back out, bringing with her a razor, towel, and shaving cream. She laid these on the table next to Alex and left silently, allowing Alex time to take in the razor and think about what was going to happen next. As she ran water into a bowl, she heard Alex muttering.

She returned to the bedroom, carrying the bowl. She set it on the nightstand and dipped the razor in it. As she uncapped the shaving cream and squirted some into her hand, she looked at Alex. "A good femme should always be smooth for her daddy," she said. She rubbed the cream into Alex's armpits and removed the hair deftly, rinsing the skin clean. She then moved down and repeated the procedure on Alex's legs, slowing scraping away the fine black hairs until her skin was silky and her muscles stood out in sharp relief.

When she pulled down the pink panties and moved toward Alex's cunt, the butch squeezed her powerful legs shut. "No goddamn way!"

Sara twisted the razor in her fingers. "It's either this," she said, "or I do a bikini wax. Your choice."

Alex allowed her legs to be parted, and Sara began the delicate job of defoliating her pussy-lips, drawing the razor down first one side and then the other. She even forced Alex to lift her legs and spread them so that Sara could shave the area around her asshole. When it was done, Alex's skin gleamed white and bare against the sheets. Sara gathered up the shaving paraphernalia and returned it to the bathroom.

When she came back, she fetched a pair of high heels from the closet and put them on Alex's feet. They were a little small, but the effect was what she wanted, and certainly Alex's comfort was immaterial. She stood at the end of the bed and looked down at the captive butch, all dolled up in femme drag and looking for all the world like a two-dollar whore.

She got the camera. When Alex saw it, she started to thrash around, screaming. "Get that fucking thing out of here!" she bellowed. "You fucking stupid bitch, I'm going to break your goddamn neck!" Her body flailed against the mattress as she tried to break free from her restraints.

Sara knew from experience that Alex could never break the cuffs' grip. As Alex bucked and twisted, she snapped picture after picture, the Polaroids fluttering to the carpet like leaves. As she did, she teased Alex. "That's it, baby, give me more. Give me more. Make love to the camera, baby doll." When she finished the pack, she gathered them up and looked them over. There were some great shots. Her favorite was one of Alex with legs spread and panties around her calves, her mouth pursed in what looked like a kiss as she arched her back and clenched her red-nailed hands. The face was unmistakably hers, but the body was all wrong.

"I really like this one," Sara showed the photo to Alex, who was huffing and puffing as she tried to regain her breath.

Alex looked away from the proffered photo. "Fuck you!" She said.

Sara went to her desk and picked up a small manila envelope. As Alex watched, she placed the photo inside and sealed it. She then wrote something on the envelope. She did the same with a handful of the other photos, then brought the envelopes over to show Alex. On each one she had written the name and address of one of Alex's butch buddies. On the one that contained her favorite photo, she had written Alice's name and address. It had taken a little detective work to get them, but the look on Alex's face told her it had been worth it.

"If you are not a perfectly behaved little girl," she

said, "every one of these goes into the mailbox outside my building. Do you understand?"

At first Alex refused to answer. The veins in her neck throbbed as she looked at the envelopes and then at Sara.

"Do you understand? Yes or no."

"Yes," Alex hissed finally.

Sara smiled. "Good," she said. "Then we can get on with it." She placed the stack of envelopes on her dresser, where Alex couldn't help but see them, and went back into the bathroom. "Daddy will be right back," she called over her shoulder to Alex.

When she came back into the room, she was wearing nothing but Alex's dick. When Alex saw it, her eyes turned hard. "You cunt!" she screamed. "You fucking cunt! How dare you wear my cock—"

"Shut the fuck up, bitch!" Sara screamed back. She stormed over to the bed and smacked Alex hard across the mouth, smearing the lipstick unevenly across her cheek. "Who the fuck do you think you are, talking to your daddy that way?"

"Give me my dick," Alex said evenly. Her hands had balled into fists, and one of the nails had broken off.

"Oh, I'm going to give it to you, all right." Sara brought the tip of the cock close to Alex's cheek. "I'm going to give it to you real good. Daddy's little girl is going to get just what she deserves."

Sara pulled Alex's panties back up around her waist. "Keep yourself covered," she said in disgust. "Little fucking tramp."

She climbed onto the bed and straddled Alex's waist, pinning her down. She could feel the rise and fall of Alex's breathing beneath her, the beating of her heart as it pulsed against her thighs. She stroked the dick between her legs.

regina

"Yeah, you're a pretty one." She ran her hand over Alex's chest. "Daddy likes you." She pinched one of Alex's nipples hard through the bra. Alex jumped beneath her. "Oh, did you like that?" Sara cooed. "Maybe I should just take this off, then."

Leaning over, she pulled a knife from her bedside-table drawer. She held it glinting in the air for a moment, before using it to cut the bra away from Alex's body. She then ran the sharp point under the mounds of flesh and up around the nipples. As she did, Alex's breathing became more shallow, and her nipples swelled. Sara was surprised.

"What's this?" She flicked one of the hardened points with her nail. "Is someone turning into a bottom before my very eyes?" She dropped the knife and pinched Alex's tits, pulling on them viciously as she talked to her. "Filthy fucking whore," she said. "Want Daddy to play with your tits, is that it? I bet you play with them yourself when no one's around, don't you?"

Unable to stop herself, Alex was moaning, the sounds of pleasure coming out as muffled barks. Her eyes were closed, and her reddened lips were parted. Sara's cunt jumped as she realized that Alex was in control. She stopped playing with her tits, and Alex let out a sigh of both relief and frustration.

"That's enough for now," Sara said. "But just so you don't forget what it felt like, you're going to wear these for a while." She reached once more into the drawer and removed two spring-operated clamps. With two quick snaps, she affixed them to Alex's nipples, causing her to scream out in a mix of pleasure and pain. Sara hoped it was more of the latter.

Leaning forward, she smacked Alex's face with her dick until Alex looked up at her. "Suck it!" she ordered.

When Alex didn't respond, Sara forced the head of the cock between her lips. Surprised, Alex didn't have time to lock her jaw before the thick shaft was pushing into her throat. She gagged as she attempted to take it in.

"Like how it feels?" Sara teased, pumping her hips a little so that the cock slid in and out of Alex's mouth. The lipstick smeared along the pink sides as the shaft glided in and out. Alex was helpless as she was fed more and more of the prick.

"You're a natural cocksucker," Sara taunted. "Now do a good job, and maybe I'll let you have this back."

Alex's mouth worked up and down the length of Sara's dick. At first, Sara simply fucked her mouth. Then she pulled out, forcing Alex to lean forward and take the head between her lips. "Tease it," she ordered. "Use that blowjob mouth of yours on Daddy's big cock."

Alex strained against her cuffs, leaning forward to take all of Sara into her mouth. Sara held herself just out of reach, until Alex's tongue was fully extended in a vain attempt at reaching the dickhead. Then she grabbed her by the hair and slammed the cock forcefully into her again, choking her. She loved the feeling of being in control, of watching Alex take her cock into her throat.

"You keep that up, and Daddy just might come down that pretty little throat," she said.

She pulled out, leaving Alex gasping for breath. "That's enough," Sara said. "Actually, it's more than you deserve."

Moving down the bed, she pushed Alex's legs apart and yanked her panties down. "What's this?" she said, fingering the material. "Feels like someone got a little bit wet. Couldn't be you liked sucking Daddy's dick, could it? Greedy little bitch."

She ripped the panties off and held them to her face. "Smells like a little girl," she said. "A very horny little girl who can't control her own pussy."

Balling the panties up, she shoved the wet crotch into Alex's mouth. "Suck on that while Daddy inspects your pussy," she said.

Forcing Alex's legs wider with her knees, she ran her fingers over the smooth lines of her labia. Alex had never allowed Sara to touch her cunt, and now Sara made up for it by taking her time. She tickled the skin, then pulled the lips open and ran just the tips of her fingers along the sensitive edges. She looked up at Alex and saw that her head was thrust back against the headboard.

Sara slid a finger into Alex's cunt and felt the walls contract tightly around it. "And all this time I thought you were a real man," she said, slamming another finger in alongside the first. A roar escaped the gag in Alex's mouth.

Sara pulled the panties out. "What was that?" she asked. "Did you ask me to use another finger?"

Alex didn't answer, so Sara began to fuck her, sliding her fingers in and out until they were glistening with juice and she could feel Alex's body begin to shake. Then she stopped.

"Do you want me to fuck you?" she asked.

Alex didn't answer.

Sara slid her fingers in and out again, keeping Alex on the brink.

"Do you want me to fuck you?" she repeated.

Alex nodded almost imperceptibly.

"I can't hear you." Sara pinched Alex's clit.

"Yes," she whispered.

Sara thrust a third finger inside Alex's swollen cunt. "What?"

"Yes," Alex screamed. "Yes, Daddy, I want you to fuck me."

Sara pulled her hand out and slammed her cock into Alex's pussy, driving it home in one swift stroke. Alex rose off the bed, a howl ripped from her throat, as Sara's dick impaled her. Sara knew nothing had ever been inside Alex before, and she imagined the pain must be terrible. This only increased her excitement.

Pulling back, she hammered Alex's cunt with vicious force, pumping away at her in swift thrusts. Grabbing Alex's legs, she hoisted them over her shoulders and toward her head in a classic porn film position. She liked the view this gave her of Alex's cunt and of her cock slipping in and out of it.

"Nice fucking pussy," she said. "Makes Daddy's cock feel good."

Alex was moaning, her head thrown back as Sara fucked her for the first time. Her high-heeled feet dangled over Sara's shoulders, and each time Sara pounded into her, the clamps on her nipples pulled, causing her to cry out.

"What a sweet cunt," Sara said. She felt her body begin to tense as she neared her own climax. "You like being fucked by your own dick? You like taking it up your cunt? Take this!"

Alex answered her by coming in a long, shuddering orgasm. Her whole body tensed, and Sara felt the walls of her pussy clawing at the cock inside her. It pushed Sara over the edge, and she allowed herself to be swept up in the tail of Alex's come. "Fuck!" she shouted, plunging one last time into Alex's hole.

When it was over, she looked down at Alex. The wig had slipped off and fallen to one side. Her eyes were closed, and her lipstick ran in smears down her chin.

Sara reached over and undid the nipple clamps, making Alex cry out as the blood rushed in. Sara pulled her cock out of Alex and unfastened the harness. She dropped the dick on the floor. Hearing it fall, Alex opened her eyes.

"Now get dressed and get out!" Sara unclasped the cuffs at Alex's wrists.

Alex scrambled off the bed. She quickly pulled on her jeans and her T-shirt. Without a word, she picked up the dick and started for the front door.

"Not so fast," Sara said.

Alex turned. Her face looked like a watercolor painting left out in the rain. The strong butch facade had been cracked. Sara walked over to her, a crisp twenty-dollar bill in her fingers. Folding it up, she tucked it into the waistband of Alex's pants. "Thanks," she said. "Let's do it again sometime. Oh, and tell Alice I said hello."

Without a word, Alex opened the door and left. Sara went back into the bedroom and began to clean up. As she threw the torn panties and bra into the wastebasket, she noticed the stack of envelopes still sitting on the dresser. She picked them up and began to laugh and laugh.

Soap and Water

Allegra Long

Connie is a fastidious woman. She is the most sensual and uninhibited lover I've had, but she insists on being totally, absurdly clean before she'll let me anywhere near her. She always smells and tastes delicious, so don't think I'm unappreciative, but I've always been a man who savors natural pussy smell, sweat, and the pungent sexiness of a body well-used and well-loved.

I've tried many times to make love to Connie first thing in the morning when her body retains its aftertaste of sleep, but she always has to brush her teeth and bathe, taking an agonizingly long time in the bathroom. Then she's mine. All mine. Every responsive and succulent protrusion, dip, mound, ripple, fold and tunnel. I began to get curious about the dramatic change in her from when she first slips shyly out of bed in the morning to when she emerges, glowing and hungry, from the bathroom. Was she really just getting clean? I wondered. What did she do to get ready for me?

So one very early morning I gave in to an irresistible urge. She was expecting me about eight, but I let myself

in to her apartment almost two hours early. Her bathroom is large and contains a walk-in linen closet opposite the tub. The closet door is slatted and a person
inside can, if the angle of the slats is adjusted, get a
striped but adequate view of the entire bathroom. The
perfect hiding place for me.

I didn't have long to wait. Connie came into the bathroom in about ten minutes and sat down on the toilet to
pee. I felt guilty spying on her, but we've been together a
long time and it's not like I've never before seen her on
the toilet. It was strangely exciting to watch her when she
thought she was alone. She hummed as she wiped, stayed
seated to examine her fingernails and hands for a while,
then her breasts, rubbing them and circling the nipples
with fingertips she'd moistened with her spit. When I
heard a delicate sighing fart, I almost spoiled everything
by bursting into laughter. Even her farts were feminine.

She stood and stared at herself in the mirror over the
sink. Her eyes still looked sleepy and she rubbed them
and stretched. It took her forever to brush her teeth, but
the jiggling motion to her breasts made the time pass de-
lightfully for me. Her naked body looked so soft and
vulnerable and touchable I nearly sprang from my hiding place right then and there. And of course my dick
was getting harder by the minute, crying for release. But
I tried to be patient.

A large blue beach towel always hangs over a chair
she has in the bathroom and I've never known what she
uses it for until now. She spread it, still partially folded,
on the chair, then reached under her sink and pulled out
a box and a bottle. From the box she removed a sealed
disposable douche, and I wanted to yell at her *no*. I
didn't want any perfume or disinfectant covering up her
natural pussy smell. I couldn't believe she used those
things, but my initial objection gave way to a deepen-

ing, aching arousal when she straddled the toilet and pushed the long nozzle up into her vagina. My dick twitched, jealous. I could hear the liquid dribbling out from its brief visit inside, and she was done too quickly with that procedure.

But the fun had only started. After having emptied the premixed douche, she filled the plastic douche bottle with soapy water, lubricated the full length of the nozzle with K-Y and, to my astonishment, bent herself over that blue-toweled chair like it was my lap and she was waiting for one of my spankings. Oh, I wanted to oblige, to make that lovely upturned bottom quiver and blush. Especially when I watched that fingersized nozzle disappear between her sweet cheeks. With one hand she squeezed the soapy water inside, and a moan almost escaped from my throat.

This part she did slowly, like she was paying attention to every sensation. When the water was gone, she stood a little unsteadily, filled the bottle again, and returned to the receptive position. I got to watch another bottle empty into her rectum. After removing the nozzle, she took her time standing, stretched again, then finally sat down on the toilet to evacuate. You'd think *that,* at least, would be a turnoff, but nothing is predictable about sexual arousal. I don't know if I'd suddenly become a voyeur or an enema freak or what, but something was stirring in me. And I was awfully pleased to have discovered her secret—how her asshole always smelled and tasted so clean. No wonder my exploring fingers always found her open and empty and welcoming whatever I wanted to put into her.

My whole groin was throbbing by this time, I wanted her so badly. But she wasn't done. She spread the large towel onto the floor, and while she waited for the bathtub to fill, she lay down, grabbed the bottle, which turned out to be oil, and covered her skin with it—neck, breasts, arms, belly, pelvis, thighs, calves, feet, and toes. Slow, tender, oily circles with her hands, all over. She spread her legs and rubbed and pulled apart her private lips. Her open pussy was aimed right at me and I could hardly breathe. *Enough,* I wanted to cry out. *Please.*

But then she rolled over, luxuriating like a cat, and reached back to oil as much as she could manage without help. *I'll help,* I said silently. As she massaged the oil into her buttocks, they pulled apart and gave me a brief, teasing view of her tiny dark pucker.

By this time, the tub was full and she lowered her glistening body into it. I watched her soap every square inch of it over and over. She gave special attention to her round full breasts. After soaping her underarms, she reached for the razor that was on the edge of the tub, and carefully shaved. Her long legs were next, the razor gliding along her skin, and I could feel the silkiness under my own impatient fingertips. When she stood, suds slid down her body and I thought, *At last, she's done.* But she put one foot on the side of the tub, squeezed some other kind of soap into the palm of her hand, and rubbed it slowly between her legs. I could tell she was rubbing her clit as she soaped herself. Her eyes were closed and she bit her lower lip. Then she grabbed something that was hanging discreetly behind a loofah pad and I recognized the joke gift I'd given her some time ago: a soap-on-a-rope shaped like a miniature erect penis. What on earth . . . ?

One foot still rested on the side of the tub to open her legs, and she bent over to wet the soap in the tub, stayed slightly bent, and reached back to rub it up and down the crack of her ass. I held my breath. What was she going to . . . ? She did. She tucked it all the way inside her ass with the help of a wet finger and left only the thin rope dangling. When she sat back down in the water, the little soap-phallus was still in place. She lay back and closed her eyes, almost motionless, and I tried to imagine how she experienced that final internal cleansing—the slippery, tingly dissolving that was going on. It obviously didn't hurt, at least not in a bad way.

When she opened her eyes she sighed and seemed to be thinking about the time. Listening for my arrival. Then she pulled the bathroom plug, stood up, and reached back to tug on the rope of her own personal little plug. Out it slipped from her bottom. She closed the curtain and turned on the shower to wash her hair and rinse her whole body thoroughly. My chance to sneak out and return at eight. But could I now pretend to be innocent of her morning ritual? If I confessed to my voyeurism, would she be furious and even inhibited with me? Or maybe . . . I stared at her muted image behind the shower curtain. *Now,* I ordered myself *Go.* But instead I waited too long, couldn't resist watching that curtain open again to present me with the next exotic scene—the slow rub of a towel on glowing skin.

Oh, what the hell. I silently peeled off my clothes and stepped out of the linen closet. She gasped, and I grabbed her steamy perfumed body and kissed her on the mouth, long and deep. The tip of my dick found her clit to tickle, and my hand caressed that heavenly ass. "I'm sorry," I whispered. "But it was so good, Connie. Watching you like that."

"Yes," she said. "It *was* good. And you're so bad." Then she giggled and I realized that, at some point, she'd figured out I was there. "Your turn to get clean," she said. "Thoroughly, absolutely, finger-licking clean." To my dismay, she began to reassemble her equipment, eventually pointing at the chair with the nozzle of her refilled plastic bottle. What could I do but submit?

How Coyote Stole the Sun

M. Christian

THE BUS DROPPED to its knees, yawning open its door. The day was burning: the sun angry at something it wasn't sharing and the wind scared to come out.

Dust swirled, friendly and clinging, around Dog as he left the cooling bosom of the Interstate Lines bus. Satisfied that its friend was out and walking safely away, No. 47—Albuquerque to Taos—closed its door and left with a belching cloud of exhaust.

The trees must have had issues with Dog, because as he approached them they shuffled and fluttered their leaves to flash pieces of the too-hot sun down on him.

But Dog was used to that kind of treatment from trees—he paid them no mind and just kept on walking along the dusty road.

After a time of walking (precisely how long being difficult to say, because time wasn't something Dog really understood and because watches, as a group, refused to speak true to him even if he bothered to ask), Dog saw some signs of man: the broken teeth of a old picket fence, the rusting mesh of its chain-link brother, the stumps of telephone poles, and, distantly, the regularity of a small house.

A few steps later, details filled his eyes: it was a small house. Clapboard painted red. A porch that was a mixture of rotting and rotted old boards. Glassless windows with torn curtains like pale moss. A screen door with more holes than screen.

It took Dog a few seconds to really see them, they were so faded into the grasses and the shadows: the two little boys were brown and furtive from running with the rabbits and the squirrels. Their eyes were as blue as the sky when it was in a good mood, and about as tame as wild foxes. They were naked and tanned from the stern sun—dirty and scuffed and uncaring, unworried. Maybe nine summers, maybe ten. Not twelve. They could have been brothers, or just kin who had been playing outside together too long.

Dog watched them, doing nothing for a while; then he dropped down onto his haunches, feeling his old blue jeans creak and stretch against his thighs. Putting two fingers on the ground, he gave the boys the gift of thinking that he needed them for balance—when Dog could have stayed there for many nights without moving.

After a time, the two wild boys decided that he wasn't a hunter, or at least wasn't a hungry one. Cautiously, they came out from the high grasses in front of the dead house and looked at him.

Finally, the one with some echoes of being civilized, or just less of the music of the wild world, spoke: "What you doing here, Mister?"

Dog spoke, slowly and without threatening timbre: "Just passing."

The boy who spoke, nodded, as if that was more than enough, or all he could understand.

Dog played a bit with the dust at his feet, careful to draw something without meaning. "Anything around here?" the drifter said.

The other boy, the one who hadn't spoken, heard a sound and leaped into the weeds in pursuit. The other looked like he wanted to join his friend or brother but was still fascinated by the stranger. "Birds. Rabbits. Mice. Squirrels. Roc."

"Roc?"

He jerked his head down the road. "He has more than anyone. Even stuff."

"Stuff?" Dog said, standing and brushing some of the clinging dust from his denim jacket.

The boy looked confused for a moment, as if he didn't have any other words. Another sound chirped from the high brown grasses, and he looked harder this time in its direction: the wild wasn't calling—rather, it was screaming for his small attention.

He looked back at Dog once more, decided that either he didn't have anything else to say, or he didn't have the means to say what he wanted to, and bounded off into the grasses to make hunting and catching noises all his own.

Dog watched the grasses shake and shush a bit, then turned and walked down the road.

Roc?

Once it was a town. Now, though, most of the houses, from lack of company or just from uncaring company, were dead: their doors hung loosely open, their only breaths from a turgid breeze that liked to play in their corpses. Their paint was either faded or completely gone, showing lots of dry boards and rotting wood.

The street was as unpaved as ever, with ruts like canyons from the breeze and occasional rains.

Dog saw four buildings: a grocer's bare of life, a two-story hotel (Excelsior) with dead air as guests, a gas station fuzzy with weeds and grasses, and a garage.

The garage was set against a low hill fuzzy with dead yellow grass. It was shaded by a sickly oak. Like the others: peeling paint, empty-eyed windows, and rattling signs. But the garage, YOU NEED IT / WE HAVE IT, seemed to have a clinging kind of life. The weeds in front might have been dead, but they were also cut back. The building, a Quonset hut, was tired, old, and cancered with pocks of rust, but it was organized: crates of Coke, motor oil, K rations, rolls of chicken wire, and drums of gasoline were placed in clusters against it. Its windows were dirty and dark but seethed with a heavy vibration of glowering intensity. The garage might still be alive, but it held its life close to its chest.

The sun was still pissed. It tried to cook Dog as he walked through the town, but Dog was used to this kind of treatment from the sun, and so its harshness just rolled off his denim-covered back. Tipping his leather hat down a bit lower over his eyes, he walked toward the garage.

Its door was open, cooling air swirling out from the dark insides.

"Howdy," Dog said to the man inside.

Dog had seen no one so far, so this had to be Roc. It had to be Roc for other reasons: his skin was heavy and granite; he was fat from storage of everything he could get. He bulged with selfish satisfaction, a statue carved from dark wood and dressed in a simple pair of torn and faded denim overalls and sitting on a sagging stool with rollers. You could see, and Dog could see, that he was fat, yes, but it was a strong kind of fat. He was big, not blown out of perspective. Roc's skin was a kind of tan, stretching to almost burnt black from days like this one. His face, what Dog could see of it from a misty beam coming through one window of the garage, was strong and not jowly. He had a stone, cleft chin, and eyes that glimmered deep, deep blue from inside the gloom of the garage. A gray and black mane of unkempt hair left the top of his head, stopping just short of his shoulders. The lines of his face, the planes and crags, told a quick story of great strength, power, and a stern attitude toward survival. He was here, and he had what he needed to stay here. He lived to acquire and to stay strong, at all costs.

All from his body and face. That and the back of the garage were a treasure trove of things: boxes of Rice Krispies, stacks of romance novels and *Playboys*, drums of fuel oil, tanks of propane, bundles of fishing poles, crates of lawn mowers, and piles of Gold Circle condoms.

Roc responded to Dog's greeting with a slow, tentative, and guarded nod.

"Someone," Dog said, walking into the freezing shade of the doorway and leaning, oh-so-casual, against the roll-up door frame, "told me that you might have some stuff."

"Could be." Roc's voice was deep and brass. It was as strong and big as his body. He obviously didn't use it often, but when it did everything that had ears paid attention to what he said.

Dog kicked back his hat with one quick flick of his thumb and smiled with his eyes if not with his expressive mouth. "Well, could be that I might be interested in something special. Especially if you happened to have some, shall we say, very special stuff."

"Could be," avalanches, thunderstorms, grinding equipment, and mine shafts. "Could be."

"Now, not just what you might call ordinary special stuff, mind you. I speak of the 'special' kind of special stuff. Something more unusual, something more rare than your typical kind of ordinary 'stuff.' You-know-what-I-mean?"

Roc smiled, the planes and inclines of his great, ponderous face shifting into a shark's grin. "I know what you mean," he said, shifting his great body back and forth and tapping his thigh.

Whatever Roc considered "more unusual, something more rare than your typical kind of ordinary *stuff*," had to be awfully small and awfully strong to fit, and survive, being under his ponderous ass.

Dog smiled his special smile—the one he reserved for virgins, people who said they didn't play poker all that well, for double-or-nothing, for "Do you love me?" and for "What you gonna do about it?"—and said: "Now that, sir, sounds like exactly the kind of thing that someone like me, who likes the really special, the very rare, the more kind of—shall we say—unusual kind of stuff might just be interested in."

Roc shook his granite head and dropped his own smile down to something that spoke "I'll break you in half" as he replied, "Not for sale."

"Now I can understand that, sir, I really can. I mean, I'm a man of the world, you understand. I'm a fella who knows what you mean, knows that kinda language means that this isn't what you would call a negotiable point. I can hear that, sir, I know that tune. Believe me, I'm not one of those fellas who would press you on this thing. I'm not one of those who'd insult you by pulling a great wad of money out of his back pocket and maybe, say, dropping it casual on the ground with the kind of understanding, unspoken of course, that if you were to, say, get up and come pick it up that would be an invitation for me to come over there and pick up that special 'stuff' and be on my way."

"No," said Roc, simply.

"I understand, sir, I really do. Like I said, I'm not one of those kind of fellas who would make such a offer to a fella like you. I'm not that kind of fella, I assure you. I'm not one of those kind of guys who make some kind of promise to a fella like you, like maybe that I might happen to know this certain young lady in a nearby town, a young pump of a girl, you might say. A certain lady who could, and would, for a special friend of mine, do special things with her bee-stung lips, strong, round ass, cushy pussy, that would make your eyes melt right in your head, sir."

"No."

"I'm not that kind of fella, sir, like I said. I'm not even the kind of guy who would simply leave it hanging, implying that there might be something in my humble ability to give you that would make you get off that most comfortable-looking chair—therefore, you might say, giving me this most special kind of stuff."

Roc was as quiet as his spiritual brothers. He sat in the cool semi-darkness and stared at the relaxed figure of Dog leaning against the door frame. Time, as was said, isn't something reliable around Dog, but it was some number of those flighty things called seconds, those quick things called minutes, and maybe even one of those heavy things called hours before he said, "Maybe."

Dog smiled. This one was his special one, the one he kept in his back pocket and only took out when someone said, "Maybe."

"Now I'm not the kind of fella," Dog said, pushing himself gently away from the door and walking into the cool dimness of the garage, "who might take that as a guarantee or something. It's just potential, right? It's just that we have opened what you might call *lines of communication*. We have something to talk about. We know that I might, say, be able to offer you something that might be attractive, say, to make you rise from that very comfortable-looking stool and therefore offer me your special stuff. Potential, that's all."

"Right," said Roc, eyes gleaming like polished steel. "We can talk."

"Yes we can, great, Roc, yes we can. Maybe, sir, I should start that I have many talents and many skills, not to mention innumerable resources at my disposal. I have many things to offer you, Roc, many things that might *interest* you." Dog walked deep into the dim chill of the garage, walking on the dirt floor till he was just a dozen or so hands away from the giant man.

Almost invisibly, Roc smiled.

Dog smiled, too, but it was *that* smile again. It was the knowing grin, a curling of the lips and the slight flash of white, sharp teeth that said (even though Dog never did), *I see you clearly now.*

And Roc was smiling, because he was seeing Dog clearly now: a tall, lanky man filling a pair of jeans with muscles. Denim jacket and stained T-shirt that promised broad shoulders and a strong chest. Dirty, battered hat. Dog looked like many, but there was an added extra that made people, and things like the wind and the sun, watch him walk by. His face was rugged and unshaven, wind-sculpted and tanned into leather. His nose was long and sharp, a nose that announced the man moments before his true arrival. His eyes were shaded by a heavy tangle of eyebrows. His lips looked chapped and coarse, though full and broad around a large mouth. He looked like many, but there was that something else: his eyes smiled, his lips promised strength yet softness. His face was tough and used, but there was a mirthful kind of experience back there: what he had been through hadn't hardened him as much as filled him. He had seen a lot of this, you could tell, and that, and it had all ended up making him smile. From wisdom or from blind stupidity, though, it was very hard to tell.

"Anything at all that might interest you. Maybe some kind of task I might perform? Now, without beating my own . . . drum, so to speak, might I propose some kind of, say, test of strength, perhaps, or endurance, say, or performance, maybe—something along those kinds of lines? May I be so bold?"

Inside the shaded, cool garage, it was remarkably hard to say—but Dog's eyes had adjusted quite a bit from the pounding of the sun outside to the dimness inside, so his perspective was a bit sharper (but then his perspective was always a bit sharper)—was that a smile on Roc's strong and adamantine face? Were those the yellow tombstones of his teeth there, in the dim of the garage? Dimples? Hard to say, but, still, Dog did smile *that* smile back at him.

The garage was quiet as well as dim. The only sound came from the gentle breezes playing outside, rattling the loose windows and rocking empty oil drums back and forth. Maybe the only thing directly audible, for Roc's mouth did open that time and he seemed to be moving his strong lips.

But then Dog's hearing was a bit sharper than most, a bit more acute (he could, just about, tell you which of these gusts playing outside were male and which were female), so he could pick out the words where others wouldn't have:

"Pick me up."

Dog smiled and bowed deep, so deep that the tip of

his battered hat actually touched the dust and dirt floor of the garage. "Ah, most humble Roc. I cannot begin to tell you how pleased you have made me by giving me this most challenging of tasks—" Then, as if he suddenly realized what he had said, he quickly added, amended: "Not to imply in any way that you are of unnatural girth, kind sir. Not at all. I, for instance, have laid eyes on many a more huge, more giant specimen of man. I have seen many others much more huge, much more grotesquely magnificent in their dimensions. You, in fact, are almost svelte in comparison, say, to some of these grander gentlemen—"

This time, for sure, that was a smile. For sure, this time Roc spoke, gravel tumbling in a steel drum: "Pick me up," he said, "*now*."

"I most humbly will attempt to perform this task," Dog said, standing back up and moving toward and then around the huge man.

Carefully, craftily, Dog inspected Roc. He saw pretty much what he had seen the first time, but this time with the greater detail closer range brought: the brass buttons on the giant fellow's overalls straining in their reinforced loops against the incredible strength and size of him, the tanned-to-deep-brown quality of his skin, the valleys and broad plateaus of Roc's well-defined muscles. Yes, he was big. Yes, he was huge. But it was the kind of size that doesn't come from excess. It was a size of natural dimensions. Roc was big, but he was also strong.

"This could be quite a challenge," said Dog, slowly circling Roc, running his thin, long fingers over the taut skin and even tighter denim covering him. He let his fingers fall into the creases of him, tracing those definitions he'd only felt with his eyes. Roc's body was a passive statue carved from tan stone, from crimson woods. "Not to say that you are too big to even contemplate moving—"

Roc's laugh was thunder rolling over high hills, an earthquake, a tide retreating from a rocky beach. There was a smile in his words: "Pick me up if you can."

Dog made a kind of sneezing *here goes* sound, saying: "Very well, kind and gentle and rather, very, extremely, incredibly, *big* Roc. I will attempt to lift you bodily from your perch and hoist you up onto my shoulder."

Roc laughed again.

Dog found a place behind Roc, where his huge ass made two great globes of muscle around the tiny roller chair he was perched on. Making a grandiose show of spitting into his hands and bending his legs and cracking his back, he put one hand on each side of the huge man and started to breathe deep and hard.

Roc, with the contact, tensed as if a minor jolt of current had flowed through him: feeling the strength in Dog's arms, the warmth of his breath on the small of his back. Dog's hands were like iron sculptures on his sides and on his chest, oak.

"Ready, big man?" Dog said, from behind him.

Roc nodded, and Dog's breathing increased. Then, he lifted.

Roc felt himself lose weight under the strength of Dog. Under him, the chair creaked from the slowly decreasing weight of him. He felt the sudden shift of his overalls and the stuff, under him, start to move. He felt his ankles leave the metal of the chair struts and his back realign.

Behind him, lifting him, Dog was a vibrant force: like the ground, the sky, the wind. Roc felt the strength of Dog, the power of the man, and it excited him: his cock strained, mighty and mighty hungry, against the thickness of his overalls.

Dog was wheezing and straining, he was panting and

heaving. Distantly, both of them heard and both of them felt Dog's back give a little pop of strain.

Almost, almost, almost . . .

Then Roc's weight returned. The chair and the container of stuff creaked and groaned. Roc felt his weight return to its normal broadness against the chair seat. In a moment he was back to his usual distribution of self.

"My most humble, profound, extreme, sincere, earnest (pant, heave, pant, heave) apologies, Roc," Dog said, his breath steamy against Roc's broad back where he rested his face. "But this seems to be beyond my humble ability. I am so sorry. Is there anything else I might do for your magnificence that might facilitate your considering me to receive the stuff in your possession?"

Roc smiled, though Dog couldn't see it.

In the garage, with the wind rattling gently at the windows, Roc's voice was shockingly strong and loud: "Empty me."

Dog, still gently wheezing from the exertion of trying to lift the massive Roc, came around to the front of the huge man. He was smiling, too: a wicked and pleased smile that stretched from slightly pointed ear to slightly pointed ear. "It would be my most humble of pleasures, dear, kind, huge, Roc, to be the recipient of you, to swallow you till only the barest of you remains. It will be my pleasure to drain you of your sweetest stuff, to sup of your delicious nectar—"

Roc's mammoth hands left his lap, where they had been calmly folded, and, with glacial slowness, undid the top right, then top left buttons of his overalls. The thick denim fell to his sculpted belly. From there, Roc pulled down hard. When the material was a faded apron over the mound of his belly, he took one of his big hands (the left) and dug down below his waist.

Dog had seen bigger cocks, for sure. On whales, definitely. On elephants, positively. On bears, on rhinos, on panthers and tigers and pumas and cougars and moose and that guy, Lou, who worked in a gas station in Memphis—but this one was damn close. It was so damn close to positively huge that Roc had a hard time freeing it from his overalls. When he finally did, after much slow fumbling with his great hands, his cock was pointed up, right up, at Dog at a forty-five-degree angle.

Roc was uncut, his foreskin as tanned and dark as the rest of his teak skin. The shaft was like—many things: a baseball bat, a fence post, an arm, a leg—but it was also lovely, strong, and powerful. Its veins and muscles played and danced with the contractions of excitement along its length and made the massiveness of it bob up and down. Dog knew that he would from then on be comparing all those things (fence posts and baseball bats and arms and legs) to Roc's cock, and not the other way around.

The base of Roc's massive cock was buried in a forest primeval of curly stiff hairs. His balls, what Dog could see of them, were the size of baseballs, of apples . . . no: apples, oranges, baseballs, peaches, pears, were the size of Roc's lovely balls.

Obviously, Roc was happy with his cock, and with Dog: a thick droplet of creamy pre-come dotted the end, and, as Dog looked from it to Roc's stern and (maybe) slightly smiling stone face, the drop fell with a weighty plop to the dirt floor.

"I shall," Dog said, stricken to short sentences by the sight of Roc's member, "endeavor to accomplish."

Getting down on his knees on the dirt floor, Dog kissed and cleaned the foreskin with wide swaths of his soft, soft tongue: licking all around the base of the head, tasting the sweat, the manliness of the cock, feeling the corona through the thick skin, and then, finally (with a groan from Roc), he put his full lips on the tip and gently swallowed the thick bead that swelled there.

Slowly, Dog opened his mouth wider and wider till his teeth were oh-so-gently tapping against the ridge of the hidden cockhead. Then, with his strong and supple lips—as well as his learned and maneuverable tongue—Dog slowly started to push himself onto Roc's cock and pull his foreskin back.

In Dog's wide-open mouth, Roc's cock was like a stone covered in silk: a great weight perfectly formed into the head of a cock. The foreskin peeled back as if wanting it as much as the cock's owner did, retracting smooth and supple till the bare cockhead was filling Dog's soft mouth.

Above Dog, Roc permitted himself a subterranean growl that vibrated through his body and dribbled a thimbleful of come down the back of Dog's throat.

Then Dog really started to work.

First he bathed Roc's cockhead with his tongue—teasing and milking it with his mouth. To Roc, it felt as if both a mouth and a hand were working on him, drawing the come and the come juice out of him like a snake charmer working on a snake.

In fact, the music of Dog's blowjob was so skilled and so well orchestrated that Roc soon felt his great reservoir of come start to boil and seethe with an impending orgasm.

Then it was too late. The fuse (in Dog's mouth) burst into pleasurable, throbbing sparkles, racing down and through the shaft of Roc's cock and straight into his belly and balls. There the gates were opened, and he started to roar out and into Dog's hungry mouth.

Cups? Pints? Gallons? Hard to say, but whatever the immense amount, Dog gulped and swallowed and consumed every last bit of it, letting it flow down his throat and into his belly. Above him, Roc flowed rivers of sweat and groaned and moaned and cried with the power of his come. He seemed to deflate, to diminish, as his juice flowed out of him.

Dog swallowed it all—save a last tiny bit: the last cup flowed over Dog's lips and splashed down onto the dirt floor.

"My apologies, my most humble, humble apologies, great and powerful Roc," said Dog, standing up and wiping his mouth, chin, and face with a large red handkerchief. "I am most ashamed that again I have disappointed your huge and magnificent self with my poor performance of the task you have set before humble ol' me. I can only hope that you will look back on this, and me, kindly and not with scorn and—"

"Shut up," Roc said, hugely, "and fill me."

That smile again. "Sure," Dog said.

Walking behind the great mountain, Dog played his hands along the broad, strong back of Roc, playing among the valleys and ranges of his skin with his mouth and hands, feeling and tasting the torrents of sweat still trickling off the huge man.

Roc had pulled his overalls down to expose his cock, and in doing so had exposed his asshole as well.

Despite his worldly experience, Dog looked and whistled: mouths, rose blossoms—all now could be compared to the puckered asshole of Roc. For such a huge and very obvious (his cock!) man, Roc had a surprisingly dainty asshole. Well, not exactly dainty—Roc's asshole was easily the size of a half-dollar: firm and tight and pink and clean—more like "cute." Though Dog was sure that if he said as much, he would be squished like jam between bricks by the massive hands of Roc.

Instead, he said, "I will (ahem) strive to accomplish this more pleasurable of tasks, this plumbing of your most intimate depths, the filling of your aching emptiness with my most humble of—"

Roc inhaled, as if ready to speak his rumbling tones—

"I'm doing it, I'm doing it—!" Dog said, fumbling with his belt. When his jeans dropped to the dirt floor, they kicked up tiny clouds of yellow dust that, as friendly as their outside counterparts, clung to Dog's hairy legs.

Dog's own member was much more . . . *sedate* than the giant's Roc's, of much more modest proportions and dimensions. When one viewed Dog's penis, and many had done so, the things that came to mind were of a much humbler variety: flashlights, ears of corn, zucchinis, and the like.

Still, even though it was a bit smaller than the giant's, Dog's cock had a lot of character. His was a cock that spoke (rarely) of wild fucks, mad fucks, quick fucks, fucks in strange and weird places, of assholes, mouths, melons, fists, and maybe even the occasional cunt. It was long and tapering, uncut, as was Roc's, but bent in a curious way, kind of down and to the side (left), and the head was bulbous and even nicked by what looked like scars—as if maybe one or more recipients had been a might alarmed by Dog's use of it.

"I will," sighed Dog, stroking his cock to a righteous state of iron-readiness, "endeavor to perform this task."

And with that, he spat into his hand and started to lube up Roc's asshole, which, being an obviously well-trained asshole, immediately started to bloom open around his gentle fingers.

When Roc's back door was quite ready, willing, and more-than-likely able, Dog carefully positioned himself so the head of his cock was resting gently against his puckered other mouth and grabbed hold of Roc's strong sides.

"Ready?" he inquired in excited tones.

No sound came, but the giant head nodded.

As asshole fucks go, the one between Dog and Roc that day wasn't the absolute. Easily, some others could have exceeded it in terms of length of time, intensity, passion, determination, depth, and resulting orgasm. Many, for sure, were far more powerful than Dog and Roc's, but none came to mind, none, especially, for either Dog or Roc, before or since.

For Roc, the slender wanderer's cock was like an iron shaft gliding in and out of his most tender and excited opening. Dog's long and strong shaft reached in and tickled and fucked him in ways he'd never before experienced. Already, after a few minutes, Dog's skillful use of his cock inside him had started the engine of his come. Already, great rivers of sweat were pouring off him, and his great eyes were fluttering with anticipation of a mind-altering orgasm.

For Dog, Roc was the perfect thing to fuck: big and wide and hot and tight and lubed and eager. His asshole was an amusement park of sensation and pressure—his skilled tissues felt like hands, tongues, and lips, all striving to push him up and over the top.

When they met at the peak of their respective comes, the orgasm that rocked and rolled through the two of them was like a stick of dynamite lit and tossed between them. Dog exploded with a spasming jerk that felt as if live wires had been grounded in his arms and legs. Roc felt as if heated lead had been squirted into his tender asshole.

Dog filled Roc with his come, almost all the way, but then—

Dog's legs seemed to give out. Dropping back onto his bare ass on the dirt floor, he jetted a last pint or so into the air and all over his shirt. "I beg (pant) your ultimate (sigh) forgiveness, great and mighty (wheeze) Roc, for I have (Ohboyohboyohboy!) failed you again in my attempt at the task you have set before me—"

Roc didn't say anything, didn't do anything but sit there on his tiny wheeled stool and pant and wheeze and gasp himself.

Staggering to his feet, Dog hitched up his battered jeans and dusted his ass off, saying all the while: "I feel so bad, great Roc, for failing you in not one, not two, but three of the tasks you have set before me. I feel so inadequate as a man and a being that I do not think I can ever raise my head again. I can never meet the eyes of another knowing I have failed you in these tasks. I feel I can never redeem myself for these failures—

"Unless," Dog added, and there was that smile again, "I might attempt one of these tasks again, say. Another, no doubt, fruitless attempt at something you know I have already dismally avoided success in. Maybe then (oh, please, oh, please, oh, please) I might be able to restore my essence of pride in myself and my abilities as a man."

Now it should be said that two orgasms (like trains entering tunnels) had already had their way with the giant Roc, and that he had few brain cells that were actually working at that time. It was expected, then, that the only thing that did come to mind for him was either once again having Dog's lovely mouth and throat on his cock or having Dog's incredible cock inside him again. With his two functioning brain cells, Roc said: "Sure (wheeze), anything."

So Dog smiled that smile again and grabbed Roc around his huge middle and lifted his now very diminished, shrunken, and exhausted form off the stool.

While he wheezed and panted and strained again, it was obviously easier this time—Roc was just light enough for him to do it. With Roc held high, Dog then kicked out with his right foot and neatly booted the "stuff" off the stool, sending it skidding across the floor of the garage.

Then he dropped Roc back onto his stool and sprinted like a wild animal away from Roc's flailing arms (like whirling stone paddles), scooped up the stuff—which was neatly contained in a battered and stained Sucrets box—and ran for the door.

Where he stopped, turned, bowed deep, and said: "It was indeed a great pleasure meeting you and taking your stuff, Mr. Roc."

Then he turned and left, leaving the bellowing Roc behind him.

Down the road, by the house, Dog stopped a moment to heave and pant and wheeze some more ("Quite a workout today"), bracing himself against one of the rotten fence posts. Satisfied that Roc was completely unwilling or unable to follow him, Dog allowed himself yet another special smile—one that said *Got ya!*—and decided to look at his prize.

The little metal box was quite stubborn, but he finally managed to pry it open and look inside.

A mirror. Reflected in the mirror was the sun, burning hot and dry and mean over his head.

Curious, dumbfounded, and more than a little pissed, Dog turned the box this way and that, trying to puzzle it out. He did this for many minutes, till, at last, he simply shrugged his shoulders as he done many times before and would do many times again, chucking the box over the broken fence and into the weed-choked yard.

Then he left, humming absently to himself.

A short time later, the boys found the box among their weeds and took it with them. A little time after that, they thanked the lanky stranger who had come and gone—leaving them such an incredible gift.

CONTRIBUTORS

ISOBEL BIRD is one of the many names of writer Michael Thomas Ford. The author of numerous books, including *If Jesus Loves Me, Why Hasn't He Called?*, he is also the editor of the books *Happily Ever After: Erotic Fairy Tales for Men* and *Once Upon a Time: Erotic Fairy Tales for Women*. His essays and fiction have appeared under various names, in magazines such as *Cupido, Mach, Paramour,* and *St*rphkrs,* and in anthologies including *Best American Erotica 1995, Flesh and the Word 3, Brothers of the Night, Machine Sex, PomoSexuals, Generation Q,* and *Noirotica 2*. His erotic fiction has been called "haunting" and "chilling" by *Publishers Weekly,* "obscene" by the Catholic church and Canadian customs officials, and "the work of a perverted, wet-pantied tweak" by femme-editrix Shar Rednour.

TED BLUMBERG, a freelance writer living in New York, is currently at work on a memoir. He gives his thanks to Amelia.

BILL BRENT has published *Black Sheets*, a humorous zine about the intersection of sex and popular culture in the nineties. He is the author of *Make a Zine!,* the first full-length book covering every aspect of how to do a zine. He also edits *Porno Pen,* a market guide for writers of erotica. Elsewhere, his writing has appeared in *Noirotica,* a collection of erotic crime stories, as well as in the zines *Paramour, Rant and Rave,* and *Anything That Moves.* His nonfiction sex story, "True Confession," which first appeared in *Black Sheets,* was chosen for reprint in *The Factsheet Five Reader,* a "best of" collection of zine writing.

LAUREN BURKA's short stories have appeared in anthologies by Circlet Press and Masquerade Books. Even though her tarot cards declared Lauren would never hold down a normal job, she is currently employed in the Internet security field, and finds Mate's technology descriptions "charmingly naive."

M. CHRISTIAN's first published story, "Intercore," was accepted for *Best American Erotica 1994.* Since then, he has published over fifty stories in such books as *Best Gay Erotica 1996, The Mammoth Book of International Erotica, Sons of Darkness, First Personal Sexual, Leatherwomen III,* and *Hot Ticket,* and in the magazines *Paramour, Black Sheets, Sexlife!, Pucker-Up,* and *Anything That Moves.* He is also the editor of *Eros Ex Machina: Eroticising the Mechanical,* due out from Rhino*ceros* Books.

NANCY KILPATRICK writes under her name and the nom de plume Amarantha Knight. She has published eight novels, one hundred short stories, and two story collections; edited six anthologies; and written numerous comics. Her upcoming work includes *Endorphins* (Macabre Inc.) and the anthology *Gargoyles*

(Ace/Berkley), and her story "Teaserama" will appear in *The Mammoth Book of Dracula,* edited by Stephen Jones. In 1992, she won the Arthur Ellis Award for best mystery story.

TSAURAH LITZKY is a poet, essayist, and short-story writer who believes that this is the promised land. For the last three years she has been writing an "Eros and Existence" page for the New York–based paper *Downtown/The Aquarian Weekly.* Her work has appeared in *The East Coast Rocker, Longshot, Davka, Ikon, Pink Pages, Breakelen, Penthouse,* and *The Unbearables,* an anthology published by Semiotexte/Autonmedia. Her third poetry chapbook, *Blessing Poems,* has recently been published by Synaesthesia Press in San Francisco.

ALLEGRA LONG is a professional dancer who considers sexual intimacy the ultimate dance form. She has conducted an exhaustive search for the most pleasing combinations and the perfect partner.

MICHAEL LOWENTHAL's fiction has appeared in *The Crescent Review, Other Voices,* and *Yellow Silk,* and has been widely anthologized in books, such as *Best American Gay Fiction* and *Men on Men 5.* He is the editor of the best-selling *Flesh and the Word* anthology series, and he has also edited *Friends and Lovers* and *Gay Men at the Millennium.* The recipient of a 1995–96 New Hampshire State Council on the Arts fellowship for fiction, he now lives in Boston.

JOE MAYNARD lives in Brooklyn, writes a weekly column for *The Aquarian,* and has been published in various magazines and anthologies, such as *Best American Erotica 1994, Paramour, Exquisite Corpse,* and others.

He collaborates with a group of New York City writers who call themselves the Unbearables. Joe edits two of the best lit-zines in the country: *Beet* and *Pink Pages*. He is currently looking to publish a collection of his short stories, *Our Hitlers, Ourselves*.

SERENA MOLOCH is the author of several famous contemporary women's erotic stories, including "The Babysitter," "I Visit the Doctor," and "My Date with Marcie." Her work has appeared in *On Our Backs* and the *Herotica* series. For their editorial guidance over the years, she thanks Susie Bright and Marcy Sheiner; for the inspiration for "Beyond the Mask," she thanks the diarist Hannah Cullwick and the makers of *Céline and Julie Go Boating*.

THOMAS ROCHE is a San Francisco writer and sex educator. His 1997 collection of stories, *Dark Matter,* is available from Masquerade Books. He has written short stories in the horror, crime, science fiction, and fantasy fields. He has also edited the erotic crime anthologies *Noirotica* and *Noirotica 2* and written scary comic books and fiction based on role-playing games.

MARCY SHEINER is editor of *Herotica 4* and *Herotica 5*. Her journalism and fiction have been published in magazines as diverse as *Penthouse* and *Vegetarian Times, Mother Jones* and the Scandinavian *Cupido*. She teaches erotic writing classes in the Bay Area, where she lives, and is currently working on a collection of essays.

SIMON SHEPPARD's work has appeared in the 1996 and 1997 editions of *Best Gay Erotica,* and in many other anthologies, including *Bending the Landscape, Fantasy, Switch Hitters, Brothers of the Night,* and *Grave Passions: Tales from the Gay Darkside.* His stories have also been published in magazines including *Drummer, Powerplay,* and *Bunkhouse.* He has traveled extensively on Indian Railways, and he loves his boyfriend very, very much.

STEPHEN SPOTTE is a marine research assistant at the University of Connecticut. A collection of his stories will be published by Creative Arts Book Company this fall.

E. R. STEWART was born in Altoona, Pennsylvania, on the 146th birthday of Charles Dickens. He began writing eight years later and publishing eight years after that. His credits include fiction, nonfiction, criticism, maps, photography, cartoons, and poetry. He's married, has three kids, and travels avidly. He currently lives in Germany.

MARK STUERTZ is a freelance writer and editor, graphic designer, and wine critic. He lives in Dallas with his wife and their young daughter, Amelia.

LUCY TAYLOR is a full-time fiction writer whose novel *The Safety of Unknown Cities* (Dark Side Press) won the Bram Stoker Award for Best First Novel in 1996. Her stories have appeared in *Best American Erotica 1996, Dark Love, David Copperfield's Tales of the Impossible, Noirotica,* and *Love in Vein 2.* She lives in the hills outside Boulder with her seven books.

Ivy Topiary is, as you might have guessed, a pseudonym. "My Professor" was penned originally for *Penthouse;* it was rejected as "too intellectual."

Loana DP Valencia is a puta jota sinvergüenza escandalosa y pervertida from east l.a., a xicanindia of multiple genders livin' en la misión en san panocha fightin' to break taboos, change rules, and defy categories.

Bob Vickery's stories have appeared over the years in numerous gay erotic magazines (*Blueboy, Honcho, Freshman, Torso,* and *Mandate,* among others) and he is currently a regular contributor to *Advocate Men.* He has several anthologies of stories out, *Skin Deep* (Masquerade Books) and *Dharma: A Gay Buddhist Anthology; Butchboys,* and *Unzipped.*

Rose White and **Eric Albert** love each other very much.

READER'S DIRECTORY

Many readers ask me where they can find outstanding erotic fiction throughout the year. Below you'll find a list of magazines and small presses that have published the erotic fiction over the past year that I found worthy of a BAE nomination. Please contact them directly to learn more about their work. Also, if you are looking for a place to publish your own erotic fiction, these are all worth looking into.

Anything That Moves
Anything That Moves is the only regularly published magazine for bisexuals in North America. Subscriptions: $20/4 issues. Single issues: $6. Sample issue: $1.50. Call (800) 818-8823 for subscriptions only, or write to 2261 Market Street, #496, San Francisco, CA 94114.

Black Sheets
Intelligent, irreverent, sex-positive magazine. Bill Brent, the editor, may be reached by e-mail at BlackB@ios.com. Subscriptions are $20/4 issues, payable to The Black Book, with a statement of legal age required; a sample issue is $7 postpaid. A free pub-

lications catalog is also available with signed age statement. P.O. Box 31155, San Francisco, CA 94131-0155; (800) 818-8823 for credit card orders.

Circlet Press

A small, independent book publisher founded in 1992, Circlet specializes in erotic science fiction and fantasy with anthologies and collections of short stories on topics from vampires to futuristic erotic technology. Send SASE for catalog to 1770 Massachusetts Avenue, Suite 278, Cambridge, MA 02140, or e-mail: circlet-info@circlet.com. or http://www.circlet.com/circlet/home.html.

Cleis Press

Publishing America's most intelligent and provocative sex-positive books for girlfriends of all genders. For catalog and further information, write P.O. Box 14684, San Francisco, CA 94114, or call (800) 780-2279.

conMOCIÓN

"Una revista red revolucionaria de lesbianas latinas" and "100% latina lesbian vision," published one issue devoted to erotica. That erotica issue is still available. They are $5.00 each and you can order them at *conMOCIÓN*, 2626 N. Mesa, #273, El Paso, TX 79902.

Down There Press

Down There Press has published sexual health and self-awareness books for women, men, and children since 1975. We look for books that are innovative, lively, and practical and that will strengthen sexual communication. In keeping with our sex-positive philosophy, we also publish literary and photographic erotica for women and men. For a catalog, write to 938 Howard Street, #101, San Francisco, CA 94103.

Libido
The journal of sex and sensibility. Published quarterly by Marianna Beck and Jack Hafferkamp. Subscriptions: $30 per year; single issue, $8. Write to 5318 N. Paulina Ave., St., Chicago, IL 60640.

Masquerade Books
World's leading publisher of straight, gay, lesbian, and S/M erotic literature. Richard Kasak, publisher. Bimonthly *Masquerade Erotic Newsletter* subscriptions are $30/year; book catalogs are free. Write to 801 Second Avenue, New York, NY 10017.

Paramour
Luscious cream-filled pansexual magazine featuring short fiction, poetry, photography, illustration, and reviews by emerging writers and artists. Amelia Copeland, publisher/editor. Published quarterly; subscriptions are $18/year, samples are $4.95. Write to P.O. Box 949, Cambridge, MA 02140-0008.

St*rphkrs
Not-so-true tales of sex with all your favorite celebrities, from Elvis to Patsy Cline to Courtney Love. To order a copy, send a signed statement of age with $4 cash or money order to Shartopia at 3288 21st Street, #94, San Francisco, CA 94110.

CREDITS

READER
SURVEY

1. What are your favorite stories in this year's collection?

2. Have you read previous years' editions of *The Best American Erotica*? (1993, 1994, 1995, 1996)

3. If yes, do you have any favorite stories from those previous collections?

4. Do you have any recommendations for next year's *The Best American Erotica*? (Nominated stories must have been published in the United States, in any form, during the 1997 calendar year.)

5. How did you get this book?

_____ independent bookstore   _____ chain book-
                                                             store

_____ mail-order company   _____ other type of
                                                            store

_____ sex/erotica shop   _____ borrowed it
                                                  from a friend

6. How old are you?

7. Male, female, other?

8. Where do you live?

_____ West Coast   _____ South

_____ Midwest   _____ Other

_____ East Coast

9. What made you interested in *BAE 1997*?

_____ enjoyed other *BAE* collections

_____ editor's reputation

_____ authors' reputations

_____ enjoy "Best of" anthologies

_____ word-of-mouth recommendation

_____ enjoy anthologies in general

_____ read book review

10. Any other suggestions? Feedback?

Please return this survey or any other *BAE*-related correspondence to Susie Bright, *BAE* Feedback, 309 Cedar Street, #3D, Santa Cruz, CA 95060, or you can e-mail me at BAEfeedback@susiebright.com.

Thanks so much.

ABOUT THE EDITOR

SUSIE BRIGHT is a writer, editor, and performer hailed by the *Boston Phoenix* as the "goddess of erotica." In addition to having edited *Herotica I, II,* and *III,* a women's erotic fiction series, she is the author of *Susie Bright's Sexual State of the Union; Sexwise; Susie Bright's Sexual Reality: A Virtual Sex World Reader; Susie Sexpert's Lesbian Sex World;* and *Nothing But the Girl: The Blatant Lesbian Image. The Millennium Whole Earth Catalog* calls her a "national treasure, right up there with the Grand Canyon, the Okefenokee Swamp, and the Smithsonian's Nancy Reagan Memorial Dress Collection." Susie currently lives in Northern California with her seven-year-old daughter.